Arcura Book One

Shatterbound Reign

Simon Leith

www.simonleithbooks.com

First published by Busybird Publishing 2025

ISBN:
Paperback: 978-1-923501-41-6
Ebook: 978-1-923501-42-3

This is a work of fiction. Any similarities between places and characters are coincidental.

Cover image: Simon Leith

Cover design: Simon Leith

Layout and typesetting: Busybird Publishing

Busybird Publishing
2/118 Para Road
Montmorency, Victoria
Australia 3094
www.busybird.com.au

What if the beat of the heart was wild?
And the soul within, unbridled.
Would your spirit grasp at the power,
or will it forever be out of its reach?

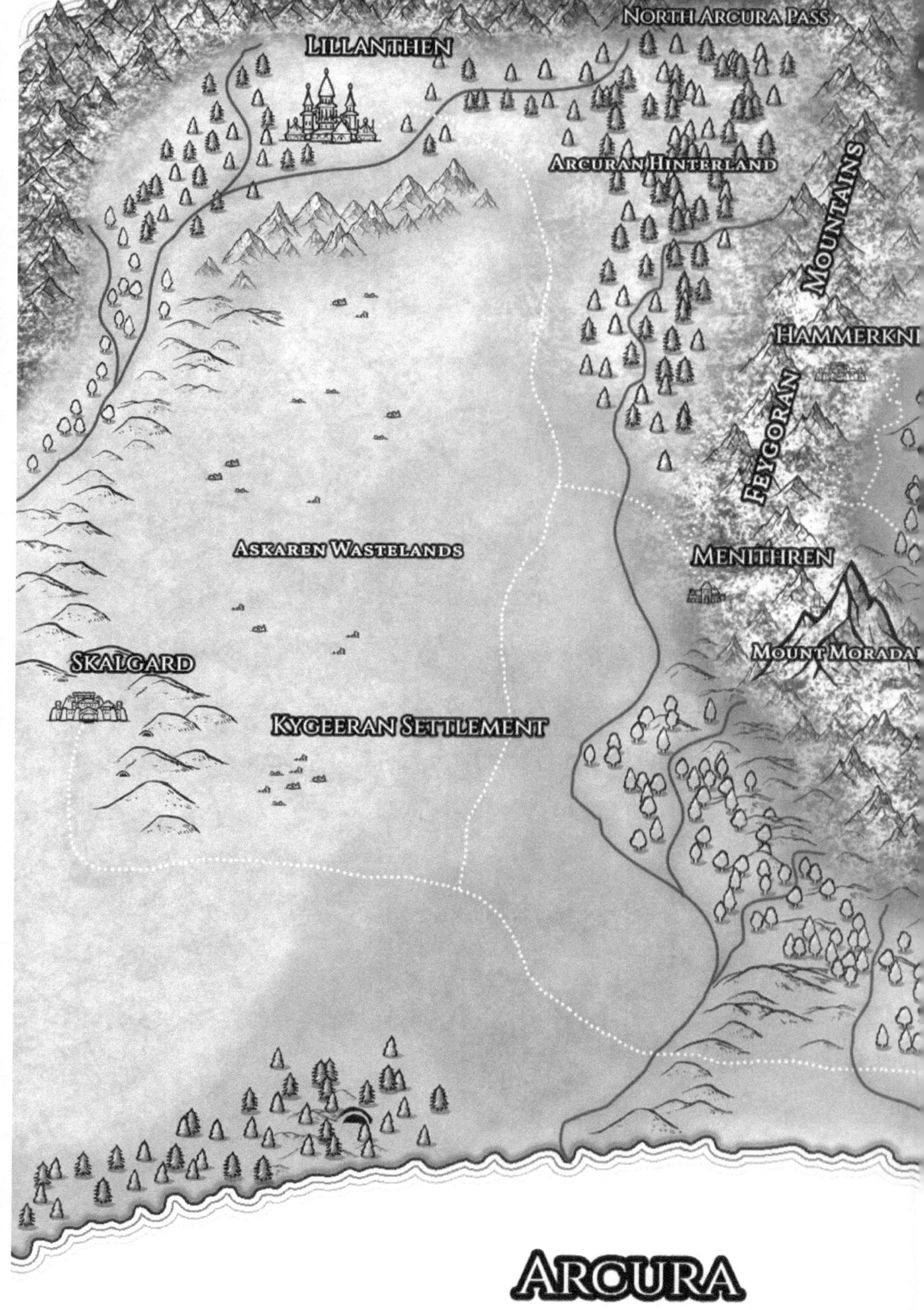

LILLANTHEN
NORTH ARCURA PASS
ARCURAN HINTERLAND
MOUNTAINS
HAMMERKNI
FEYGORAN
ASKAREN WASTELANDS
MENITHREN
MOUNT MORADA
SKALGARD
KYGEERAN SETTLEMENT
ARCURA

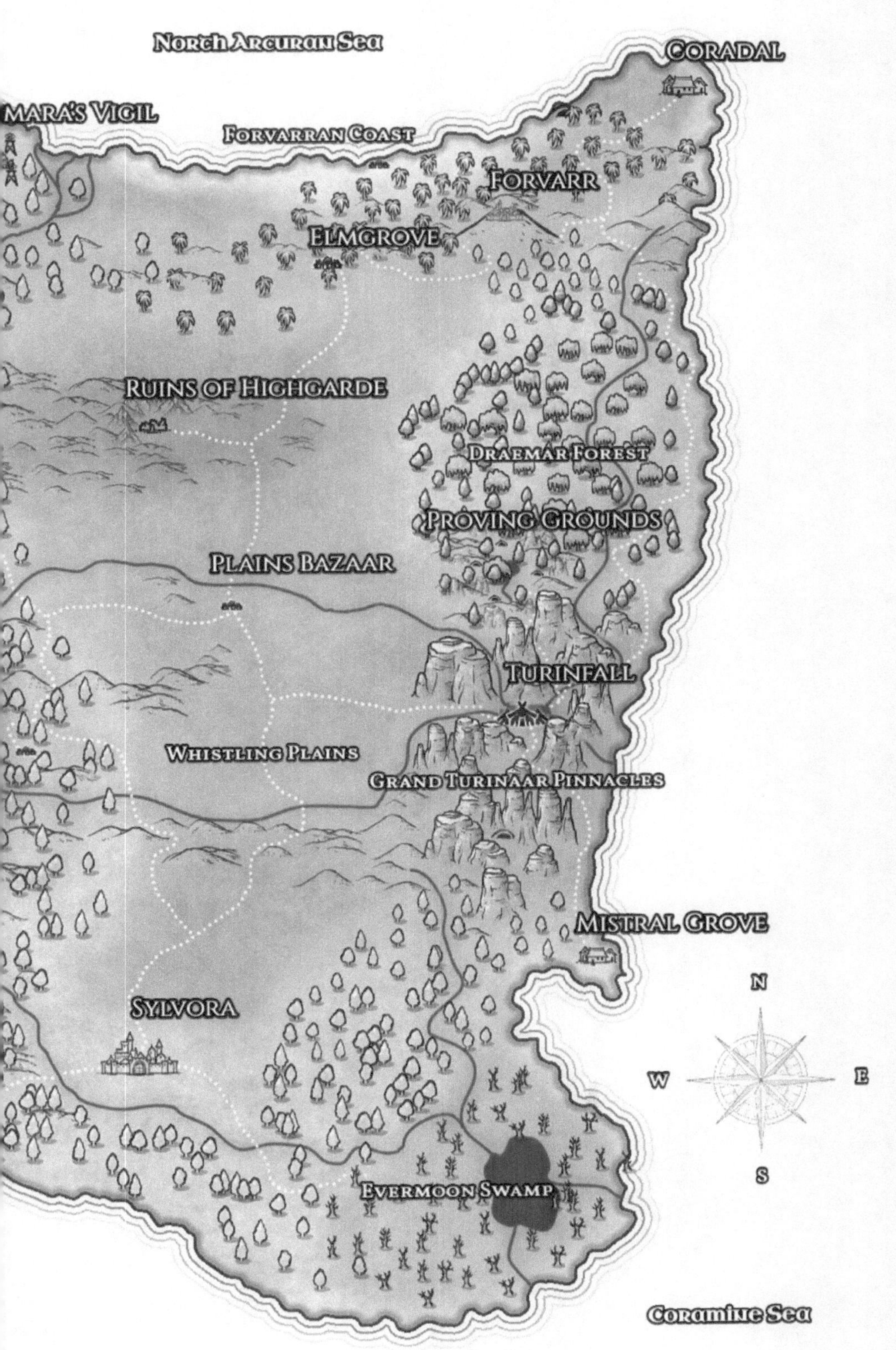

North Arcuran Sea
CORADAL
MARA'S VIGIL
Forvarran Coast
FORVARR
ELMGROVE
RUINS OF HIGHGARDE
Draemar Forest
PROVING GROUNDS
PLAINS BAZAAR
TURINFALL
WHISTLING PLAINS
GRAND TURINAAR PINNACLES
MISTRAL GROVE
SYLVORA
N
W
E
S
EVERMOON SWAMP
Coramive Sea

One

ARATHYN

Thundering echoes reverberate through me; I run, swinging my head around as far as my neck can stretch. An obvious danger lurks, invisible to the naked eye. The ground trembles, my feet fail me and I fall.

"We must get home!" My determination is enough to lift me to my feet with Draygar's help.

Wind shears as rocks topple down from an overhanging shelf, doing everything to hinder my advance. My sanctuary appears in sight as Rangers ready their bows.

With a final burst into the awaiting hands of salvation.

I am home.

A Ranger stares me down. "Are you alright, boy?"

"Something was after me!" I find myself staring back, only to find faces full of confusion as they peer out beyond me. I muster the courage to look, cringing at the thought of what I might see.

Nothing.

No rockfall. Air is calm. My heart is still pounding at a million miles an hour.

The Ranger lowers his bow; his look, perplexed. "You … had best get some *rest*."

I check over my shoulder once more, scratching my head. "Did I anger the lumberjack?"

A memory instills. A memory when I was only ten.

My hands shook, I lost my bearings as my feet stumbled into a desecrated place where none should tread. Echoes of darkness whispered to me, dread set upon my soul, and a dark grasp on my very being made my bones clench. I ran as fast as I could, as far as my ten-year-old legs could fathom. A strangeness washed over me after I made my way back to the path alongside my companion, Draygar. We ran for our lives, back to the company of my parents once more.

I escaped from darkness …

"Arathyn Lycanheart!" The booming voice of my father jolts my twenty-year-old body from my bed. "I was informed of what happened earlier. Do not cause trouble around here! For all we know, another group of bandits was tracking you."

Words take a while to coalesce as I shrug off the hostility in his voice. "I am sorry, Father."

"Get dressed please, your mother is out on the eastern fields. Give her a hand, will you? Take this basket and no more nonsense. Attacks have been frequent lately as you would know."

The journey out to the tilling fields eases my mind as I pass through the tranquil beauty that Turinfall has to offer. Bridges high above a lake of pearlescence, constructed in a heavy weaving of rope and log, connect several parts of the village. Cascading waterfalls between towering flat-topped spires of rock. Rivers that snake their way through the landscape. It is beautiful this time of year, snow-melt from the Feygoran Mountains runs as pristine water out toward the Coramine Sea.

Draygar paces beside me as I hurry my step. The amber-eyed wolf-like beast covers the ground effortlessly, his near-black fur whipping in the breeze.

Stopping briefly at the crest of Greenscale Hill, I regather my breath, marvelling in the magnificence of mahogany buildings that lie before me. Buildings belonging to none other than Argora herself.

Huntsmaster Argora Turinaar. The head of the Turin bloodline, ruler of our tribe. An elegant woman who dearly loves nature and preaches our cultural heritage. Animals and humans are one.

The Turin bloodline. With a wealth unimaginable for people like us. Argora often sends bands of Rangers on missions to serve surrounding towns. Protection from pillagers and outlaws is what they offer, often gone for weeks on end before they return with a small fortune for their services.

My father, Relgyn, is the Turin's choice builder; just a scratch upon their prestigious buildings is enough to request his services. Prestigious. Not for us. Small, insignificant huts are what we call home. Oak sourced from Draemar Forest, rounded into shelters. Families are grouped together, one hut for each.

My mother, Elraetha, forages for food. As an only child, I spend a lot of time with my parents. Our daily lives are labour-intensive; however, our companions are built for such a burden.

Memories of my childhood rush back. The excitement in my parents' eyes when I first laid mine upon Draygar, knowing the Amandryr would be mine forever, before a rush of nervousness hits me at the sense of responsibility. An animal that must be captured and tamed when a child reaches the age of ten. The mother passes down the beast and thus begins our journey toward an extreme bond of companionship.

The sight of a woman dressed in pale white pants, a vibrant red jacket and gnarly pink gloves catches my eye as I reach the fields. She stands out amongst the villagers that forage here; my mother always dresses bright.

Upon grabbing her attention, her blonde hair whips around as she turns to face me. "Quite the collection today."

"It is the rains, my boy, look at the beautiful colour." My blue eyes race through the vast assortment of berries encased in a basket before me. Black berries and blue, just like her eyes which embed excitement.

"The morning harvest is done. The bakers will love these. Oh, you brought one too." Her eyes make out the basket in my hand as I struggle to find anything to fill it with. "Some exercise at least."

Something has a grip on our way of life, darkness stirring beyond one's sight. I try to redirect my thoughts. My eyes drill into the weaves of the basket as I need somewhere to look. Draygar questions me with a look of confusion. I recall our journey west all these years ago, to the ruins of Highgarde. Darkness calling to me. *Warning* me.

Uneasiness grips my body.

———◆———

A few weeks after my birthday, a sudden desire strikes deep within to acquire my own bow. My father's older, worn shortbows are plagued with problems. I can't think of anything I want more. My desire to hunt and provide for Argora, whom I idolise, fills me with excitement.

Upon visiting the bowyer, who has just received a delivery of fine maple and the highest quality bowstrings, I worry that indulgence will set in and I'll pay whatever she wants.

Auriella's young daughter is dusting the racks with a brush. "You can finish later, go take a short rest," Auriella says to her warmly, before turning to me.

Approaching her, my face awash with curiosity and excitement, she spots me immediately. "Hello, Arathyn. How are you today?"

My eyes are fixated like a hawk upon the maple bows before me. "Ah, I see you are after our best. Quite hard to resist? Yes? These are the finest we have had in a long time, our shipments have been ransacked as of late."

The table that stands before me gleams as I unload silver coins from my pocket upon it. I run my eyes back and forth amongst the traders, Auriella's excitement doesn't seem to sway anyone's attention.

My eyes pick out a bow before discovering a crate of ivory stashed away below the crafting bench.

"I also see that you have an interest in ivory. That one is three hundred coin and I can assure you it will last a lifetime. Should you wish to part with more, I can work wonders with it." The barterer in Auriella convinces me, she doesn't miss a thing, likely why she is so successful.

Once again, I find myself unsure. The Turin have ivory statues carved into perfect sculptures of vicious, menacing creatures that you would dare not challenge without a heart of steel. A testament to battles, trophies if you will. These giant constructs mesmerise me and I want a piece of that material for myself.

"I'll tell you what. Give me until morning. Five hundred coin and your dream of an ivory-laced bow becomes a reality."

A proposal I can't resist, every part of my being is exploding with excitement. I bellow back. "That would be amazing!"

Now I've drawn the attention of others. "I'm sorry. I will accept your offer."

A dashing smile grows across her face. "I will see you tomorrow, Arathyn, and bring those riches with you."

Heading back to my hut, doubt begins to convince me that my parents will not approve; however, it does not stop me storming through the door exhilarated.

"Auriella is personally handcrafting me an ivory bow. It will be finished in the morning!"

My father lowers a flagon onto the bench and fixes his gaze upon me. "Don't you storm in here like that. Where are your manners, Arathyn!"

My lean body stands frozen as if I've been buffeted by a blizzard, cast forth by his ice-like blue-eyed gaze. "How much does that woman want you to cough up? You will receive no more than what we gave you."

He stands like a brute under a short head of hair and I am just able to muster enough courage to answer. "Five hundred coin …"

"All of it? Well, who am I to stand in your way … if that is what you really want." His approval is a weight lifted off my shoulders. "Are my bows not good enough?"

My mother laughs. "You must show me tomorrow."

My stride is once again comfortable as I brush past the smooth wooden exterior of my hut only a few paces away, to find Draygar fast asleep.

"Draygar, we are going hunting tomorrow!" A snort is all I receive in response as he lies there bathed in the comfort of a woven Reygyre-fur rug.

⟡

Dawn breaks over the Grand Turinaar Pinnacles, my entire night tossing and turning forces a yawn from my weary mouth. All that occupies my thoughts are the bow and the adventure that will follow. Draygar shares my excitement, sitting next to me in wait as if he knows what today holds for the two of us.

Opening my old wooden chest, an eerie creak pierces the air around me as I reach in. With silver coins in my grasp, I rampantly push open the door that provides no barrier to my eagerness and brush aside the shawl, only to be blinded by the rising sun. A glare I'm not prepared for, I should still be asleep.

Regaining my eyesight, I head out to the pathway that leads down to the bazaar, Draygar in tow. The wonder of the village at dawn stops me momentarily. Glinting waterfalls to the west. Thunderous roars of water plunging into the lake below. Shadows that shoot through the valleys between the Grand Turinaar Pinnacles. Turinfall, nature's canvas of tranquillity.

A completely deserted central square welcomes my presence. It is a good hour before Argora expects the villagers to commence work, although there is some leniency on that matter.

Draygar and I sit upon cold ground before overhearing a rustle that catches our attention, originating from the bowyer's tent. Moving cautiously, we head over only to trip upon a pile of loose stones. Feeling like a stalker that just lost his cover, Auriella whips open the shawl with excitement.

"Arathyn! You are very eager. I finished your bow upon nightfall yesterday; however, I felt it rude to visit you after dusk. Did you bring that wealth with you?"

My hands find the coins in my side pocket. "I have it right here. Do you supply arrows?"

Auriella eyes off our surroundings as if she's tracking a thief before whispering into my awaiting ears. "A secret between you and me. A name I shall not speak. Your eagerness was noticed. Arkryn saw to it that your bow was … let's just say, *glorified.*"

Excitement explodes throughout my body. My lengthy blond hair whips around my face as I nod.

"As per your previous question. Of course. My bows come with a quiver and ten of the finest arrows. With Arkryn's steel-hardened crafted tips, you have everything you need."

The bow is finally in my hands. "Thank you, Auriella. I will take extremely good care of this!"

As I begin my journey back, my hands make out the fine craft of smoothly rounded maple, bent into a perfect recurve. The cooler, smooth texture of embedded ivory pleases my senses as I run my fingers along it. The bowstring is taut and snaps back as the resistance of my fingers gives way to the pressure. Arrows with heads of steel at the end of hardwood shafts that can pierce the thickest of hides. Feathers from the manes of Featherkin grace the ends. Lightweight, renewable and extremely durable, they provide the best quality of flights.

Featherkin aren't killed for their feathers. Anyone found guilty will surely be executed by Argora herself as they are sacred to the Turin. They are plucked from the mane of a select few as they regrow naturally after a few weeks.

Then, I notice it: a *diamond*, encased within steel. Recessed into the arrow rest. Twisting the bow in my hands, the gemstone finds the sunlight and gleams like a star in the night sky. *Exhilarating.*

A target is set and practice begins. Not by any means am I the most accurate marksman, but I hope my father will train me further.

One last arrow finds the makeshift target before it splits, the sheer power of the bow has all but destroyed the weak and weathered construction.

"Good day, Arathyn." Startling me is my father as I ponder what to do next. "I see that you need a new target." The expression on his face fills me with satisfaction.

"Let me see what you have there … This is a work of art. Auriella definitely knows what she is doing!" My father's eyes notice the diamond, a stern look is thrown my way. I tense up before the look recedes. "Throw me an arrow, would you?"

The instant he catches it, he nocks, spins around and draws before bulleting an arrow right into the centre of the target. It is nothing more now than a pile of mangled wood on the grass.

"That'll do it." My father sports a grand smile. "Very impressive. Be careful of the power within that, I am sure it can pierce solid bone. Just don't hurt yourself!"

My father pulls a note from his pocket. "We have received a request from Argora, we will leave shortly. Show me what you can do with that bow and bring us home some kill!" My father disappears inside, clearly impressed with what he's done.

The time for adventure is upon us.

Two

ARATHYN

The morning graces us as Draygar and I head south. I haven't ventured down this way for a few years, most of our work lies north around the Featherkin Grounds, sometimes even as far as Draemar Forest.

An adventure awaits. A test of my capability. The ideal place is here, around the southern edge of the Grand Turinaar Pinnacles. These grand formations of rock dwarf everything else around, giving the feeling of a maze that you have to navigate your way through. I am sure it will be teeming with beasts. One thing I was taught is to always remember the positioning of the sun. The shadows cast will indicate direction.

I scour the lower lying rivers that slalom to the Coramine Sea. Striders and wild Reygyre call these areas home and are fairly easy to hunt.

My eyes fix upon a small pack of Reygyre trudging west in a small clearing. These beasts are similar to Featherkin in shape and size; however, they adopt more of a reddish hue within their fur, a very light hide that is easily pierced with the worst of arrows. A grey head and tail complete their unique look. They feel destined to be the first real test for my bow and Draygar himself.

Amandryr, Draygar's breed: a breed on the brink of extinction, develop an instinct to stalk, to strike first. Young cubs, however, up until a year or two of age are much more relaxed. The process of capturing one, the alpha protecting the young cubs, is first subdued by an experienced handler. It is considered by some to be a cruel act, but Argora herself believes cubs that are taken away have a much stronger chance of survival as a companion. A companion that will grow into a majestic beast and become one with their owners.

We are ready to strike. Draygar recognises my hand signal and begins to move through light vegetation toward the pack. My experience in watching my father instructs me that since there are three, I could kill one, Draygar will take one down and the last beast will flee in fear.

Nocking an arrow, I draw my bow. Draygar stares at me from within the opposing bushes, waiting for a command.

Fear grows inside me. After shaking my head, I aim again. Blackened ground grasps at my boots. My body, battered by a wind that shears through the Pinnacles. My name is whispered as a flash of a ghostly entity darts through my peripheral vision. My eyes shift to track it.

It's gone.

A grey sky descends as an ear-piercing cry rips through me. Huddling over on the ground, I clasp my head. A feeling that I'll fall into an abyss of shadow right below my feet drenches me, an inevitability that the ground will open up and swallow me entirely. Darkness rakes at my soul as I try to resist.

Gloom fades. Reality comes rushing back.

My eyes frantically glance around for answers. Breathing heavily, I turn at every angle, my mind racing to try to piece together an understanding.

Draygar returns to my side, sniffing me and our surroundings. An incessant growl plays for my ears. I find surety in only two things. The fortuitousness in having Draygar watching over me and that our prey is long gone.

Time is at a standstill as I try to comprehend the mysterious event. Strange feelings have crept up before, things beyond the realm of possibility: darkness enveloping the world, only to dissipate just as quickly as it strikes.

Draygar seems worried, his eyes leer back at me with confusion. The feeling is mutual. The inability to recall exactly what just happened frightens me.

We're here to hunt. The pack of Reygyre are still out there. Surely enough, they have left tracks which we can follow that lead to a nearby cave on the opposite side of the valley. There is a chilling, eerie feeling about this place. The mouth at the entrance beckons us in.

Draygar leads at my signal, entering the cave exuding extreme caution. We descend. Light erases itself from the surroundings.

A growing sensation of fear leads me to command Draygar to hold. But I don't. A rustle, then a howl catches my ear, the origin of which is not far ahead.

Light emits through large cracks overhead as sunlight seeps through. Moving cautiously into a large open cavern, my eyes find vines that drape down limestone walls that encompass the area. A faint but constant dripping of water adds an extra edge of uncertainty.

As we creep further inside, we nearly jump out of our skin at the sight of a large animal. A gore-drenched, wolf-like beast with claws of extraordinary length. Bloodshot eyes and orange fur as rough as a jagged rockface. Lying there as if in its den, it holds a

Reygyre within its jaws. Others are frozen in fear, their attempt at escape would be futile.

Reaching for my bow, I prepare myself for the unknown, but as I turn away, something isn't right. Draygar isn't by my side, he must have anticipated a command.

Frantically, I peer in every direction, but shadows plaster the walls. Finally, I notice a tail that disappears behind a rock opposite me.

A fiery head lifts, somewhat spooked, peering in Draygar's direction. Without a moment of hesitation, the beast leaps to its feet. Roaring with the fury of a thousand storms, it forces me to cover my ears. Powerful legs spring the beast forward and with one malevolent swipe, the remaining Reygyre are catapulted into the wall.

"Run!"

Draygar speeds out from behind cover, narrowly avoiding a slash. Hastily retreating toward the entrance of the cave, the beast gives chase. Adrenaline pumps through me, enough to fuel my escape all the way back to Turinfall. Death lurks as we hear thundering footfalls echo behind us. We run for our lives.

Fresh air and the warmth of daylight greet us once more, but it's nothing more than a brief reprieve.

All of a sudden, I stop. The foreign grip returns.

Rage takes over my body as I turn around to face the glaring black abyss of the cave. Draygar darts to my right, concealing himself within large bushes.

"Kill it … Kill. Your soul … demands it." Whispers of something unknown deep within my mind call to me.

I can't resist. With a face awash with anger and determination, my body prepares and the bow is drawn.

Suddenly, I feel full of ability as if something needs me to succeed.

The beast appears in the mouth. Sunlight brightens its already terrifying features. Jaws sink into its neck as Draygar leaps upon it. With one rabid movement, my companion is thrown to the ground a few paces in front of me, landing with a thud and a sob. An aggressive stance is assumed, the beast roars with bestial wrath.

"Kill … Kill … You are—" A beastly eye is pierced with an arrow. The beast's head snaps back before its body slumps to the ground.

The hold on my mind is released. Rage dissipates.

I am myself once more.

Draygar regathers his feet, stumbles toward me and lies down. Thankfully, he isn't injured.

I approach the slain beast with caution, it isn't breathing at all. A few prods at its rough hide, then I step back in case of a violent reaction. There is no response, the beast is dead.

How I am going to bear the weight of this huge animal and bring it home to Turinfall, I have no idea.

My efforts to drag it singlehandedly are futile, the beast is ridiculously heavy. Draygar sinks in his sharp teeth and we labour the corpse behind a large tree. We are a good hour from Turinfall and I don't want to leave the kill here.

I spend a moment pondering my encounter with the strange, unexplainable force. It was trying to tell me something, then cut off. This is not the first time, although I have no idea why it is happening to me. Thoughts of my childhood travels emerge once more. What happened before feels linked to those thoughts. It is growing stronger.

Mistral Grove lies to the south. There is a path that runs to the coastal town from Turinfall, it can't be too far. This kill cannot go to waste, it is too valuable. I know the land fairly well, or at least from what I've been told.

Historians visit Turinfall every so often, sharing their stories with the villagers. They tell of other civilisations within Arcura. Arcura, a region upon a greater island. Argora believes that knowledge becomes power and she encourages parents to send their children to the ceremonies when they visit.

The tales of Lilanthen, one of the favourites. The man described the city as a diamond in the peaks. Spires of crystal and gold shoot up amidst city walls and the entire domain shines brighter than the stars in the night sky. A warrior race with a kingdom of riches.

Skalgard, a settlement created entirely of stone, is tucked away within the hills on the Askaren Wasteland. Iron mines run deep and vast.

I have dreamt of visiting such places one day; however, the journey seems too far. It would take days with little navigation.

The path isn't far. We stumble upon the rough cobblestone trail sooner than I expect. The sun is starting to hide away to the west. My parents will begin to worry. But not as much as the thought of me becoming the next meal to a pack of rabid night prowlers.

The flicker of a dancing flame catches my attention: a lady upon a white steed which draws a cart. Unsettling creaks cry out with each rotation of its neglected wheels forcing Draygar to his feet immediately.

A woman's voice carries over the creaking. "Oh, hello there. What are you doing out here all by yourself? You never know what might be lurking around."

Relief rushes over my body. "I thought I might try my luck and here you are! I have a favour to ask of you."

The woman frowns, her eyes are fixed upon Draygar who isn't feeling hospitable. Then she makes out my impressive bow. "What do you ask? Seeking coin for that lovely bow of yours?

That could fetch quite a few."

I could never. "I am afraid not, I have slain a beast only a short way to the west. Would you help us with the task of transporting it to Turinfall?"

She lifts her head to the sky, then back to Draygar before piercing me with a questioning look. I can sense that she wishes to give her name, but her hesitation suggests caution, given the nature of what *we* slayed. "Very well. We don't have much time and Gelari must eat. Don't try anything, boy, I have weapons at the ready."

Without too much thought of her threat, we begin our return journey to the beast.

Gelari trots with elegance, they must have been riding together for years. Alongside its grey mane sits a sheathed sword with a hilt of gold and silver. That alone keeps me in check as she likely knows how to use it.

"Here!" Gelari stops in an instant and the woman gestures to me to hurry. Draygar and I drag the fire-orange furred corpse from behind the tree and out into the open.

The woman draws her sword with the precision of a veteran fighter. "You killed that thing?! How in all things mighty did you manage that!?"

I rack my brain for an answer. "Not easily. It was either us or it."

She gazes around uneasily, quickly sensing that something isn't right. "That is a Moltecern you have slain there, boy, I've heard stories of such fire-like branded beasts."

She strokes her jaw. "Quickly, there should be enough room by the back of the cart. Do not try to steal anything or it won't be the only thing to die here today!" A chuckle carves apart the air.

Draygar and I manoeuvre the beast behind the cart. "This beast weighs more than a mountain of iron. Care to lend a hand?"

She scoffs. "I am a woman of class. I will not touch that dirty thing."

I examine my surroundings for a fallen branch to use to lift the beast. The old ghostly tree that hid the Moltecern for quite some time has a few limbs still barely attached. Snapping one off with ease, I head back to the cart. Surprisingly, the limb is of hardwood, it must have rotted at the joint.

With all of my limited might, I push the beast onto the branch, just far enough so that Draygar can grab a hold of a leg. After countless attempts of pushing and pulling, we have the slain beast loaded. Our bodies, with energy no longer. The task is done.

Draygar and I are wheeled back to Turinfall as Gelari walks us home. I lie down before gazing at glistening stars as my body begins to recuperate. Our relaxing journey is frequently interrupted by Gelari's forceful exhales, brought about by the heavier burden the horse has to bear. The wheels of the cart creak loudly, straining with every turn.

Finally, the sound of crashing water fills the air and the light of a thousand torches chases away the darkness.

We are home.

As we approach Turinfall, Rangers stare inquisitively at the contents of the cart. A half-interested shrug from one's shoulders and once again they peer out into the wilderness. Rangers are posted on every entranceway to our village, Argora leaves nothing to chance.

Stopping in the central square, a crowd gathers quickly as Draygar and I drag the lifeless beast from the cart. It falls to the ground with a massive thud.

A voice full of surprise speaks up. "A Moltecern! Argora will hear of this at once!"

I am thrilled, yet terrified at the same time. *Are these beasts sacred?* That is not a conversation I wish to have with the huntsmaster.

"Arathyn!" My father rushes through the wall of bodies. "We were worried sick. Who is this woman you rode in with and what is that beast?!"

I feel as if I'm being beaten by every rule and tradition. "I killed this … Moltecern. It nearly took our lives and this kind woman offered to bring it back to the village."

It takes a lot to surprise my father but this does it.

"I'm glad you are alright. You killed this? It is bigger than the two of us bound together! What did you say it was? A Molte—"

"A Moltecern." The crisp voice of a woman interrupts as everyone in the village goes silent.

I spin around to see Argora herself, trimmed in an ivory-infused pristine leather jerkin and chausses draped in white bone. Earthy-brown eyes leer at me through a helmet made from the skull of a wolf-like beast under which jet-black hair flows down her back. She passes by me and crouches down to examine the corpse. I cannot help but notice a fine jet-black mahogany longbow littered with small skulls as ornaments resting upon her back.

"Arathyn, you say this beast was slain by yourself and your companion?" It feels like an interrogation rather than a conversation and every eye in the village is upon me, awaiting my reply.

I try to sound confident. "Indeed. We lured the beast out of hiding. Draygar dared to fight and my aim was true."

"These beasts do not know death, I have known many to fall to the Moltecern. Survivors of such an attack are extremely rare." Her statement echoes with a heavy heart, it strikes emotionally within.

A leather glove rests upon the Moltecern's head. "These beasts instill fear into the mightiest of men. Men who have seen glorious battle. They freeze in horror. Do you not, Arathyn? What makes you any different?"

I remain silent. I feel as if any answer will offend.

My hesitation prompts an immediate glance towards my companion. "Maybe within Draygar lies the answer?"

A shrilling whistle pierces the air before thunderous steps edge closer from beyond. An onyx beast appears in the firelight almost as big as the Moltecern itself, its yellow eyes gaze at Argora. Merciless white fangs protrude from its mouth. Everyone takes a step back. I know what is coming.

A whisper of elegance hits my ears. "Miratharl. Come to me."

That elegance is not mutual, however. "Summon your beast, Arathyn."

Fearing not to be disrespectful, I motion a terrified Draygar out into the open. Not only has he faced a Moltecern, surely Argora's choice companion is at least as deadly.

"Charge!" Miratharl lunges at Draygar, the latter only narrowly avoiding a rending swipe as he ducks under.

Draygar looks at me, expecting a command and I indicate with a forceful gesture. My beast darts around searching for an opportune moment to strike but the onyx beast stands firmly in control.

Draygar eventually pounces, only to be caught within drooling jaws and held. With one rapid lurch of its head, Miratharl hurls Draygar aside before finally coming to rest against a stack of lumber next to the carpenter's tent.

"Enough!" Argora's voice hits me like an arrow. "Raegyla, tend to Draygar's wounds immediately. This beast shall suffer no more."

My heart sinks, I have failed him. I know what this means.

She sees right through me. "Arathyn, as much as I wish to believe that you and your companion stood firm against this beast and slew it, I cannot fathom such an outcome. My dear beloved was taken by a Moltecern. Your companion, Draygar, although aggressive and loyal, does not have the power for what you preach."

Her words draw the interest of the gathering, inviting her to continue. "His name was Morathaen. We were pursuing a man who committed crimes against our people before we encountered one of these beasts. I could only watch in horror as he froze in fear before his body was ripped apart. I retreated, injuring the beast enough to escape. The only remnant that remained of him was this pendant."

Argora holds an onyx stone within a tight grasp. She is emotionally defeated. "So I pledged as Rule of Turinfall, such beasts were never to be hunted."

A pledge forgotten. Although I was the one being *hunted*.

The crowd disperses upon hearing the devastating recount of Morathaen's death. No one knew exactly what had happened to him until now. *Had I slain a beast that a man in such high regard could not?*

Only I know what happened.

Three

ARATHYN

A snap slices through the air as the tree falls, it has taken every ounce of my energy to hack through the hardwood. My heroic feat several days ago has led me here, they think I'm invincible. *Maybe it's my punishment.*

Arkryn, the village blacksmith, has gifted me an axe. It splits the wood with ease, the day's felling is done. I don't feel overworked. Draygar transporting lumber to and from the village is a massive help in that regard.

"Arathyn, my dear. You look parched!" My mother's eyes are staring at me from the confines of a Starberry bush. Bushes that provide silvery-white berries that give an instant boost of energy.

My mother worries about me too much, but the feeling is mutual. She hands me a flask and a few berries. The caressing feeling of cold water hits my mouth as I drink vigorously.

Dusk is settling beyond the horizon, warning us that it's time to gather our tools and head back to Turinfall. Our last supply of lumber is loaded.

Terariat and Delbura are my father's and mother's companions respectively, larger and stronger than Draygar. Beasts that are built for hauling, they relieve us of the burden of drawing the cart home.

Trained to wear a harness attached to a hardwood frame, they are very muscularly built. Muscular, sure. Behavioural? Rumours have it that you can tell of a person's maturity by their companion's behaviour. I believe that. Draygar and I are like twins born into completely different forms.

Our feet find Turinfall once more. We pass right by Argora's stead on our way to the central square. The fire-orange head of the slain Moltecern, looking like it could start a blaze, rests prominently on a post nearby. It towers above other ivory statues, stuffed and cured.

There is a large ceremony planned at sundown. A portion of the lumber we gathered earlier lies amassed in the firepit, ready to be set ablaze.

Butchers hastily portion meat. Poorer villagers look enamoured at what they're about to dine on.

Our final collection is offloaded into the storage yard. A yard bereft of space, occupied with an abundance of wood.

Rangers ensure we stay productive. There is almost never a time when resources at hand are scarce, large amounts of which are traded with neighbouring settlements in return for iron, stone and coin.

Iron. A luxury we have to pay through the teeth for.

A bustling Ranger approaches. "Arathyn. Argora has sent word for you to visit her at once. You must leave your companion here. Come with me."

Immediately, I dust myself off. My parents wave goodbye with nothing more than worried looks on their faces.

Strolling through Argora's courtyard, passing by the numerous statues, excitement is an afterthought knowing that she refuses to accept my story. I grow anxious, but I do my best to hide it.

"Argora waits inside, Arathyn."

A huge mahogany door stands before me, surely worth more than my entire family's living quarters. The handle of which, a jewel-encrusted skull, turns effortlessly as I grasp it. The layout within is a secret to many, no doubt. The beautiful scent of Thistle Reed hits me immediately. It feels as if I'm on the shores of the lake once more. A crisp, floral essence with hints of fresh rain eases my mind. My worries retreat.

Under firelight, cast from burning braziers, sits furniture of the highest quality. Majestic bows and numerous skulls of all shapes and sizes line the walls. The interior is mesmerising, it wouldn't be out of place in a palace.

Hesitating a moment, I feel that I don't possess the significance to be here. Argora sits upon a granite bench, hunched over before a warm, crackling fire.

"Arathyn, do not be alarmed." Her calm voice subdues what is left of my worries.

"I do not believe the events that you speak of; however, the people believe in you and as a tribe we must celebrate such an achievement. After my betrothed had fallen, there wasn't much to believe in; I had lost all hope. Your victory will help to restore that anew."

Argora motions for me to approach her. "Come, Arathyn. I have something for you."

Slowly walking over, I notice Miratharl fast asleep in his bed of silk and feathers.

"Turn around please." The smooth texture of cut gemstone falls upon my skin as Argora rests a beautiful piece of onyx jewellery around my neck. Embedded with quartz and citrine, it is marvellous.

It's almost as if her emotional burden lifts as it leaves her hands. "Wear this wherever you may travel. Morathaen wore this pendant, it was all that remained of him. I cannot bear the pain of keeping it any longer. He instilled hope into others, Arathyn.

Maybe you can too."

I have to pinch myself. This is far from what I expected. "Thank you."

It doesn't end there. "I have one more gift for you. However, you must return home."

A Ranger posted outside her door escorts me out. A heroic feeling grips my body, although I am not worthy. My parents are anxiously waiting outside and upon first sight, my mother gasps in disbelief. "Oh, Arathyn. I believe that was Morathaen's pendant. What an honour! My hero."

"I must return home. Argora has another gift for me." My mother's jaw drops further.

As I run back uphill with Draygar, people are beginning to make their way to the ceremony, turning their heads as I pass by.

Returning so quickly, I have to rest for a moment to gather my breath. I whip away the shawl that covers the entrance. My eyes rest upon a crimson fur-hide coat, ornamented with the teeth and trimmed claws of a Moltecern. A coat made from that very beast.

I am in disbelief. Not only has Argora herself donned me with her beloved's pendant, she has gifted me one of the finest garments I have ever seen. Within moments, my body is wrapped perfectly. The coat initially feels quite cool to the touch before a deep feeling of warmth takes over.

He instilled hope into others, Arathyn. Maybe you can too. It all begins to make sense.

Draygar looks up at me with eyes like a peasant seeking acceptance, a look I have never witnessed before. I know I am going to arrive to a grand reception. Argora said so herself, that the people believe in me.

Her disapproval of the situation with the Moltecern still reserves a place in my thoughts. This ceremony is just a façade over a hidden truth.

Upon opening the chest, I gather my bow. My want to be perceived as a hero has me gathering everything of importance.

Anxiety finds a way past my pride. I am just a young man of a timid nature who just takes every day in his stride. The whole situation is just so overwhelming.

Exiting through the shawl, I begin the return journey to the central square. I lock my anxiety away. Looking back at Draygar, there is nothing but excitement in his eyes.

As I crest the hill, torches flare up under a gust of wind. Huts are swallowed in a vortex of shadow. Out of the void appears a rift, depicting a glimpse of the monastery seen years ago. Whispers grow louder as the vision lingers before my eyes. Growls and roars join in chorus right before the rift snaps shut.

The blaze retreats. The vortex clears. Turinfall appears under torchlight once more.

Resting momentarily with my body forced into submission, my head turns in every direction to make sure it is over.

Three villagers on the opposite side of the river are standing perplexed with gaping mouths. One is a young child. Terror forces their retreat.

Argora will certainly hear of this. *What did they see?*

Guilt washes over me. Rising to my feet, I make my way down as if nothing had happened. *Ignorance is bliss.* My focus remains locked on the events that will unfold on the most glorious of nights.

The people believe in you. Not those.

I become the focus of a few prying eyes as I press on. The river turns, as does my mood, to one of satisfaction. Drinks are raised. Cheers of approval ring out.

Young children tug at my coattails, almost rendering me immobile. However, I manage to continue my stride.

My father is full of pride as he approaches. A thumping hand crashes down upon my shoulder. "This is for you, my son. Revel in what is to come."

A massive bonfire explodes into flame as a torch strikes the doused wood. Small braziers around the square dwindle into nothing more than a dying flame in comparison. My mother hands me a flagon of mead.

Dark thoughts re-emerge. My bout of insanity. The three witnesses are nowhere to be seen. It appears as if everyone has now gathered. Bodies that sit upon a large ring of rocks that encircle the firepit.

Song and dance erupt around the bonfire. Teeth rend and tear at the delicacy of the Moltecern's meat. I seek out conversation with a few others nearby, burying my thoughts in the process.

A scream disturbs the aura of excitement as a lean figure appears, pushing through the crowd. "I have seen the end! Darkness will consume us all!"

The Rangers grab the man awash with anguish, pulling him aside. Celebrations shift into distress. I recognise the horrified man, he is one of the three.

"Him. Him. Take him!" A finger points directly at me. "I saw it all. The madness! Utter madness! My family is sick. My child is frozen in fear!"

My father comes to my defence before I can even fathom what is happening. "This is my son, Arathyn. Are you deluded?! How dare you insult one of my own!"

Some villagers cheer and echo my father's words. I say nothing as two Rangers hold onto the man.

"Silence!" It's Nelathryn, Argora's High Ranger, the head of enforcement throughout Turinfall. His eyes narrow with a frown to match. "This is a time for celebration."

"We witnessed it!" The man is adamant and rightly so.

Nelathryn stares down at the man – "Who's 'we'?" – before turning to the two Rangers.

Time stands still as I anxiously wait.

"Argora will decide on matters." Nelathryn walks directly to her quarters. My heart sinks deeper than a stone in the sea.

Argora appears in her doorway, fully draped in leather attire. She must have been planning on gracing the audience. Nelathryn walks back toward us in her company. Words are exchanged, I feel as if a council is imminent.

"I see it fits you well, Arathyn. Quite a sight to behold." All I can manage is a wry smile.

Her eyes pick out the complainant. "What is your name, troubled one?" Her voice somehow seems to calm the situation.

"My name is Sevoryn, milady. My family is cursed!"

Argora's eyes flick to me briefly. "What did you see, Sevoryn?"

His eyes turn on me with a look of pure terror. "I saw him fighting with himself. Dread washed over us all. His companion was aggressive toward him. He didn't seem afraid, but … possessed."

Possessed. The word resonates with a thought Argora seems to have in her mind. "You say he showed no fear?"

"No, milady. Full of anger. Out of control. Just laying eyes on him has haunted my youngest. She is sick and with her mother. We had only a short rest before we awoke from night—"

My father interrupts. "This is preposterous. How can you believe any of this!"

Argora shoots my father a glare. "Silence, Relgyn!"

It takes a lot to silence my father, but that does it. Her words cast an icy chill over her people, she has broken her usual character. My interrogation will begin shortly. What Sevoryn is saying must be true.

Am I that volatile?

Argora's gaze burrows right into my brain. "Arathyn, are the words of Sevoryn true?"

All of my thoughts are fixed on the young girl and I can't escape them quickly enough to not arouse suspicion that I know about it. As my words fail to coalesce, the mood changes dramatically. Everyone retreats.

"I don't know what happened." I'm drenched in guilt.

My father looks at me with puzzled eyes. "You are not evil, my boy. I will not believe that you are cursed!"

I can only return a heartfelt glance, assuring my father that his concern is appreciated. For the first time, Argora is completely lost for words as she looks around in dismay.

The moment of silence is interrupted as a woman as pale as snow strolls into the square.

"Ciela, my dear. You should be resting!" Sevoryn's words fall on deaf ears, without even a hint of acknowledgment. Ciela continues to walk unabated, her eyes glazing over.

"Ciela!" Sevoryn's face wears a look of complete terror. Once again, his shout receives no answer.

"No!" Screams escape his mouth as she jumps right into the blazing bonfire like a moth to a flame. Rangers run to her aid, but it is too late. A burst of flame engulfs her white dress. Agonising screams ring out as she tries to shake the flames that lash at her body.

My eyes cannot bear to look, so I redirect them away until the screams subside. Her corpse, now a smouldering pile of flesh within the raging bonfire, is nothing but further evidence of my plight. The smell alone draws cries as people turn and run.

"That boy killed my beloved! He is evil. He is death!"

Before one more word is spoken, a dark figure shoots upward from the blaze. It barrels toward me before fading right before my very eyes.

I stand defeated.

Argora orders her Rangers to extinguish the blaze. "Release Sevoryn at once! Have him return to his child. Seek Raegyla in the hope to have this demonic taint purged from their bodies! Arathyn, take that scourge with you and never return! You are hereby banished from Turinfall!"

My rage-fuelled father steps in front of me. "You will not banish my son from our home!" He rips the bow from my back and draws an arrow. The Rangers in turn draw their weapons. Bows are drawn in one synchronised movement.

Argora regains control of the situation with a look of distaste. "Relgyn, you would challenge my order?"

"I would rather die than have my son cast away!"

"No one will leave with Arathyn, except for that beast of his. I will not risk another soul. Not you, nor his mother. He will never harm us again." Argora's perception of me has transformed from one of admiration to that of hate.

My efforts in conjuring up a few words are drowned out by my father's bolstering voice. "I will leave with my family, that I assure you." He refuses to stand down. My mother is a grovelling mess, finding comfort in the arms of a few women.

Relgyn, you do know what an act of defiance means?" Argora's words turn concerned, she cannot go against tradition.

"I do." My father stands determined. Our cultural law will have him fight for our freedom. Turin rule is not swayed lightly. Most submit.

"You are hereby summoned. Please take a moment, we will make the preparations."

Hostility recedes as Rangers lower their bows. Argora departs with her enforcement close behind. "Watch them. Be sure they do not escape."

Nelathryn and his senior Rangers escort onlookers away as my mother is ushered toward us. We are surrounded by an impassable force.

"Relgyn! Arathyn! I will not lose you! I will not be bereft of my family!" My mother is soaked in sorrow as she holds me in her arms.

My father oozes confidence. "Do not worry. I will be victorious and we will leave this forsaken place for good!"

Words escape my mouth as a tear runs down my face. "I love you both."

Nelathryn will be my father's adversary. His companion is no doubt savage given its master's demeanour. A Ranger's beast is a very rare sight, almost secret. Their presence is only requested during pressing matters.

Like this one.

"Escort Relgyn to his living quarters, his companion must be present."

Nelathryn's order is promptly followed. The majority of the Rangers follow my father. Time stands still as I anxiously await his return before he emerges with Terariat.

The moment of destiny sets in as the Rangers reform into two parallel lines leading in the direction of the courtyard.

"Move!" Nelathryn ushers us forward like prisoners. His rude nature has me imagining his demise.

An orange hue lights up the courtyard brightly. Shadows dance across the grounds in flickering firelight. Argora, now dressed in her battle attire, sits above her home on a balcony overlooking the field of battle.

"Relgyn!" Her commanding voice shoots over the grounds, sounding more sincere from an elevated position. "Do you still wish to challenge my order?"

"There is nothing that will stand in the way of my family!" My father is full of confidence, signalling his intent.

"Very well, take your position." Argora gestures toward a vacated spot. My father and Terariat are escorted over to the western side. My mother weeps as her hand evades his touch.

"Do not worry, my dear." The last words my father may speak do not seem to have a calming effect.

"Nelathryn, take your position."

Nelathryn walks stubbornly over to the opposite side with a glaring smile on his face. Whistling a long tune, a beast prowls toward him with thick, black fur. Gilt-edged claws and fangs that reach halfway down its legs signify a killing machine. Down its back are not feathers, but scales of solid bone that trace to the extremity of its tail. It stands ready.

I've heard stories that Rangers have to prove themselves able to be protectors by taming much more vicious beasts in the wild as their companions.

I wish it killed him then.

"Relgyn. If you are victorious, your family will be granted safe passage out of Turinfall. If you are not, then your son will be banished and your beloved, a widow. Do you accept these terms?"

My father's determined eyes bounce between us, Argora and Nelathryn. The latter, still beaming with confidence. "I accept these terms."

"Very well. Arm Relgyn. Rangers, take up your positions!"

My wrists and my mother's are bound tightly. The trial is about to commence. My confiscated bow and quiver find the hands of my father. The formation is set. The perimeter is established.

Nelathryn's arrogance is the first impression. "Relgyn, I have fought the strongest of men and beasts. You are but a mere, simple test. You may proceed first!"

Argora studies the battlefield before her voice wishes forth the inevitable. "Begin!"

"The only place you will visit is death, along with that boy of—"

Nelathryn is interrupted as my father quickly fires an arrow. Unfortunately, it narrowly misses.

"Oh, Garorla." Nelathryn's gaze turns towards his menacing beast. Within an instant, his companion roars up before bone-hardened scales form a shield in front of its master. Deflecting off its armour, a second arrow embeds into a wooden post.

"Well well. Now prepare to die!" Nelathryn's arrogance shifts into determination.

Garorla lunges forward, curling up into a ball of solid scale mid-air before landing in an aggressive stride. A remarkable action. However, the growing realisation that this beast may kill my father purges my admiration. Terariat stands before my father, digging in its claws.

"Steady …" Never have I seen my father so focused.

With careful calculation, they part, jumping aside moments before Garorla arrives. The palisade behind feels the wrath of the onyx beast. Garorla finds its feet instantly before spinning around, bellowing a roar that pierces the night sky.

Nelathryn laughs. "Oh, you didn't want to do that!"

There is hesitation in Garorla's steps. The beast examines Terariat as it returns to his master's side. A caution not shown earlier.

"Do not retreat! Destroy them!" Nelathryn grows frustrated.

My father draws the bow once more before aiming at the beast, eyeing up a weak spot in Garorla's armour. Nelathryn mirrors but with two arrows.

Garorla speeds off in an assault, only for Terariat to intercept. My father's companion sinks its jaws into the beast's head.

It is unlike my father to be distracted, but his lapse in concentration is detrimental. Turning back to the High Ranger, he looses the bow before only having enough time to lift his arm to block his Nelathryn's arrows. One pierces his forearm, the other penetrates his lower body. But it's not in vain. Nelathryn also takes a direct hit, his shoulder pierced. Cries of pain ring out as my father takes a knee to brace his weakened body.

"Relgyn!" Emotions overcome my mother. Comfort is all I can give with the belief that Father will not give up.

Nelathryn's arm is disabled; however, he manages to draw a short blade with the other. His eyes don't leave my father for one second as he walks across the arena. With the beasts preoccupied with each other, this is now man-to-man.

Nelathryn edges closer, clutching at his shoulder. Arrogance no longer, only hatred.

"Relgyn, will you just give in? If you surrender, your beloved may leave with Arathyn. But you will not!" Argora remains unmoved, it is likely just a taunt. A look of disappointment is cast toward her High Ranger at the attempt at her rules.

My father doesn't give him the satisfaction. His head hangs low. Muttering under his breath, he laughs at the proposition.

Nelathryn spits. "You would disrespect me?!"

My father lifts his head. "I will kill you."

Garorla finds a second wind and lunges at my father. Terariat's attempt to intercept misses, jarring its fangs on scales. My father's lower leg is the target of menacing fangs, but pain does not stop him. Like a veteran warrior, he does not show weakness.

Terariat sprints around, drawing its claws before pummelling them between the scales on Garorla's back. Both beasts rear up in a show of dominance as Garorla, in turn, whips its stone-edged tail into Terariat's head. My father's companion is knocked to the ground, its remaining strength all but beaten away.

Garorla withdraws its fangs from my father's leg, sensing an opportunity to finally best Terariat. But as it shifts its head towards the beaten-down beast, my father grabs a loose arrow from the earth before piercing Garorla's skull with a forceful thrust.

"No!" Nelathryn screams as he finally stumbles up to my father before lifting his head so their eyes may meet.

"You! My poor Garorla. Such ferocity in battle. You have destroyed half of my being. Now, let the other half destroy you!"

Terariat whimpers. Beaten, clinging to life. There is nothing the beast can do to aid its master. Nelathryn plunges a dagger into the chest of my father. My mother faints in my arms. Memories take over.

He worked so hard to provide for us. He mentored me. Taught me everything I know and was a loving partner to my mother. Rousing on Draygar when my beast was too rough.

Tears roll down my face as memories of my childhood flash by. *What would my life look like without him?* I wish for nothing other than the darkness to come once more and swallow me whole.

Boastfully, he walks away from my father's body before a faint murmur of laughter catches in the air. Nelathryn freezes solid.

"Should … have finished … the job … Fool." Within the excessive panting come words that force Nelathryn into desperation.

The High Ranger spins around in a crazed rage only to be struck through the heart with an arrow. He falls to his knees before crashing to the ground.

Breaking free from my captor, I run over to my father as blood trails from his mouth. I know we still have one final moment to share. "I will never forget that you gave your life for me. I love you, Father. I promise to always be the strong man you have raised me to be!"

He grabs my arm. "Shhh … Arathyn. Of that … there is … no doubt …" Wishing I could make out the detail on his face, tears cloud my vision.

"Here … have this bracelet … It was my … Father's … Be strong, my … Son …" One last embrace is shared before his grip on my arm releases.

I close my father's eyes.

"Arathyn. Your father was victorious. You should be proud. However, we will have no evil here. I will give you the choice. You may leave with or without your mother. Respectfully, I will give you the night to mourn and come to a decision by sunrise. Raegyla will tend to your mother during the night."

My swollen eyes peer up at Argora. "Look after her, please."

All I receive is a nod and that's enough. "You must rest outside Turinfall until dawn. Return Arathyn's belongings and his companion. We will not have a curse here."

As I am escorted out of Turinfall alongside Draygar, I take in one last sight of glistening waterfalls. The picturesque sunset above the Feygoran Mountains.

My mother will be looked after and cared for, beyond what I could ever offer myself. The thought of never seeing her again tears me up inside. I slip my father's bracelet over my wrist, feeling a sense of his presence.

Turinfall. My home. Albeit, no longer. It will remain true to my heart.

Forever, I will long to return here one day. I decide not to return at sunrise.

Four

VEXXYRA

Cool water presses against my skin, enveloping my body. *I can't believe I jumped.* My eyes stare back once I surface, finding the image of my friends standing atop the cliff. Even from this distance, I can make out the sight of Mira's jaw nearly at her feet.

Luckily, I can swim. Then come the waves from Oran's plunging body. *I need to make it back to the beach first.* I can't have him boasting. Bulky arms push through the water with ease, he's gaining. Wet sand grips at my toes. I'm drenched, but I'm back. *Of course, the Coramine Gales would whip up now.*

A fur rug is thrown over my body as I hear Mira's voice, "Are you crazy!" *Possibly.*

Peer pressure is horrible. Oran welcomes my eyes from time to time, but the feeling that I need to impress him is daunting. Mira is keen on him too, I just wish he were more mature.

A scream cries out before it is muffled by the sea. It's Arix. Water encapsulates my body once more as we rush to his aid. Oran dives under as we reach his location. Arix hasn't surfaced. *Oh god, I hope we're in the right place.*

After what seems like an eternity, a head surfaces, followed by an arm around an upper body. *Lucky.* Arix's eyes flutter. Teeth clenched on his lip. Thankfully, he has a light frame. *I wouldn't want to be pulling Oran's body through the waves.*

Adrenaline fuels our return.

"It's my leg … It's broken …"

I gulp. It certainly is. Bone as pale as his father's horse splits through skin. My brain gets to work. *Vines and sticks. Why do we have to be at the damn mine?*

My pack! The cloth-woven satchel beckons on the nearby rock shelf. I'm there before my legs catch up. *Marshvine! Who would've thought stringing up a new balcony for my mother's parlour would prove so beneficial?*

Driftwood. Enough for the task, lies scarcely about the shore.

"If you can clench your teeth any harder, now is the time." Fearful eyes peer back, but I need to straighten it.

The sound is enough to make Mira vomit. Screams through closed lips don't make me hesitate. *At least it's in a better place.* Lining the wood down both sides of his ravaged leg, Oran holds it tight as I bind the Marshvine around itself and hopefully what will keep his leg steady. *It's the best I can do with what I have.*

Hoofs thunder toward us. "What are you doing to him!?" It's Vilriyan, Arix's father.

"Saving him from further pain." Vilriyan's eyes peer through me as if I'm invisible before observing his son. A look lingers long enough as if he's deciding to reprimand us. Emotion may as well stay on the moon.

"In the carriage. Now!" His authoritative voice carries so much weight that we're almost spared from doing the lifting.

No one speaks as we begin our return to Coradal. The carriage suddenly stops. "Your ignorance will not go untold! My son's disability is on your heads." Sentries are the target of Vilriyan's wrath.

A wrath that doesn't sway. "Move along!"

A sign, freshly painted, draws my hazel eyes: "Mine Collapse.

Do Not Enter!" The sign belongs to Deepsalt Mine No. 2, which has been closed for as long as I can remember, looks recently replaced.

My thoughts quickly shift to Arix, then my eyes follow. The brace is holding, as is his face that holds a little more comfort. Oran is staring at me, my drenched clothes as if his eyes want to remove them. I'm not going to give him the satisfaction. *I just wish he were more mature.*

Coradal lingers in the distance. A town spread throughout with neat wooden homes and stores. Gulls circle overhead. It's mid-morning. Bodies bustle about, trying not to be flattened by horse-drawn carts. *I need to get out of these clothes.*

The carriage stops at the door of the physician, Quincy Faraday. His figure, dressed in a white coat, strolls outside. A saw in one hand, an axe in the other, below a gleaming smile. "Two limbs for the price of one!"

Arix dies inside momentarily before a laugh injects a heartbeat into his defeated body. "Do not worry, boy. I'm just after the one." *Is that any better?*

Quincy is very likeable. I have learnt much from his tutelage. If it weren't for him, Arix's leg would be much worse. With our help, Arix's limp body is escorted inside, awaiting its fate.

The tailoring parlour. My mother is the expert on fashion. Honestly, I don't care what I look like. Clothes like glue, my body half-drowned in garments that hold water like a prisoner.

White stone steps leading up to its entrance are unmistakable.

My mother, Harriet, spots me immediately. "Dear me! What have you been up to?"

I'd answer, but she's already rifling through a rack of beautiful dresses. *She knows.* Visits to the beach at the Deepsalt Mines are frequent enough.

Brown eyes examine me further. I hold their gaze before slightly shifting my own, making out her beautiful black curls that line her head perfectly.

"Here. You can't have yourself looking like you've been pulled from the well." My mother hands me a blue homespun dress.

It does look amazing. But I press my lips. "Mother. This is far too fashionable to wear on the streets. I will not get two steps before someone is grovelling at my feet."

"Oh, please. You need a man. I married young."

I'm twenty.

The garment fits me like a glove, making out all my features. No longer am I cold, but bathed in the warmth of wool.

A hand briefly covers my mother's mouth, an expression of jealousy likely hiding behind. "Oh. My girl. You look beautiful."

"Thank you, Mother." An embrace as warm as my dress is shared.

An expression of jealousy. Mira's jaw nearly hits the floor again. "Vexx! You look stunning!" *If these walls let sound escape, I'd have Oran lined up on the steps already.*

Waves swell before crashing on the eastern beach. The Coramine Sea, vast beyond. A beverage is offered as Mira sits beside me on a wooden bench. "The finest."

A cup of water. Mira's company is a breath of fresh air. She lets me escape my thoughts. Our toes play in fine sand beyond the furthest reach of grass.

Reality hits. Tomorrow is one of the most important days of my life. I'm reserved and she notices it. "Shall we play with fire?"

"Absolutely."

A small chest is unloaded nearby. Reagents and tinctures fall to the ground. Flint and steel find Mira's hands followed by a coil of Marshvine. "Ready?"

My eyes narrow. Then, I laugh. "That's Marshvine! Why do you think houses are made with such?"

"Oh. My foolish hands." Mira sifts through the spilled contents once more. "Ah ha." Drapeweed. *Perfect.*

A weed with an extraordinary rate of growth ignites. Flames travel up its stem with ease before finding the yellow bloom at the tip. It fizzles and cracks before exploding in sparks that light up Mira's face.

"Pass me one!" Another Drapeweed finds my grip. A vial with Crimsonbloom mixture catches my eye. "Your eyes will not forget this!"

The yellow bloom is doused red. A flame ignites before the bloom burns. Flames turn a deep red until the mixture in its entirety is consumed. *Pop.*

We're left alone. Everyone is used to our crazy antics.

"That's cute." It's Oran. My body is heaved from the ground and I smile.

My thoughts shift to the stricken. "Is Arix okay?"

His sarcastic tone answers. "Well, he gets to keep his leg. I guess that counts."

Mira rushes off; perhaps she forgot. *I did.* The wonders of alchemy can drive out all rational thought.

My body is jerked around to face his muscle-ridden body. Oran's eyes run over my body before he leans in to kiss me. I turn my cheek which feels the heavy pressing of his lips. Matters beckon that are of far more importance. An apothecary, I may just be one tomorrow. There is so much studying to do, so many words to prepare.

"We must wait."

Five

VEXXYRA

I sit and stare out into the ocean, sand curled up between my toes. My excitement is hard to contain. Coradal rarely advertises for an apothecary understudy. But here I am, moments away from possibly becoming one.

I run the names of every herb and root I can imagine through my gridlocked mind. I want to impress them. I *need* to impress them.

"Vexx." It's Mira. Hours were spent this morning, quizzing me on the many different reactions and tinctures one could make.

She takes in my demeanour. "You're not worried, are you?"

"No. Overenthusiastic, I guess." I pull my hands through my long brown hair and get to my feet. "I was born for this."

The bell tolls and one of our emissaries begins to gather up the candidates. I am selected first and I can't help but blush. My tall, somewhat muscular body strides over and I take my place in front of the beautiful hall. I have my father to thank for my build, his broad-shouldered ego mirrors his physique.

My eyes peer up at the large sign atop:

Coradal Apothecary's Guild

The line is growing, and with that is my chance of failure. They only ever take one. The last was five years ago, just after my fifteenth birthday. Not much of a present, I know.

The old wooden doors part and I need to wish my feet back to stop them from moving out of sheer excitement.

"Vexxyra Laybrook." I nod.

I stride through the doorway, and immediately I'm hit by the sweet scent of Azurebloom. Pots and pots of it, like jars of sapphires.

"Ah. The first. Don't be too cocky now." An old, withered man forces out words under considerable effort. Maybe this is why they are looking for a new understudy, he looks like death is waiting for him. I abruptly redirect my thoughts.

A woman sits beside him, the one they chose last time. I do my best to hide my jealousy.

She gestures toward the table they're sitting at. "Tell me. What are you looking at?"

"Coradal Root. Azurebloom. Starberries. Thistlereed. In that order." She grows a look of interest, then her eyes narrow, glancing toward another table to her left.

"Seasnap. Silverwisp. Eldenmoss. Duskwart and ... a pitcher of water."

The old man chuckles, then coughs heavily. "Maybe you could cure my sickness, young one."

"It would be an honour to try." I try to sound remarkable, but the truth is, he looks terminal.

"That will be all. Thank you." I am dismissed by the woman. I'm burgeoning with knowledge I want to bestow upon them but I think better of it.

Hours pass and Mira knows it's the only thing on my mind. She offers me a beverage which I drain too quickly.

"Calm down, there is no way you didn't impress them." She scowls at my actions.

Worry creeps in. "Was I too much for them?"

"There isn't a single person in this village with your knowledge.

You said last time that you wouldn't miss out again."

She's right, there isn't.

Clouds begin to roll in from the Coramine sea. Drops of rain begin to fall upon my homespun dress before my name is called once more and I nearly jump from my seat like a frog.

"It's yours to take. I've been rooting for you." The emissary whispers in my ear and I grin.

Entering the hall once more, I hide the smile, not wanting to look too confident.

There are four of us.

"The four of you have been selected to progress but as you know, there can only be one. I don't need to tell you how much renown you will gain with this position. Coradal's apothecaries are known all over Arcura." Great. That is all I needed to hear to cast a little more doubt upon my mind.

The other three are all men of different ages. I know Renfry, he must only be fourteen or fifteen and I have seen him dabbling around in medicine here and there. The other two are much, much older. One is sporting grey patches of hair and the other looks very confident with numerous glass vials upon his belt.

"You may call me Sophia. I will be testing you this afternoon." Now that we are on name-based terms, I feel closer to my goal.

"Anders Willoughby. Make a brace from these," Sophia says, gesturing toward a bundle of Silverwisp on the table.

"Braces are made by physicians." I raise an eyebrow at the audacity of his statement and Sophia notices. She presses her lips. Eyes fire back at Anders, looking displeased.

"Here we don't just make remedies and the like. One would expect us to know how to treat people with ailments."

"Very well." Anders looks confident, but it's a trap. I look around, there is no sight of chain-linked gloves or any protective apparel. He walks forward and begins to reach for the thin, reedy strands and I can see the look on Sophia's face. She glances at me briefly again.

He clasps his hand around the bundle and I wince. He is going to deserve this for his former statement. He exasperates heavily and withdraws his hand immediately, you may as well grab a sword by its blade. Blood trickles down his arm from several cuts on his palm before he wipes it on his linen shirt.

His eyes leer as sharply as the strands. "You tricked me!"

"I cannot allow an understudy to not know of the dangers most reagents possess."

A guard storms in. "Is everything alright, Miss Sophia?"

"He was just leaving." Sophia's look is stern. Anders returns a look of disdain and hurries outside.

I gulp, then focus.

"Forgive the interruption. May I have your attention please?" Sophia redirects us back to the matter at hand as the guard follows Anders out.

"Renfry Holsworthy. Azurebloom. Name its two uses." Oh, how I wish I was asked that.

"Burn treatment and water purification." He replies with such confidence for a young man, I may just have a challenge after all.

"Excellent."

"Gordon Higginbotham. Coradal Root grows in three places. Where?" He hesitates like he only knows two and you can see him racking his brain.

"The Plantation. Deepsalt Mine. And ... and ... the Hearthweed Farm?" I feel the disappointment within him, he is so close.

"Thank you, Gordon. I admire that you know two of those. Hearthweed Farm is in fact ... well, Hearthweed. The Living Grotto is the third."

Indeed.

"Thank you for the chance, Miss Sophia. Good luck to you both." I smile and it is refreshing to hear someone with such grace. He proudly walks out into the rain.

Renfry already answered correctly, so now I have no choice but to do the same. Upon looking over at him, he smiles with such juvenile joy.

"Vexxyra Laybrook." Her eyes narrow as if she is about to throw down a gauntlet of a question.

"Ghost's Grip. How is it collected?" Renfry looks over at me, I can tell he has no idea.

I actually need a moment to place it, I have only seen it once or twice before. It grows at night behind the stone sentry towers. "Cotton or silk. Anything slightly rough will make it crumble, unusable. It grows extremely fast. Also, it must be picked at night or the sunlight destroys it."

Both of the apothecaries' eyebrows are raised. "No one has answered that correctly before, let alone know that."

Renfry swipes his arm before him and clicks, he thought he had it. However, the look on his face is one of admiration.

"Miss Sophia, may I concede? Vexxyra deserves this." My surprise almost makes me fall over.

"And you don't?" Sophia replies.

"I do. There is absolutely no way I knew that question and she has been after this for as long as I can remember. I will win next time."

"You may concede." The rush of excitement fills me with so much adrenaline that I nearly knock Renfry over as I hug him.

"Thank you, Renfry. I will take you with me when I forage. If you would allow, Sophia?"

"Of course. How can I not?"

I do feel a sense of guilt, but Renfry is so humble. He didn't deserve to be beaten, maybe that is why he conceded. Also, I didn't want to be the one who did that to him.

"Vexxyra Laybrook, understudy to the Coradal Apothecary's Guild. My name is Leronas Braithwaite and, of course, you have met my granddaughter Sophia. Congratulations on your appointment, please sign—" The heavy cough returns, forcing Sophia to comfort him. "Sign your name here, please."

I take the fine-inked quill from his hand and sign my name, which I haven't done before. It just looks like a mess.

Sophia's sternness evaporates. "Please report at sunrise tomorrow. I'd love to know how much knowledge you already possess."

"Thank you." We share a smile and then I'm out the door.

Finally, after all of these years.

Lines and lines of mounded dirt lay before me. I've visited here before, but not one of duty. The Coradal Root Plantation is vast, teeming with herbs and roots alike. I place my basket upon the cold earth and begin to delicately cut away at rough twisted roots that congeal at the slice of my blade.

It doesn't take long at all before I'm hauling back a full basket. It's only an hour's walk back to our oceanside home.

"Stop right there!" My body freezes as a raggedy voice reaches my ears. Three men dressed in rough leather attire walk toward me as I find the courage to turn around.

"Hand it over."

Thieves. On my first day. I can't fail my first task.

A blade unsheathes. "Did you hear me!"

"I did." Rather than focusing on the matter before me, my thoughts are directed at why the sentries didn't see them coming. These fields are patrolled night and day.

"Well, hand it over!" Another speaks up. "Sammy, should I take a precious finger off her hand?"

My father is tilling the fields nearby. That thought alone has my feet in a flurry. Bounding into stride, they chase like a pack of rabid dogs.

"Hey! Come back here!" No thought is given to their threat. I'm still focused on the lack of enforcement as they continue to chase.

Roots begin to fall from the basket as I reach unfavourable terrain. In the distance, I can make out the unmistakable barn of Hearthweed Farm.

My legs begin to tire. I'm no slouch, I can run. Extremely desperate, the thieves reach the building only a moment later.

"I'm going to kill you, Miss." There is no one here, the barn is empty. *A trap.* The only exit is behind the thieves who are staring me down.

"Kill her and torch the barn. Coradal needs to pay for their ignorance."

Tears begin to form. The best day of my life, followed by my worst. Ambition is going to lead to my death.

But there, in the large open doorway, my father stands heroic, wielding nothing but a pitchfork and a look of pure anger.

Bewilderment flashes across every face before bursting into synchronised laughter. "What's your name? So I can tell the others how ridiculous your attempt was."

"My *attempt?*" My father is completely unfazed.

Sammy remains confident. "We will kill you first. Then get the girl."

"Vorathen Laybrook. And I'll have you know I intend to write my name on your tombstones when I bury you all in this very barn." *This man is definitely my father.*

"Is that so?" Sammy is full of intrigue.

"Oh, hurry up. I have tilling to do."

A crazed rage boils inside them, they charge. Cutting off their joint advance, the barn door is hastily ripped ajar. My father is as bulky as he is courageous and these men are nothing more than malnourished pillagers.

A strike is easily deflected upon the tines of the pitchfork before one of the thieves finds himself forced to the ground by a heavy bash. Swift strikes from a heavily-laced boot crash down upon his leg, forcing anguished cries.

A keen slash slices my father's arm, catching nothing but the left sleeve of his shirt. Continuing unabated, he dodges a further strike before pinning the outmuscled against the door with one hand. His other hand, gripped upon the pitchfork, thrusts with a sound that makes me cringe.

Sammy eyes my father, sensing his defeat. Having lost one of his mercenaries, the other disabled, Sammy draws a blade before backpedalling. His boots find the thick covering of hay on the barn floor. My father continues toward him, no longer with a pitchfork, but the blade of the one he just killed.

A knife suddenly pierces Sammy's back.

Mine.

His body jerks before crashing to the ground. My father stares at me, knowing what this means.

Adrenaline is pumping through my veins. My hand trembles and I lose my grip, the bloodstained knife drops to the hay. "I'm going to need to clean this. I can't have blood on the apothecary's knife."

My father looks around, his medium-length blond hair whips at his neck. "Is this going to be an ongoing part of the Guild? I just cleaned the barn."

His ocean-blue eyes take in the sight of me struggling to function. A hand is placed on my shoulder, I take it within mine. "You did what you had to. We all do what we *have* to. Now I have to tell your mother, unless you want to, of course. Best not keep these things inside."

"Hands over your ears, dear." Turning away, I close my eyes as he finishes off the previously disabled.

Reality snaps back as my fingers find the handle of the now half-filled basket of Coradal Root.

I hope the Guild will believe me.

Six

ARATHYN

"**D**raygar!" A sheer drop beyond the bushes has me worried. *It had to run into there, didn't it?* He searches further before emerging with a rabbit skewered by an arrow.

Exiled, we persevere. Everything must be fought for. Collected by my own two hands or we go without.

Rain begins to fall, immediately I seek shelter. One of the wettest seasons of the year adds to the difficulty of living alone.

Draygar is all the strength I need, with an eye for battle and a cunning that would make a seasoned warrior uneasy. Danger is everywhere out here. Howls in the hills. Even the sun can't drive away the bugs in the damp.

Camped upon a rock shelf for days, the outlook is grim. A path up from the lower reaches is quite staggered, but with a steady foot, one can climb up to this beautiful overlook. The western face is the best option, providing shelter from the incessant wind that whips up from the sea. Fire, food and water. Maybe we just have a chance out here.

My head rests against smooth windblasted rock. I can't drive out the thoughts of my mother. Taking comfort in the fact that she will be much safer in Turinfall, I still miss her greatly. She won't have to worry about the dangers that I'll face out here.

Perhaps myself.

Surveying the land further, I find it somewhat familiar. A path weaves its way through the buttes to the west before it seems to head out to a clearing. I gather my thoughts for a moment: the growing realisation that a return to Turinfall is prohibited, my curiosity is going into overdrive.

What life will I have if I just skulk around the outer reaches? Living off rabbits. Quenching my thirst with a cup of water. There must be other wanderers. Ones that will likely take everything I have and leave me for *dead*. But Draygar seems excited. I wish I shared his enthusiasm. For now, that's all I need.

A voice splits the misty silence that hangs over the landscape, the sound of which doesn't disturb Draygar's slumber. "We're getting close to treasure, boys. I can feel it. There's a village to the east."

Creeping out upon my perch, I notice a band of crudely dressed men in ragged clothes with sheathed swords belted over their shoulders. The immediate danger brings about caution. *Bandits*. Quite possibly the same ones that have hands in Auriella's shipments.

There are three. I stay safe and out of sight.

Crawling back toward our cave, my body freezes solid and I can't move an inch. My mind shifts and I lose control. I'm forced back out, exposed. The heavy mist, not white, but now drenched in a purple hue. Draygar begins to stir behind me.

Voices grow louder. The river roars. The monastery flickers in front of me. The vision of such and the cave behind grows larger, inviting me in. A rage boils inside. My bow is drawn, aims high towards the mountains and fires. My willpower battles the foreign grip, trying to release whatever has a hold on me. It's of no use, I lose my balance and tumble down the slope.

"Look! Up there! We've been spotted!" Each of the men draws a sword and charges towards me in a frenzy, however the sheer ruggedness of the terrain hinders their movements.

With a steely determination, they hurdle over towards me unabated. My eyes grow fierce. I stand my ground, completely enveloped in rage. My hand grips a second arrow before I am knocked aside like a disfigured ornament.

Draygar roars with bestial wrath, the sound of which makes the ground tremble. Amazement arrives briefly before confusion strikes.

The mysterious clutch lets go.

I lie immobilised by a pain that races through my entire body. I crane my head around in an attempt to spot the bandits. To no avail, they have fled.

Draygar stands to my side, nudging me with a worrying paw. Ruffling his mane, I struggle to find my feet. *Did Draygar just try to protect me?*

Or kill me?

Nevertheless, I am alive. My companion has warded off our assailants.

It takes every morsel of strength in my body to climb back up to our hideout. With Draygar whimpering by my side, he occasionally nudges me forward. He still has my best interests at heart. I devour a portion of cooked rabbit and drain an entire cup of fresh water. Such a common meal has never tasted so divine.

Draygar sits beside me, peering up at the majestic ranges of the Feygoran Mountains. His fur ragged, his mane knotted. He has seen better days.

I need answers. This nightmarish hold on me will soon drive me insane, one way or another.

That first arrow.

Why did my body fire with such a wayward aim?

The gloomy haze that dispersed in that same direction leads me to believe that I'm being guided by something.

Having forgotten most of the places to the west of Turinfall, I find myself wandering. But a path must lead somewhere.

I remember running off after Draygar, my parents were livid when we returned. He was nothing but a small cub. I felt as if I was being chased by something while searching for him. Thinking nothing of it at the time, I brushed it off.

These memories feel linked to my episodes at Turinfall that ultimately led to my exile. And now here again. Are these visions trying to lead me back to Highgarde, to what had happened all these years ago?

What is happening to me now?

It is time to face the truth.

We leave our temporary place of solitude. I stumble upon a satchel at the base of a tall palm. What luck, one of the bandits must have dropped it: a canteen, one poorly drawn map, and a purse filled with a few hundred coin.

An outer pocket is stubborn, I do my best to slip my hand in. Upon shaking the satchel vigorously, to my amazement, out falls a sapphire pendant trimmed with gold.

If Morathaen's pendant could feel jealousy, it would glue itself to my skin. No doubt the golden jewellery would look better on a woman. Turning to Draygar with excitement, I am met with a questioning gaze. A smile flashes across my face. The satchel is repacked, finding a place over my shoulder. The newly acquired pendant falls into my coat pocket.

We head off in the direction of the arrow's flight.

Travelling west, we leave the confinement of the pinnacles. Oaks dot the surrounding landscape, finally with room to grow. Reygyre prowl around on rolling hills. Draygar is larger than all, they never grow too formidable in size. Most of the orange beasts turn their attention to us, but the sight of Draygar quickly quells their interest.

The Feygoran Mountains inch closer as we wander, appearing much more tranquil with every step. The air becomes cooler, crisper. No longer feeling damp.

A fork in the path beckons. The Grand Turinaar Pinnacles are well in our wake. I take out the crumpled map. We appear to be within the Whistling Plains. That thought is bolstered by evidence of a raging gust that whips through the swales, blowing up from the southeast. A chilling blast from the Coramine Sea. My beastly garment and Draygar's winter coat do well to counter the chill.

"Hello there!" I jump in fright.

To my amusement, I realise it isn't me being greeted. Draygar has already snuffed out our new acquaintance. Several paces away, a man crests a hill.

"Hold!" Draygar stops, leering back at me. A horse appears behind the man, through a haze in the wind, completely covered in a fur blanket.

An elder voice cuts through the gale. "That is quite a beast you have there and quite tame!"

He seems friendly enough. "It's my companion, Draygar."

"Companion. You mean your pet?" It dawns on me rather quickly that he is oblivious to our way of life.

"Of a sort." I save him from any detail.

"I'm on my way to Sylvora. A castle to the south. Still a day off."

"Oh. I have never been there. Where are you travelling from?"

"Coradal. The north-eastern point of Arcura. Even more than a couple of days. The name's Lorelth, I frequently travel this path. Nothing more than a merchant trying to make ends meet. That pendant you wear, boy, would you like to part with it?"

Morathaen's pendant. Not a chance. As much as I would love to offer Lorelth the sapphire pendant in exchange for something useful, I can't trust someone I just met.

"It is a gift from our huntsmaster, I could never trade it."

The tone of his voice becomes a warning. "Very well. I wouldn't get caught out here too long, you'll freeze to death!"

"Have you heard of Highgarde?" The words just jump out of my mouth.

Curiosity peaks on his face. "The old monastery, you ask?"

"Yes."

"That place has been abandoned for centuries. If you take this path leading towards the Forvarran Coast, it is nestled in the northern end of the Whistling Plains below small peaks." Lorelth points toward a set of rocky spires reaching far above the surrounding landscape.

"Best be off, young one. These old weary bones can only endure so much." Lorelth climbs onto the saddle. Hoofs clap upon the stone surface as his steed canters off.

It is easy to get lost out here, the land is scarce in the form of habitation. Most man-made constructions have either been destroyed, or look long abandoned. My only sense of direction is the mountains to the west, the fortunate map I stumbled across and Lorelth's guidance.

Draygar and I head for the peaks. Underfoot, it is anything but comfortable. An uneven construct of quarried stone, traced with hardened earth, doesn't offer much comfort. We find an alternate route on more forgiving grassland, keeping our vigilance so as not to wander off course.

I catch a glimpse of a watchtower rising above a wooden palisade. We conceal ourselves below the crest of a hill before circling around to take up a better vantage point.

We watch in wait, eyeing out the gale-spared fortification. A plume of smoke rises every so often from a chimney. Two guards patrol a rampart upon the top of the wall. The gates are slightly ajar.

Sensing a lack of hostility, I approach, having eyed off the guards who are none the wiser. Upon nearing the small breach in the gate, I am spotted. A wave of appreciation is shared. These people can't be at all dangerous, they are too neglectful.

Entering the fortification, I discover tents and stalls of goods. This is a bazaar, a marketplace for travelling merchants. Positioned centrally on the plain where a number of paths converge, an ideal location to capture the attention of roaming traders.

Wares in every nook and cranny. Wooden tools, iron blades, and whetstones. An abundance of food and clothing. Livestock, just waiting for the chance to break free. There are families here that have taken up residence inside the tents. They likely move around with the seasons.

"Hello there! You must be from Turinfall!" A young woman shouts in excitement, pointing at Draygar.

"Indeed."

Her excitement rises once more. "Can I purchase your entire garment? That crimson red is beauty to my eyes!"

"Sorry. It is a gift. I also need clothes." The woman giggles behind the hand she tries to cover it with.

"I will take a flintstone and dagger." I think it best to carry a hidden blade.

"Oh. Straight to the point, are we?" I'm not sure if the joke is intended or not.

The young woman walks enthusiastically to a weapon rack beside the forge before plucking a stone from a wooden crate. "Fifty coin please."

The weighted coin pouch finds my grasp. Much to her delight, I place roughly stamped silver coins into her youthful hands.

Suddenly, she grabs my arm. "Will you take me with you?"

Draygar growls aggressively, catching the attention of the guards. My wrist is released.

"Hold fast, boy!" I swing my head around to see two men upon the rampart with blades drawn. I usher calm upon Draygar and the guards sheathe their swords.

I turn down her proposal. "Where I am heading, I am sure you would not travel."

"Goodbye then!" Her mood changes quicker than a flame would perish in these winds.

It is apparent that outside Turinfall, things are much different, requiring a guile and understanding that I will need to attain. Seemingly enough, I am considered a threat. Only a glance in the wrong direction is enough to draw attention.

The wind-whipped landscape becomes peaceful once more as a melodic sound of running water fills the air. It seems that we have left the Whistling Plains as there isn't much more than a breath of wind that lingers. Our strides continue along the bank of a rushing river, one that likely flows all the way to Turinfall. I stop to examine a small cluster of bushes, littered with silver spore-like berries.

Silver Stars, as they are known. Berries that grow at the base of waterfalls in Turinfall. Safe to eat, they provide a high burst of energy. Severe dehydration is what one can expect if liquids are not consumed in tandem.

We wander down to the river, washing ourselves off before sharing in the delicacy. We drink so much that we risk drowning ourselves, we know what to expect. Upon stuffing extra berries into the satchel, we're off.

Silver Stars are also used by Raegyla to treat the sick, but with a more medicinal process. Ironically, the berries cure their own sickness. Memories of bad days re-emerge. We hoarded them for intentional misuse.

The land flies by as Draygar and I journey toward our destination. Our strides are effortless. The mountains look like they are moving toward us, such an illusory feeling, spurned on by our questionable choice of food.

A faint outline of shaped stone catches in my peripheral vision as we scour the mountainside. The ruins are in sight. Only a short distance separates us and a possible answer for all the trouble that has led me here.

The path starts to incline with the surrounding land. Numerous striders squawk at us from possible nesting grounds at the base of the peaks. These flightless birds are quite large in size, some even bigger than me. They differ in colour, with a beak that can swallow smaller game whole. We keep our distance.

Nightfall is nearly upon us as we take to the mountainous terrain. We press on.

An eerie feeling begins to claw at me. Caution sets in, our feet no longer sure of where to tread. We have arrived at Highgarde.

Draygar and I move cautiously as we creep forward into the grounds. Bow is ready at hand, I crack apart the wrought iron gates entwined by a dark creeper.

The monastery. No longer just a vision. Stands only a mere hundred paces away.

"Come …" A chilling voice falls upon my ears. I no longer fear what is happening to me, although this desecrated place feels soul-withering.

Five runes proceed to glow faintly in colour upon a large, rounded stone dais.

Blue. Green. Red. Yellow. White. In strange, yet simple arrangements of circles and lines.

"Arathyn …" Louder and louder the voice grows as my name is repeated, becoming more distinct as I approach.

How does it know my name?

Within an instant, rust-encrusted iron torches ignite around the space. Grasping my bow tight, I harden my stance, peering around for movement.

Draygar is acting strange, almost disinterested. A small crevice behind the monastery keeps his focus. After only a brief moment of hesitation, my companion walks off.

"Hold!"

No response.

My efforts to chase after him are useless as I am suddenly rendered immobile by an invisible force. Struggling to break free, I cannot move more than an inch as attempts are made to escape the grasp on my body. Draygar disappears into darkness before a terrifying howl originates from within. Worry displaces my thoughts. *What is happening to him?*

Torches burn out and a gloom descends. A figure emerges from the cave. *Draygar?* Only he is enveloped in a grey shroud and his eyes burn as orange as the setting sun. Trice-sized and granite-hardened, he prowls straight towards me, snarling.

Draygar moves to the centre of the dais. Almost like an arena, I stand opposite the transformed beast.

My body is dragged before being held above the white rune that shines brightly. Amazement displaces my fear as I peer down upon its strange arrangement. The only arrangement to contain a central square. Draygar stands in a central position, but not directly over a rune.

A shock rips across my body before reaching out to the extremity of my hands. Light surrounds me, but only for a moment, before receding to reveal a white sigil upon my wrist.

Torchlight flares up once again as I am released from the hold, empowered, evolved.

Draygar roars with so much force that buildings rock. Old, withered trees shake violently. A spirit of pure darkness shoots out above him, emitting a terrorising cry before returning into his body.

Lunging into a stride, the beast speeds toward me. Raising my bow to bear the brunt of the incoming onslaught, a direct hit is taken. No pain, but I find myself standing well behind where I was struck. Force, incredible. Draygar spins around, retreating before facing me once again.

With such haste, I fire my bow. Again and again. Draygar dodges, weaving his way through the barrage with cat-like agility. Movements I cannot even comprehend. My back finds the earth as I'm knocked off my feet, taking a battering once more. Thunderous roars toy with my eardrums.

Feeling like a castle gate trying to withstand a battering ram, whatever is protecting me is obviously outmatched. Jumping to my feet, I draw three arrows at once, firing them simultaneously. They fan out slightly. Draygar jumps into the air, higher than I thought possible. Arrows pass haplessly below his frame. One pierces a thick oak tree, the others embed into a stone wall. Circling around, the beast snarls at me, waiting for a moment to strike.

My voice just wails as I attempt to command Draygar to stop. A voice that pierces the night sky. It seems to startle him. Energetic legs take the beast back.

His eyes grow brighter. A wispy haze grows darker. He leers at me, paralysing my body. In one final swift movement, all force and being are thrown into me. The wrought-iron fence feels the full force of my hurtling body.

Draygar ejects the darkened spirit once more. Leering into my soul, it stares at me. Another spirit within me cries in agony as it is exhumed from my body, drawn towards the darkness as it tries to resist. A white spirit defeated. They begin to coalesce into one.

An entity shines brightly above Draygar, brighter and brighter it grows before it begins to convulse. My eyes dare not look at it any longer. Colourful energy courses around blindingly for a brief moment, before a monumental explosion of energy hits me with a concussive force.

Seven

VEXXYRA

There is commotion stirring nearby. I watch through dark, stained-glass windows while gently grinding away at Azurebloom petals with a mortar and pestle.

It's Vilriyan. He's arguing a point about a weakness of Coradal's. He isn't a part of the Captain's Guard but he sure thinks he is. Numerous sentries converge around the stoic man, but it's still him doing the talking.

I can just make out the words muffled by the glass.

"Tell Edward it isn't good enough. We are weak. Guards like yourselves have no mettle. Just last week, a group of you were struck down by nothing more than *hired militia*.

"When *I* become captain, the lot of you will be given your marching orders." Vilriyan's act of defiance doesn't sway the sentries one bit. *I think he is digging himself an early grave.*

A sudden shear of wind followed by a flash of pure white light rocks the town. Vials shake violently before coming to rest in different places. Glass windows crack. People on the streets now find themselves lying on the ground in sheer bewilderment.

I run outside and peer up into a blue sky. Frantically, I look around. Everything appears normal.

Then, like a cascade of small rainbows, colourful objects begin to rain down upon our people. One impacts on and injects itself into my arm. Sudden pain forces a cry.

Fighting at the anomaly, I feel a strange energy using my body as a hiding place. Suddenly, the pain lessens. A tingling feeling gives me back the use of my arm. My eyes stare at my wrist. A wrist with a strange, luminous, blue rune-like depiction etched into it.

Are my eyes deceiving me?

Vilriyan is hit by a much larger ball of energy, knocking him flat on his back. Twitching and convulsing, he looks as if he's going to die.

He doesn't. In no time at all, he's up on his feet, gazing wondrously at an even brighter etching than mine.

"She's dead!" A woman screams. "They're all dead!"

I blink, trying to reset my wayward vision. *This is real.* Many of our people lie lifeless on the ground.

Another yells, keeping his distance from an encroaching sentry. "Stay away from me!"

They're all different. An assortment of colours glows from wrists alike. Accusative, a guard runs towards Vilriyan. A wispy trail of red light stops him in his tracks as something is siphoned from his body. A siphoning that seems to empower Vilriyan, forcing the guard to perish.

Eyes flick back and forth like a standoff, waiting for who will make the next move. No one does.

"Dad!" A young boy, no older than eight, runs toward Vilriyan with a look of sheer terror. My eyes divert away, I can't look. The poor child knows no better. Vilriyan clutches his youngest within his arms.

Nothing. No reaction. Vilriyan grabs his wrist. Blue.

Vilriyan's eyes find mine, which triggers a thought. *My mother, in the tailoring parlour.* My body moves with such desire.

Disbelief embeds itself at the forefront of my thoughts. Bodies are strewn everywhere. Tears well as I identify Mira. *Arix? Oran?*

"Mother?!" The parlour is deserted. Shedding tears, I run for Hearthweed Farm.

I'm there before I can even comprehend how fast I make the journey. My father sits against the wall of the barn, staring at his arm.

Green. He is the only one here. *Lucky.*

Our eyes meet. Relief washes over his face, as does mine. Legs begin to stride over.

"No, Father!"

Stopping immediately, his look changes to one of confusion.

"They're all dead! Coradal. They're dead!"

Astonishment grips his face. "What?"

"You're green. I'm blue. We will die if we get too close!"

Without even needing to question me, he nods.

Rushing back to Coradal feeling as far apart as we've ever been, Vilriyan still stands in the town square, only now he has amassed a following of people with blue markings.

I drop to my knees. A sensation of a knife piercing my heart reduces me to a grovelling mess.

Mother. Lying dead at his feet with a puncture wound.

I scream at Vilriyan. "What did you do?! She wasn't here before!"

It's the first time I've seen tears on my father's face. But like a snap of lightning, it starts to bleed hatred.

"What did you do?!"

A moment passes, no words. My father then grabs a blade from the dead hands of a guard nearby before pointing it directly at Vilriyan.

"I'll ask again. What did you do?!" If my father's blade doesn't kill him, the gaze from his death stare will. All I can hear is a faint murmur of conversation through clouded ears. Focus I cannot as my mother's body is in my arms like a vice.

My father is going to explode. "I will take your hesitation as guilt. Believe me, I will rip you apart and feed you to the hounds!"

"No … no, you will not." Vilriyan walks forward confidently. My father charges at him without sparing a single thought for the armed contingent of blue behind.

But it's futile. My father is forced to his knees before Vilriyan. Life begins to be siphoned.

"Stop! Stop!" Vilriyan takes in my emotional state and backs away. A sigh and a thud are all I hear. My father is clinging to whatever life is left within him.

"Take her!" Strong hands grip me as I'm ushered away. In a crazed rage, I strike at my captors as the grip on my mother is lost. Screams rip at their eardrums before my strength is all but sapped.

Weakened protests from my father are faint in my ears. Nothing but a weary arm is shaken, he is too stricken to move.

—◆—

I'm ushered forward like a prisoner, my wrists in chains. I walk with others up a damp stone path through a dense gathering of palms. Seagulls squawk above. A fresh breeze from the sea is the only respite from a mouldy stench.

"This way!" Vilriyan shouts.

We reach a sharp incline that rises further to a huge fortified gate at the crest of the hill.

It's the castle, Forvarr. Seemingly abandoned, one can tell by its dilapidated look. The perfect hiding place for Vilriyans' treasonous crusade.

"Lock them below until I decide a use for them." If my heart could sink any further, I'd trample it.

The gate slams shut behind us. I'm led below, down winding staircases, through damp corridors. I heave at the stench. I'm stopped before the iron door of a cell within a small room. Firelight reveals a skeleton, hunched over in a sitting position against the wall of the adjacent cell as a lamp is lit.

This all feels too planned.

I'm shoved onto a small, bowed, mould-ridden bed. Moments later, the cell door slams shut before the turn of a rusted lock emits a sharp creak.

I'm alone. Broken.

Eight

ARATHYN

Sunlight streams down on me. I must have been out all night. This place seems … different.

My head is still spinning, my vision blurry. I try to regain my feet only to stumble over. Leaning back as I sit up, my body yearns to find support in the rusted gate. I fall on my back again, it is no longer there. Several paces away, in fact, mangled and strewn in pieces.

My senses recover and I'm able to stand. I reach for the satchel and drink profusely, gazing at a white sigil on my wrist.

A line. Five circles, one struck through.

Gathering my bow and quiver, I dust myself off before walking back toward the dais. The buildings that once stood here are reduced to rubble, the trees flattened. The dais floor is cracked right through and all but the white rune are dull.

Draygar is nowhere in sight. I can't fathom what has happened.

This sigil?

That beast?

The spirit?

I recall the day that we were here, a long time ago. The cave Draygar had wandered off into, did that ignite all of what has happened here just now? Maybe the answers I seek lie within the eerie opening before me.

Descending into the cave, it isn't far before I reach an open cavern. The air is cold. An entire village could fit within its damp walls. A shrine stands almost dead in the centre, littered with cracked remnants of ceramic ware. At the foot lies Draygar. I can see the rising and falling of his chest.

I can feel his pain, his thoughts, as if I were inside his body. Our minds, strangely connected. I know we share a bond but this is a heightened state, a weird telepathic energy. Still slightly morphed into the form that battered me the night before, he is much weaker. I don't want to take another step, having seen with my own eyes the rage of the beast that lies before me. He needs time to recover. How we survived that explosion, I cannot even begin to imagine.

He starts to whimper, his pain runs through every part of my body. The urge to resist I can no longer help.

"Draygar!" He lifts his head briefly to see me before dropping it once more. Upon grabbing the canteen from the satchel, I fill it from a stream of water that runs down the cavern wall. I reach for Silver Stars, forcing him to swallow them. I make sure that he drinks the entire canteen, then I lie next to him and wait.

I spend much of the day worrying sick. Draygar is improving, I can feel him growing stronger. There seems to be lingering energy sitting stagnant in the air, the hair on my skin stands. Nothing stirs in the surroundings. However, there is no doubt that something extremely unusual has happened here. Draygar musters enough strength to rise on two feet. He takes one look at me and rubs his head against my side before standing.

The feeling of corruption I had recently experienced in Turinfall, which ran rampant through me then, now feels long gone.

We retreat from the cave, back once again under the peacefulness of a cloudless sky. Highgarde lies in ruin. The runes lie dormant below our feet as we stride back toward the path. I further leer at my wrist, the sigil has a faint white glow, nothing more than the brightness of a dying flame. It has etched itself into my body somehow, painless.

Far in the distance, I can make out billows of smoke rising in the vicinity of the fort we had visited earlier. Much more distinct and darker than what one would expect to see from a furnace. Deciding to investigate, we head back, tracing the path towards the plains.

The wildlife has vanished, the wind has abated and the feeling of lingering energy is replaced by a fresh wintry chill as if the sun has repealed its warmth from the land. We gather momentum, not just to warm ourselves, as these people are surely in need of help.

The fort, now in sight as we round the slight slope of a rolling hill, smoulders as the palisade wall has all but been destroyed by fire. We err on the side of caution as we approach even though there is no one in sight. All appears quiet, there is nothing to suggest that anyone remains here. Maybe they have been assaulted and left to die.

Drawing my bow, I creep through gates that stand ajar. Smaller tents have been reduced to ashes.

"Get away from me, murderer!" yells a woman as she runs for her life with a handful of wares.

Another gives chase. "You thief! Give that back at once!"

Watching in disbelief, they close in on each other, a blueish-green wisp of light connects them. Bodies entangle briefly for a moment before the wares drop to the ground with a thud, as do they.

Light disperses. Death is all that remains.

Numerous bodies lie around within the bazaar, still with burnt-out wooden torches in hand. Strangely, there is no sign of a fight or even a struggle. Weapon racks are still complete with armaments, garments hang over wooden railings. Kneeling, I take in the situation in detail. *Who would raze such a small trading establishment and take nothing for their efforts?*

A small movement from a body draws my attention. Hurrying over, I'm halted by a trail of wispy light that connects us, pouring out from a faint green sigil upon his wrist. Similar to mine, but with fewer circular marks. Awe envelopes me as a cloudy greenish-white bond begins to link us.

"Stop … please …" His skin turns pale before I jump back to break the link between our sigils. The man is close to death.

"Get away from me! The others. They were taken."

A Silver Star is caught in one hand, the canteen in the other. "Here. This will restore your strength."

"Thank you, young— Wait … You again?" Realisation hits the guard as I'm placed as the previous visitor.

"Rest for a moment."

Walking around the fort, I discover more bodies, guards within reach of each other. Sigils are also etched on them, of different arrangements, completely dim. Taking a step toward them, expecting a reaction, nothing happens. Within a larger tent that has escaped the fire, the bodies of a man and a woman lie together upon a woollen bed. Fates, shared. One body adorns a sigil matching mine. Looking around, there is no sign of the girl I met before.

Pacing back toward the guard, ensuring that I keep my distance, I ask, "What happened here?"

A puzzled look is an answer. "A blast tore through us. Embers from the forge engulfed the tents. Others turned on us before killing each other. Life was drained from them, like you were just doing to me."

Upon the guard's wrist lies the slightly more luminous green sigil. An understanding knocks at my brain; however, I am unable to fathom it and to what extent it could happen further.

Bewilderment encapsulates the guard as he racks his brain for something that makes sense. "They did not perish at the same time. It appeared that the strongest were more able to … *resist.* The girl ran to me, screaming for help … I tried to stop her, but she drew too close. It wasn't her who was in danger. I felt her … light draining the life from me. She must have known and fled. Had she stayed a moment longer, I'd have likely perished just like the others …"

Information bestowed upon me requires time to decipher.

Strongest? Something determines our fate.

"Thank you." A forceful thrust of his arm throws the canteen back to me.

"Hold right there!" A booming voice cuts apart my thoughts. *Bandits.* At the southern gate of the fort. Men stand in leather jerkins with blades drawn and green sigils etched upon their wrists.

"Stand aside or we will cut you down! Everything now belongs to us!" His figure cuts adamance.

Draygar pounces in front of me as I ready my bow, a rage boils inside him.

My keen eye keeps focus on the lone survivor to my side. *Not this time.* I'm sick to death of thugs running their agendas. "Don't take another step!"

Hesitation grips my adversaries, they don't expect our resistance but it only hinders their advance for a moment. "We will tear you apart!"

An arrow pierces the right shoulder of one and he staggers. Continuing to advance, he rips the projectile from his body, forcing a painful cry. All I have to do is think aggressively and Draygar responds, lunging at the other and knocking him back several paces without even having to give him a verbal command.

Draygar snarls as his target regains their feet. A hand clutches a bitten arm. An advance by the other is halted, indecision is rife.

Another attack surges and Draygar lunges with retaliatory claws that lash the man's arm, slicing through leather with ease. Quickly focusing, I fire at his chest that barely misses his heart, but enough to throw off his thrusting blade harmlessly past my right shoulder. Crashing into me, our bodies are thrown to the ground.

My sigil begins to overpower his own. Pain flashes across his face, his life departing.

Reaching for the dagger at my side, I find a firm grip and thrust it into his lower torso. His grip loosens and I manage to roll away.

The eyes of the one I helped stare me down before Draygar is the target of an onrush. *Defection.* With a weapon drawn, a flanking path is taken.

Draygar parries an attack from another with hardened claws, slashing his attacker across the chestplate. The metallic shrill pierces my eardrums. Stumbling backwards, a body with an aura of uncertainty peers back. Roars stun him temporarily. Hands are forced to my ears, it is deafening.

A wispy essence is ripped from the one I had wrestled with as he perishes. Strange energy shoots into Draygar which empowers him in a fury. A ghostly aura flares up. Eyes burn with the light of a thousand torches. Surges of energy run through his muscular body which strengthens beyond belief. Aggression takes over his mind.

My companion, transformed, lunges at the immobilised. Spinning around mid-flight, a stone-edged tail impacts upon him in a crushing blow. Lifeless, he lands at the base of a cracked palisade wall.

My eyes are glued to Draygar. My jaw collects dirt. *What has he become? Am I next?*

I struggle to find the energy to regain my footing.

The defector remains. Attention is turned to me, sensing a weakness. Raising my bow in an attempt to defend myself from a final onslaught, he fails to reach me as Draygar leaps with might, catching him airborne within drooling jaws. Fangs pierce through metal like a blade through cloth. One swift jerk of my beast's head launches the guard some distance before his body comes to rest against a stone wall.

Unworthy.

Draygar roars resoundingly before returning to my side. We are victorious. My companion has just saved my life numerous times. His aggressiveness recedes into compassion as he returns to the companion I know and trust.

Formidable. Absolutely. Draygar has developed some kind of strange ability that resembles the form he took back at Highgarde. He appears to remain loyal to me and the thought of riding such a beast fills me with unbridled excitement. We could become such a significant force together, aiding our chance at survival.

I take a blade to numerous pieces of hide that lie untouched on their tanning racks before gathering buckles from leather straps and girdles. A saddle is my goal, but a lack of craftsmanship hinders that. Something that will hold me steady upon Draygar's back, one that bears the movement of his muscular strength as he moves.

Meanwhile, I ponder the fate of the young woman I had met before. Her body, I cannot locate. Surely she will struggle to survive out in the wilderness on her own, she has likely taken supplies with her. So much loss within the aftermath of the event. The sigils, the choice of which seems somewhat random, maybe it is humanity's fate.

⁕⟴⁕

It is time to test out my craftsmanship. Draygar doesn't move a muscle while I bind the makeshift saddle onto his onyx-coloured hide. I double-band the straps for reinforced strength, trice-fold a large segment of reinforced hide, shaped into a seat on his back. Upon jumping in, he grunts and sways his head back and forth as if to check that I am ready.

I'm not.

My mind is full of indecision as I try to think of what to do next.

With thoughts of rushing around the fort, he takes a few steps forward, then halts as I change my mind. This telepathic bond is so foreign and challenging; all that floods my thoughts now is what we could achieve given time.

Draygar knows basic commands that I taught him at a young age. These commands now feel obsolete as he can sense my thoughts.

Now that we are alone together in a land of great mystery, the bond that we share will need to grow if we are to survive.

We continue at a walking pace, circling the fort. It doesn't take long before I am comfortable with his steady pace. The saddle beneath is surprisingly quite comfortable.

⊰⊱

Night begins to set in as we end our training for the afternoon. The cold prompts me to start a campfire. Luckily, everything I need is within reach.

Ironically, we have a fort all to ourselves that is laden with resources. Upon my exile, we had nothing. I have no intention of leaving before we are ready. An aroma graces my nose, the meat is ready. Just one bite has Silver Stars paling in comparison.

Gates are shut and barred, I don't wish for another ambush. However, lingering around here won't draw out any satisfaction.

Time is what I need to figure out what I want to achieve.

Is there enough time for that? The mental burden is so exhausting.

A large, beastly figure stands gracefully before me, not physically but in spirit. Mostly opaque but distinct in its features, it shines a silvery-white that gleams in the firelight. Walking toward it, drawn by anticipation, the beast doesn't move at all. A gaze locks on that doesn't leave me.

I draw within the grasp of the white beast, reaching out without any hesitation. My hand passes right through it as if it isn't there, slightly disturbing its wispy shape before it reforms. There is a marking inscribed along its neck. I attempt to examine it just as the beast leaps at me.

I wake in fright, jumping up. It was nothing but a wild dream. The campfire has burnt out. Draygar lunges to his feet and prowls around, sensing my uncertainty.

Nothing.

Dawn can't be too far away. There is no evidence of further visits, nothing looks out of place. The presence of the majestic beast lingers like it has some form of strange connection with me.

⸻ ❈ ⸻

The river rages, just as our energy does within us. Draygar carries a few small barrels of water with ease as we return. Gleaming with excitement, I want to further our ability while in a mounted position. My eyes find the watchtower, and we climb. Scouring the surrounding landscape, we identify the flattest ground nearby. The wind has died down, the weather is ideal. To the west, hills rise to a flat segment of land. The location is decided.

Securing a hold on the saddle, I throw myself onto Draygar's back. He roars, which draws a smile on my face.

This time, I don't hesitate.

I brace myself and clutch his hide.

With thoughts of us bounding across the plains, I hold on for dear life as he throws himself forward, leaving the ground momentarily. He runs with thundering footfalls as the force of his movements pins me in my saddle. We turn left and right, drop and rise as we travel unabated by the terrain. A guided projectile.

The fort whizzes past as we circle it numerous times, I could do this all day.

We slow as we return to the fort. After dismounting near the campfire, I throw him a bone. My bones ache, I feel like I just ran through a gauntlet of punches. At least I didn't fall off, that alone is enough of an accomplishment.

The art of mounted combat is an experience I crave. My thoughts draw knights that ride into battle on horses enveloped in plate armour, the idea of which has me excited beyond imagination.

Targets are set. I fire at them, finding myself horrible at first. Draygar's movements throw me off balance and the palisade wall behind them feels their impact instead.

Regathering my arrows, I repeat. The clink of metal tips hitting armour becomes more and more frequent as time passes. My aim improves dramatically, like I was born for this. Finally, I perfect my stance within the harness, being able to resist Draygar's energetic movements as much as possible.

It is time to leave our newfound home, something just fails to sit right. People have perished here, the thought of which still haunts me. The threads of our rucksack are stretched to their limit. It is impossible to take everything. I bind what we can carry on Draygar's back.

A new adventure awaits. Now that we are ready, it feels like the perfect time to explore Arcura.

We stride out of the fort one final time as one, sitting prominently in my saddle. With a bow upon my back and a beast capable of unbridled rage, I feel as ready as ever. With ample supplies to last us for days, my heading will not be for Turinfall. I respect Argora's decision, I have caused too much suffering.

Suffering. I am still afflicted with something. This ever-present sigil.

North is where we head, mainly to avoid the howling winds of the plains that will likely hinder our journey south. The sight of palms far in the distance trains my vision. Insects buzz, creating a unique ambience.

The distinct howl from a Reygyre catches my ear and at the thought of hunting for it, Draygar immediately reacts, changing course so suddenly that I nearly fall out of the saddle. My thoughts force me to understand his desire. An empowered bond that will take a long time to master.

Palm trees creep ever closer. The Forvarran Coast lies just beyond.

Nine

ARATHYN

Sounds of battle fill the air. Clashing of weapons, cries of pain. I dismount, being more confident in my ability on foot for now. Curiosity grows as we come across a small town, much bigger than the fort we had occupied. My eyes catch a glimpse of a man who turns the corner of a small building, yelling with a weapon raised. Scouring our surroundings, walls and a main gate are constructed from oak. Two watchtowers stand at the sides, unmanned. After a moment of consideration, we throw ourselves into the fray. Numerous bodies lie strewn around, not all with obvious fatal wounds.

Four men confront us, standing before an inn. Green sigils glow upon flesh. A young boy, accompanied by an elderly woman, is pinned down on a balcony above. Wide-eyed, they stare at me and on their wrists, a sigil the same as mine.

Screams of a frail nature from a figure scared half to death reach my ears. "Help us!" Everyone's eyes turn on me.

Draygar roars from a crouching position, sending shockwaves that ripple through my body from the power. Feet step back. Questioning glances are shared within. Cheers of excitement pulse from the balcony, forcing a smile on my face.

"Quiet you!" One turns his attention back to my admirer, quelling his happiness.

Another speaks to me whimsically. "What are you going to achieve? There are four of us. We've struck down this entire town."

My hand pats Draygar's head. Adrenaline courses through my veins. "Draygar could take you all. *Alone.*"

A cacophony of laughter ensues. "Draygar, hah. Is that your pet? You are going to hand that thing over to us, it looks fearsome enough and we can use it."

Drawing my bow, I lay down a stern warning. "Leave now and leave these people alone. I will not ask again."

"Oh. You will not ask again?" My threat falls on deaf ears as they approach us.

A body collapses onto the cobblestone, struck by an arrow. Curses split the air as the remaining men charge. Draygar leaps forward in fury, flattening one in the process. A dull blade strikes him on the shoulder, but fails to pierce his thick, resilient hide.

Firing at another, the arrow embeds into his lower torso. Agony grips his body as he stumbles. A fourth reaches me. A rush of air disturbs my cheek as a sword slices through it, agonisingly close to flesh. A cloudy beam of white light finds him. As pale as a ghost, his flesh turns.

"What … are … you?"

"Tell me what happened here." Answers are all I want.

"Death." One mutters through his pain. "Men. Women. *Children.* Different … Divided … There is nothing more to say."

Training my bow on him, I revel in the fact that we've overwhelmed them. "Tell me why you killed these people!"

"Make me. I am dead anyway."

All it takes is one glance at Draygar. My companion rears up, siphoning the spirits of the slain. The remaining strength is ripped from the third in the form of a wispy beam. Draygar morphs into his strange form, his eyes burning brightly.

Horrified hands cover the young boy's eyes.

He responds curiously. "You would spare me, lad?"

"I will spare you if you tell me everything you know about what is happening here."

A story unravels. "I was just a farmer living on the Forvarran Coast. Coradal was decimated. People stood with these strange markings upon them, some perished as they ran to loved ones, some perished in their sleep. I was the lucky one, away at the Hearthweed Farm, shovelling damn dirt. Our entire way of life became one of utter disorder and within an instant, we were all divided. A group was formed, *these* men." He gestures at the bodies before us. "I didn't know what else to do ... but *you* are something else ..."

His recount has me lowering my bow. Draygar peers at me, awaiting a command. I am sure he can sense my hesitation. I shake my head.

My gut leads me on. "You have endured enough. You have knowledge, I will take you with me. What is your name?"

After a moment of no response, I glance at Draygar. The wounded man turns his head to see the snarling beast, bearing drooling fangs that move ever closer.

He sighs heavily. "My name is Vorathen Laybrook, I led these men from the east. There is no need to show further hostility."

"Vorathen, tell me. Why did you leave your home?"

"Home ..." Defeat once again is perched tightly in his throat. "Vilriyan began culling our people immediately, anyone who was different from him. I returned with my daughter from Hearthweed Farm none the wiser. We found her mother slain at his feet."

He looks away. "People believe he is the mastermind behind what happened. He grabbed my daughter and led her away. I tried to resist, to do *anything*. I found men, ones that Vilriyan didn't get. And here we are."

All that I can think of is Turinfall and my mother ... has the same thing happened there?

My past home.

I kneel as thoughts flash through my mind, this is much bigger than what I have witnessed. *Did my actions at Highgarde cost hundreds of people their lives?*

"A lot to take in?" Vorathen grows a smile and I have no idea why.

Guilt rains down upon me. "I did this, Vorathen. I was too weak."

"You did what?"

"You wouldn't believe me."

"I don't know what to believe, lad. The love of my life is dead, she had the same marking as you. My daughter is likely being held prisoner somewhere." Tears run down Vorathens' weathered face.

Feeling terrible, I want to comfort him. I know enough now that if I get too close, he will soon be dead like the others.

The young boy sprints out of the house toward me with the elderly woman frantically trying to keep up, yelling at him to stop. Immediately, I rush over to him, noticing his sigil as he draws closer to Vorathen. The boy is oblivious to the danger. I wrap my arms around him and hold him tight.

"You are my hero!" His joy is a breath of fresh air.

"I also like your dog." Vorathen and I both let out a chuckle. This boy has a confidence far beyond his years. Draygar begins to recede into his original form.

The elderly woman is livid. "Jepp, what did I tell you about running off like that!"

"Everything is dangerous." Vorathen is direct.

The old woman gives him the look of death. "Nonsense. We do *not* believe in nasties."

Vorathen rolls his eyes. "Look around you. What do you see, old one?"

She quickly realises her efforts at hiding danger from the boy are pointless. "Elmgrove is ruined! You destroyed everything!"

"Now you're beginning to understand."

I take a moment to decide on how to proceed. Vorathen is fearless, I'm convinced of that just from his words.

We need to move on. "What is done is done. We need to rest and gather our strength. Let us find what we can within the ruins. Stay away from Vorathen, your life depends on it."

The woman sighs. "If we have to be civil, then I'd rather be with two strong men."

Although Vorathen is inscribed with a green sigil, I feel that we have reached a mutual understanding that we need to work together. At least for now.

"What is your name?" Jepp asks me.

"I am Arathyn, from Turinfall."

The elderly woman grows a smile. "Oh, I've heard of you folk. The ones with the pets."

Vorathen ushers caution. "Even though you share the same colour, I'd be careful with your words, woman."

"Quiet, dear." She's just as robust as Vorathen. "Arathyn. That pet of yours, what do you feed it?!"

Draygar lies slumped upon a weathered timber floor, taking up a large portion of the floor space. "He eats whatever he wants. Not a pet, but my *companion*. I have had him since I was ten."

She hesitates. "Is he … *alright?*" She peers around to see if anyone thinks she is crazy at such a suggestion. Vorathen doesn't take his eyes off his food, he eats as if he has never had a decent meal in his life. I choose to avoid details, they have not yet earned my trust.

"He has always been a little different." I lie. But to be honest, I am unsure of what he has become.

We stay put for the night. Jepp sleeps next to me. It is nice to feel needed, this young boy admires me. Just like my father, I once too held the same feeling. I still do, even after his death. I wouldn't be the man I am today without his guidance. There is a feeling of duty to keep Jepp safe. Our world has turned cruel and he is beyond the safe reach of his grandmother.

* * *

As we leave behind the war-torn town, a question Jepp has on his mind is finally let loose. "May I have a ride, Arathyn?"

A request I need to decline. The excitement on his face is a weakness. "Jepp, it is extremely dangerous out here. I need you to stay alert."

I gaze at the elderly woman. "May I ask your name?"

My question draws a smile. "Call me Grelda."

"Very well, Grelda. Please keep Jepp close, we cannot afford any mistakes."

"What is your plan?" Vorathen asks as he leads our group north through the jungle.

"We will find your daughter, lead me to your homeland."

"Are you crazy, lad?! Vilriyan will have us all killed!"

I know what Draygar is capable of so my concern is minimal. "Do you have any idea where they took her?"

"There is a castle within view from Coradal, it sits upon the highest point within the coastal palms. Forvarr is long abandoned. It may just be the perfect place to hide his traitorous crusade."

"Then we will be careful. If Vilriyan is there, he will be expecting you."

The palms of the Forvarran Coast grace us. Grelda and Jepp do not seem at all concerned with our plan, they must feel safe with us. We stand upon the crest of a hill, the sea glistens in the sunlight beyond. I take a moment to survey the land ahead: all is quiet. Surely danger lies ahead, we are entering Vilriyan's domain.

The coastal areas of Arcura are magnificent. An abundance of wildlife throughout the surrounding landscape makes the deadly situation feel all but a ruse. A vibrant array of melodic sounds from the many different species of birds and insects fills the air. I have never travelled this far, the sights and sounds are breathtaking.

"Ah! There it is." Vorathen points in a northeasterly direction. Through small gaps in the fronds, I can just make out the unmistakable sight of stone rooks that rise on the corners of the castle. "I'm surprised it isn't red with all the blood he has spilled."

"Where is Coradal, Vorathen?"

"If we continue to the coast, then east, it lies on the very tip of Arcura. I very much doubt there will be anything left of it."

"Let's press on." I keep the thought of him possibly betraying me in the back of my mind, although he seems trustworthy. His daughter is in jeopardy and if there is any chance at all she is still alive, Vorathen will need all the help he can get.

As we continue down toward the coast, we are once again thrown into lush vegetation beneath rows of palms. Vorathen takes point, my way of navigation will do us little help now.

Vorathen stops suddenly and raises his fist before pointing a short distance ahead. He ducks behind some bushes and we do the same.

"These battlements were not here before," he says, almost a whisper.

I make my way to higher ground, backtracking around and over a small rock formation. Draygar remains by Jepp's side.

Four men patrol a timber balcony fixed upon a stony incline. We are close enough to make out a blue sigil upon a set of arms. I raise my hand and signal to Vorathen. His soldierly figure climbs up behind me.

He runs a hand along his jaw. "Vilriyan has increased his defences, we need to get through if we are to reach the coast safely. I cannot ask this of you. If we are caught, we will be executed."

"This is my responsibility, their blood is on my hands too."

"Lad, you cannot blame yourself for his actions. Ask yourself. Is this the person you want to become, one of guilt and sorrow?" His wisdom hits me right in the face. He's right. I need to stop blaming myself; however, that seems extremely difficult.

"I was exiled from Turinfall. Forced out by our huntsmaster. My father was killed in his efforts to overturn her order. All of these moments have led me here. These *sigils*. I believe this has all begun as a result of my actions." I pour out the stories of my recent past, overcome with guilt.

"You are not just any young man. You bested me and our band, unlike all the others we struck down. That companion of yours is as deadly as it is loyal. I have seen enough to put my faith in you, I don't really have any other option." My guilt is replaced with courage and determination as once again his words find the mark. "You have my blade."

Vorathen believes in me. Jepp and Grelda believe in me. Whatever happened at Highgarde, it is my destiny, my journey henceforth.

"Enough words. Now give me something to do, my blade thirsts for blood." Vorathen's want for revenge is exactly what I need, I just hope it doesn't blind him.

Vorathen creeps around closer to the fortification. He is a skilled melee combatant, a weak point of mine. I feel a newfound ease from a distance with him and Draygar protecting me.

Returning to the others, I instruct Grelda and Jepp to stay hidden. Jepp looks worried, his guardian is just what he needs right now.

I take a deep breath, Vorathen is waiting for my move.

Draygar launches out from behind the bushes into the clearing below. I fire my bow, hitting a soldier in the chest. The impact knocks him off the narrow structure.

An officer responds immediately as if he knows we are here, peeping through a small aperture on a watchtower. "Fire!"

Draygar leaps aside as an arrow finds the earth beside him. Soldiers retreat from above before emerging once more below, bursting through the gate before us.

Vorathen charges out of the scrub, slicing through the torso of one of the men. His blade quickly deflects the strike of a second. I'm impressed. He can fight.

I fire once more toward distracted soldiers, Vorathen's emergence renders them vulnerable.

"There are two of them!" A cry carries through the air as I release another arrow that plunges into the upper arm of the foremost jostling with Vorathen.

Vorathen takes the opportunity to thrust his blade through the disabled man. "That's two!" His lust for vengeance must be profound, he is revelling in every moment of this.

"Watch out!" My shout reaches Vorathen as I notice the officer leaving the comfort of his hideout before straying out onto the balcony with a crossbow in hand.

He fires. Vorathen stumbles over as a puff of dust kicks up near his flailing feet. I fire in return, striking a knee. A cry of pain rings out as the officer falls between the railing before crashing upon the hardened earth below.

Vorathen parries a final attack from the last of their resistance. Draygar charges, sensing an opportunity to strike. He lunges into the man at pace, knocking him off his feet before Vorathen delivers a fatal blow.

"We can defeat anybody!" Vorathen's morale is burgeoning. His excitement breeds hope in finding his daughter. Tilting my head toward the officer, it brings Vorathen back to reality. He trudges over before lifting the man by his neck. The officer, now slumped on his knees, is at one end of a wispy bond that emerges between them.

"I know who you are, you bastard! No doubt you stood next to Vilriyan while you watched her die!" Vorathen tightens his grip on the man's collar. "You are going to tell me how to get to him!"

"Over my dead body!" Both refuse to back down, they might both still lose if they don't part soon.

Vorathen tears the arrow from his knee, forcing yet another anguished cry and then throws the arrow back to me. "Where is my daughter!"

"Oh, that young thing? Probably locked up in the dungeon like the rest of them!" It's enough to give us a target. *Forvarr.* She is likely there.

Vorathen kicks the officer in the chest, forcing him to the ground. His anger-enriched eyes find mine. "He is all yours!"

I approach the officer with Draygar by my side.

"And who might you be? Come to escort me to my death in that nice coat, have you? Maybe that swine can see his daughter after they're both dead!" Vorathen is going to explode.

Vorathen takes back his offer, spinning around in a blaze of fury which draws a laugh from his adversary. He raises his blade with a damning look before running it through the officer's heart. Dying eyes gaze back for a brief moment before the link between them forces a retreat. The blade withdraws.

Vorathen rests, leaning against a smooth rock wall below the balcony with his bloodied greatsword beside him.

Emotionally beaten, he exhales. "My daughter, I fear the worst. How many more does that tyrant have in his ranks?"

"We will find her, Vorathen." He lifts his head, there is mutual agreement in his eyes.

Jepp and Grelda remain under cover as we circle back to check on them. A cheeky grin on his face quickly quells the tension of battle.

We continue through the first line of Vilriyan's defences and beyond the gates.

The coastline nears and there is no further sight of Vilriyan's men, but we are heading away from the castle. His forces must be spread thin.

The sand beneath our feet begins to hinder our movement as it envelopes our boots. Trudging through to the edge of the treeline, the sound and sight of crashing waves upon the sea bring us to a beach. Our journey has reached its northern end.

With the Feygoran Mountains now exposed far to the west as the palms thin, my eyes spot numerous people playing about on the beach. A few small buildings sitting on the perimeter of a central village show no sign of preparedness for conflict.

Their sigils must be aligned, they are in too close proximity. I find it hard to imagine that such a congregation of people could be so lucky as to be undivided. They are far too exposed out in the open. *How have they avoided Vilriyan's forces?*

"Should we approach?" Vorathen asks.

"We need answers. They may have some. Lead the way." Vorathen moves with a hint of nervousness due to their numbers.

We flank around to the south as it offers higher ground. A building outlying on the edge is covered by a canopy, cast by giant palms. My eyes make out at least five sentries patrolling about. A small group of children plays in the sand beyond. It looks as if this village doesn't belong here. *Everything seems normal.*

It is approaching dusk. The sun still provides light as it splits through the clouds. There is no obvious point to infiltrate, the buildings are exposed from every direction. We will need to cross a clearing from here and we will be spotted. Grelda and Jepp stay hidden, backs to the wall.

Bow at the ready, Draygar prowls by my side as I round the corner. Suddenly, I catch a glimpse of the sigil on the sentry my bow is trained upon. "Vorathen. Stand down." I point in the direction of the closest figure.

"Oh. *More of you.*"

"Stay here. It is best that you go unnoticed. Keep an eye on the others." He obliges.

"If it turns sour, I don't need an invitation." Vorathen's words are armour enough that I don't feel the need to wear any.

I leap onto Draygar's back before strolling casually into the clearing. Within a short distance, just as I suspect, several eyes lock onto me.

"Halt!"

A dozen eyes examine me. Children freeze on the spot. Sentries converge as if they are trained Rangers.

"You … Are you one of us?" one asks, noticing my white sigil.

"Indeed. I am Arathyn and this is Draygar." I try to sound like one in command as I brush Draygar on the shoulder. Moving closer, the men begin to fan out, stepping back cautiously with their eyes fixed upon my companion.

"Thank the lord! I was about to run!" In an instant, all but a few gazes turn on the outspoken. The cowardly statement is not well-received.

I get straight to the point. "Have you encountered Vilriyan's forces?"

The mention of his name has an alarming effect. "The name on the tongue of their assaults? We have fought off a number of his raids. Lost most of our men. It is only a matter of time before he sends an army."

Upon hearing his recount, a thought flashes across my mind. *How can one man create so much human suffering, so soon?*

How did I?

I narrow my eyes. "We will fight. He will be defeated." For the first time in my life, I feel in control. A newfound courage and the will to make a difference, I have Vorathen to thank for that.

My statement draws a laugh. "You?"

"You should see Draygar in battle. I have another, will you join us?"

Suddenly, his attitude changes, knowing that we are offering a chance to take Vilriyan out. "Very well, the more the merrier. Any chance to rid Arcura of his evil, I will take. We have ample supplies. Take what you need."

There is no time like the present. "Vorathen?"

"Yes, lad. We are still here!"

"Grelda. Jepp. We have a new home for you! You will be safe here." Jepp immediately spots the children and he's off, quicker than a bird in full flight. The responsibility I feel for his safety lifts slightly, he will be protected here.

"Wait!" A sentry seems to stop time. "He's green!"

I try to smooth this over quickly. "Fear not. He is with me, you do not need to worry."

The one in control stands unconvinced. He runs a hand across his jaw. "You would side with another? How can we trust you?"

"Vorathen has lost just as much as you have. His daughter was taken by Vilriyan. You should see him in battle! He will fight with a vigour one can only hope to match." Vorathen nods before picking up a loose stone, then runs it along the edge of his blade.

"This is preposterous!" The man looks around, knowing full well that he has no better option. He sighs. "I will, however, accept your proposal. Who are we to turn down anyone who appears able to fight? We will keep our distance, as will he. We are well aware of what will happen."

"Hello! I'm Grelda …" A faint elderly voice trails off into a nearby house that she enters as if it were her own.

⚊⚊⚊◈⚊⚊⚊

Five enormous ghostly figures emerge in front of me. Once again, the same white and four others that shine uniquely in separate colours.

My hands reach out, beckoned by the sigils inscribed on their arms, sigils that match the runes upon the dais at Highgarde. The beasts prowl forward, forcing my retreat. My beast rears up, forcing the rest to come to a sudden halt. Cries echo back in return.

A roar like booming thunder echoes throughout. The beasts disperse right before my very eyes as I jolt awake to moonlight cast through large chequered windows.

Draygar is wide awake, staring into my soul. I start to draw a connection between my dreams and reality. What are these strange beasts? I can no longer sleep as a million different thoughts cloud every part of my mind.

Ten

ARATHYN

Jepp and the other children play joyfully on the beach under a constant watch. I find it extremely lucky that these people are all aligned. *How did they even find each other, let alone make it here safely?*

They are the lucky ones.

There must be other settlements, people forced to live together: families suffering dearly, children scared out of their minds, others not at all affected by the situation.

Draygar and I wander along the beach to survey our surroundings. A mass grave entrenched in the sand stops me abruptly, my heart grows heavy at such a sight. A stench plays with my nose, negated infrequently by a whipping of a sea breeze. A battle must have taken place here, what armaments haven't been salvaged are strewn about the sands within pools of spilled blood. Most of the sigils on the bodies match Vorathen's. This looks more of a culling than a battle.

"No!"

I swing around to see Vorathen rushing up to the burial site.

"Our people … murdered. That bastard will pay dearly for this!" Some of the slain he knows. Thoughts of my father come rushing back and what Vorathen must be going through. I glance down at my gleaming silver bracelet. A sense of comfort hits me, knowing that he is still here in spirit.

"Let's regroup. We need to strike as soon as possible before Vilriyan sends another execution party."

I rally the men together as we return to the settlement, finding a newfound confidence. "Who among you are brave enough to fight Vilriyan and avenge your loved ones?"

"Boy. Are you *mad?* You want to lead a few men against his brutes?"

I am considered a fool but I don't stand for it. "If we wait any longer, he will send another party and you will end up like everyone else in that hole over there!"

Three villagers step forward. "We will accompany you, Arathyn. Our blades are yours to command."

"That's more like it!" Vorathen gleams with admiration.

The shot of morale avoids its target. "Your enthusiasm will surely spell your death. I will defend what we have here when you do not return."

I give up trying to convince him further. With that amount of hesitation, he will be of no use in a dire situation.

"Very well. Vorathen, take point, we will see you all before too long."

Forvarr is our target. Some grunt at our choice of strategy; however, cheers begin to outweigh the negativity. Oblivious children and most common folk raise their hands in respect for our bravery, or more so, our journey to death.

"Fear not. We may be few, but we are many." I find myself questioning my words, although I do feel powerful. I'm certainly not the same young man who lived in Turinfall.

Am I too headstrong?

Maybe. But my will is true.

"Be ready. They know we are out here. Expect anything." We find ourselves back in the confines of the coastal palms. My gaze finds Draygar, who leers back at me assuringly.

"Yes. Keep on your toes," Vorathen says.

A sharp incline in the terrain rises before the castle, stone battlements tower above the surrounding bushland. Watchtowers emerge as we creep through the dense undergrowth. These fortifications almost look ancient, surely not recently erected. A testament to Forvarr's past, no doubt.

"Hold. Look." Vorathen has us all stop in our tracks. I break through what is left of the remaining cover. Numerous sentries patrol a rampart and the grounds below. The watchtowers are manned. Ahead are soldiers wielding longswords, adorned in mail armour. Archers take up higher positions.

Vorathen curses under his breath. "Blue bastards. Look at them all."

He turns his attention to me. "What is your plan? They must be twenty strong and that is from what we can see."

"We can make a statement here." *At least I hope we can.*

"You want to draw Vilriyan out?"

"From what you've told me, he is determined and likes to take matters into his own hands. It may be our best point of attack." Looking back to gather the thoughts of the three that have accompanied us, they nod, looking uncertain.

Draygar and his empowered state are what we need if we have any chance of victory here. That only seems to happen upon death and the beast consumes their souls.

"Vorathen, attract their attention. We need to get some of them close."

Before I can further think of how to proceed, the sharp crack of a stone impacting a wall rings out nearby.

No turning back now. Immediately, we take cover, just enough to stay out of sight.

"Over there. Check that out!" What must be a commander patrolling the lower section orders a group of men to investigate. Clumsy frames labour over to the wall, only a few paces away from us. A shrug is all that is returned.

My intent-filled thoughts are the trigger. Draygar lunges from the concealing undergrowth as I swiftly release an arrow from my readied bow. Finding the chest, the projectile pierces right through a leather jerkin that provides no protection. Draygar dashes towards an armoured soldier before knocking him to the ground, opening up a path for his jaws to do the rest. My companion thrashes further at the last of the group, whose armour stands no chance against the beast's lashing claws.

A kite shield emerges from cover with Vorathen standing behind it. A blade of great proportions occupies his other hand. The man is the embodiment of strength.

"You can come out now!" Vorathen looks back as our three brave followers emerge from cover cautiously. *Maybe not so brave.*

"Kill them!" An order is given before several men leave their stations, racing toward us.

This is to be the answer to my doubt. *Are we really ready?*

Draygar roars as souls are ripped from the slain. Cover is taken as arrows rain down around us. Draygar stands firm.

One by one, they fall as Draygar storms his way through a faltering resistance. Arrows ricochet off his stone-embossed hide like they are striking solid steel. Every death invigorates him. A body that grows stronger with every soul he siphons until no man can even dream of besting him. Another earthshaking roar forces us to brace ourselves to keep our footing.

A dumbstruck look is plastered upon the commander's face. "What is this … thing?!"

Reinforcements arrive, soldiers dressed head to toe in forged armour with longswords in hand. Ranks are formed behind the commander as they stand ready to engage.

Draygar is now heavily enveloped in a ghostly haze. My mind suddenly becomes awash with rage, a beastly instinct drives out all rational thought. Our wills are entwined. I can feel him calling for me, *wanting* me. Drawn to him like a magnet, Draygar turns his head as a small army looks on in disbelief.

"Go. This is your moment." Vorathen speaks as if he somehow understands what's going on.

I don't.

Our followers retreat into cover. Draygar stands before me, alluring. My feet are willed forward, I dare not resist. Almost as if something is walking my body.

But not this time. Not the possessive presence. No darkened whispers in my head. I am controlling my own feet.

Time seems to stand still as I leap onto Draygar's back. My sigil immediately brightens, shining with such luminosity that it starts to crackle. Looking through the haze as if my eyes are ignorant, surges of energy snap around as if I'm caught in a thunderstorm.

"Charge!" A muffled command reaches my ears. *But what can a mere human achieve here?* Ranks of soldiers rush forward as arrows continue to rain down around us. Some strike me but it's nothing more than the tap of a raindrop.

Firing my bow, I watch in amazement as five projectiles leave its string: not *arrows* but pure-white bolts, concussive pulses that slam into and tear through the entire first line of men. My eyes lock onto the embedded diamond that pulses with such luminosity that they yearn to look away.

Draygar leaps forward and I ride on him with ease. A heavy swipe targets the commander, who narrowly avoids the attack out of pure adrenaline. Drawing another arrow with haste, it splits into five. Projectiles strike the armoured men with a blinding energy that courses through their bodies as they fall to the ground. Spasms of pain riddle their bodies before they pass. Souls rise from the slain like mushrooms in a damp field which dissolve into the beast's fiery eyes, fuelling Draygar as we ride by.

"Retreat!" A voice echoes across the battlefield from nearer the castle. Archers as well as a few remaining soldiers run. Following suit, the commander does not. Laughter leaves his mouth as he stands before us. His time is wearing thin.

"So, you're the one we were warned of. I must admit, I did not expect *that*."

I return a questioning glance. "Warned?"

"I see you do not know *what* you are. Do not worry, you will learn soon enough."

"You! You bastard! I remember you!" Vorathen emerges. "Of course it's you, grovelling at Vilriyan's feet for years. No surprise I find you serving that dog!"

"Calm down, Vorathen. I chose to be a part of something great, you chose a path to death. Your daughter is quite feisty. Vilriyan locked her up deservedly in that cell of his."

Vorathen looks around, astonished. It's not his path to death, quite the opposite. "*Death?! Are your eyes deceiving you?! And you dare speak like that about my daughter, you filthy rat!*"

"Well. Did I say she is a rebellious—" In one swift movement, the commander's head is sheared off and topples to the ground, crashing right before his lifeless body.

"We're close. Let's not let up." Vorathen throws his blade over his shoulder. We follow.

An eerie silence grows over the battlefield, my human senses suddenly return as our empowered states wane. Fighting has ceased. The sound of crackling energy still emits from the steel-armoured fallen.

A faint mumble catches my attention. I spin around to see two of our followers laying the other to rest. An arrow has hit its intended target, we have lost one.

One turns to me after finding his feet. "Arathyn, there may be hope after all."

A loud boom echoes through the trees, the sound of a stone gate slamming shut in the direction of the castle above. Our goal, not far off now.

"We've hurt them, lad. What do you propose?" Vorathen no doubt wants me to order him into battle once more as he kicks the slain commander's head aside into the bushes.

Surveying the battleground further, I'm convinced of a full retreat. "Vilriyan will be prepared. Let's salvage what we can and return. We may be able to convince others to follow. Gather what may be of interest, anything to aid our assault. Draygar will bear the load easily."

Vorathen gathers a bounty of armour and weapons, but his steps do not approach Draygar, likely for good reason. The spoils of war are thrown to the ground. "All yours!"

"Easy, boy." Draygar's weight shifts as I load armaments upon.

Our return to the coastal village is exhausting. Relief finds me as I notice it's in the same state as when we left. Moonlight gleams off the steel trove of armaments as night falls upon us.

Approaching the village, everyone has retired inside. For the first time, Draygar feels fatigued. I'm looking forward to a well-dressed bed. Something comfortable enough so my thoughts may wander.

"Who goes there?!"

Not everyone. A sentry alerts a number of armed villagers who storm out of a two-storey building which must be used as an observation post. Three men draw their blades.

Vorathen gestures toward Draygar with excitement. "Throw those crude swords away, we have much better."

A jaw nearly finds the ground. "What in all things mighty happened over there, you've brought back an entire armoury!"

"If you weren't cowards, you'd know." Vorathen looks unimpressed, his words changing the mood abruptly.

We have no time to waste, I set forth my expectations. "We will begin our assault on Forvazr tomorrow as promised. When dawn breaks, let us endeavour to convince whoever we can to join us. We have what we need to mount a challenge."

Their moods have changed, I *can* make a difference. One's respect is beginning to find me. "Very well. We will knock through the town in the morning and see who we can enlist."

All but one nod, another questions me. "Do you think we can best Vilriyan?"

One of our courageous companions steps forward and relieves me of the uncertainty. "We lost one of our own, but with numbers, we can fight for a future instead of living in fear! Once you see Arathyn's beast here, you will not doubt our chance at victory."

"What of the women and children?" Caution is still on the wind as well as in the lead sentry's head.

"Let us see our numbers in the morning. We will take our best men. I sincerely doubt that Vilriyan will attack given our earlier victory."

Vorathen is full of admiration. "You would be crazy not to fight for this young man!" He briefly drops his hand on my shoulder in the form of a heavy-plated gauntlet. His face wears a gleaming smile before a wispy hue follows his retreating hand which brings back the harsh reality.

An agreement is struck, the morning awaits.

Vorathen chuckles. "You will need to unload all of this. Then we can rest."

Sleep eludes me, I have so much on my mind. The commander's last words, my plan or lack thereof. Knowing that a lot of questions will be answered tomorrow, it is all so exhausting that I drift off into a slumber.

⎯⎯⎯❖⎯⎯⎯

Draygar chomps through a slab of meat. I peer out through a half-misted window: the sea is picturesque, it does wonders for my drifting mind.

"Oh, Arathyn, you're awake. You must have slept well." Grelda walks in, accompanied by the smell of a prepared meal, watching me as I stare out into nothingness. "I was contemplating skipping your breakfast given the time of day. But Draygar saw meat and I didn't dare walk out with it."

I don't question anyone's reluctance in possibly angering Draygar, the thought even crosses my mind from time to time.

In front of me rests a large platter of meat and fruit. "You will need to eat, the whole village knows of you. You have quite a reputation. Vorathen and the others have been very busy."

"Thank you, Grelda. You didn't need to."

Maybe she did, given what the day holds.

The meal is the best thing I've ever eaten. My body perks, ready for anything.

Vorathen and the others have been very busy. I very much doubt he's the one knocking on door after door.

Upon gathering my crimson garment and bow, memories flood back of Turinfall and the events that have led me here: my mother and the hope that Argora would care for her, Vorathen's family, broken, much like mine, and I try to imagine the voice of my father, telling me that he couldn't be more proud.

Swinging the front door open, Vorathen turns to me with several men in armour behind him.

"We are yours to command." Vorathen speaks with confidence as several men kneel behind his powerful figure.

Draygar stands by my side as we both peer around. Our soldiers now resemble the look of Vilriyan's forces, donning the armour and longswords we have salvaged. Ten men form a back row behind them, adorned in embossed leather vests, holding fine bows.

Vorathen is dressed in fully plated armour with his head encased in an armet. A greatsword in hand that gleams in the sunlight, razor-sharp as if it could lop branches of a hardwood tree in one blow. A shield in the opposite, embedded with metal arrowheads as spikes. How he has the strength to even lift them from the ground, let alone wield them in one hand, astounds me.

Our formidable resistance strides forward to the tune of heavy thudding warboots and the clanking of armour. A large crowd gathers as we depart.

I run a hand across my jaw. "Vorathen. Do you know of a way into Forvarr that may seem less obvious?"

"She is old and brittle. We may be able to break into the dungeon cellars below. I'll punch through that stone wall if I have to!" Vorathen flexes his arms.

With a plan concocted, it is time to set off on our conquest. Cheers ring out as people wave and celebrate. As we march our way along the war-torn sands, thoughts of tactics fill my mind. I now know of Draygar's mysterious transformation and how it manifests itself. Never in my life did I think I'd lead a band of mercenaries, or more so, forcefully-armed militia following my will. *Is this who I am destined to become?*

Vorathen is my armour, my men are a shield. Draygar is my sword.

Our feet are relieved of the gritty burden of sand as we press ahead. A feeling of uneasiness begins to wash over me. Vilriyan will have scouts concealed to report our movements, expecting our return. I'm certain of three things. We no longer have the element of surprise, we are too many to hide and too loud to be silenced by the ambience of our surrounding environment.

Forvarr sits perched on top of a hill which makes approaching it difficult, a stone path seemingly the only way forward. The winding nature of which gives us more time to be spotted. Castle gates loom large at the top.

It would be foolish to attack the main gate but it would appear there is no other option. Just as I struggle to make a decision, a loud blast of a horn drives out all my thoughts, stopping us in our tracks. Quickly, I motion my men into cover below a vast canopy of palms.

I glance at Vorathen. "Do you think we have been spotted?"

He rubs his jaw. "It appears they might be planning an attack of their own."

A villager speaks up. "We heard the faint sound of that horn right before the first attack on our village."

It is decided, *they are advancing.*

A few tense moments pass, followed by the mechanical sound of a large gate opening.

Vorathen chuckles. "What's your plan now?"

Confidence is key. "We will wait. They may pass right by us. That gives us the element of surprise."

The sound of heavy jangling footfalls starts soft before growing louder as they find their way down the path. Our enemy marches forth. We stand ready, determined to *avenge*, determined to *fight.*

Three heavily armoured warriors come into view beyond a row of palms, followed by a body of swordbearers in chainmail and at least a dozen archers. This will prove to be a much greater test than the battle before.

More blue sigils, on every wrist I can make out.

Draygar and his morphed form are what I crave. Guiding him into an advantageous position, another angle of attack is attained as the rest of our men settle into position. The beast roars as I beckon, simultaneously ordering my men to attack.

The enemy is transfixed as they gaze in our general direction, looking at nothing but a green barrier. I fire an arrow with the complement of others through breaches in the vegetation. Vorathen leaps into battle over small shrubbery, alongside our soldiers.

"For Vexxyra!" Vorathen bellows loudly as he closes in with the enemy. He's irrepressible at this point. Multiple arrows whistle past him, piercing through the archers he has nearly reached.

Draygar lunges out of the undergrowth, barreling down at one of the warriors. My companion is bashed aside by the fierce resistance of a gilded shield and left in a daze. Vorathen swings furiously, knocking two archers aside before they can even react.

Draygar is dazed, his movements are sluggish. One of the heavily-armoured assailants moves in, but he is hindered by a row of soldiers that come to Draygar's aid. We fire our bows once more as archers return fire, shooting aimlessly into the undergrowth.

Draygar is in need, I have to get to him.

Vorathen dances his way through ranks of their swordsmen, his armour taking a battering. With nerves of steel as sturdy as his shield, he is a walking fortress. Wisps of colour trail around him like a rainbow dancing in ocean mist, weeping from the sigils of his enemies as well as his own.

My men are standing firm, blocking and parrying swing upon swing from the enemy.

Dashing towards Draygar, adrenaline courses through my veins as the last of the enemy archers are defeated. They stand no chance so exposed.

One of their swordsmen breaks away from Vorathen and slashes at Draygar, catching him on his back. My companion's laboured attempt to dodge it fails, his pain shoots right through me. A pain shared.

I refocus, targeting the man who now races at me. An arrow fortuitously whistles past my head and thuds into him. He falls. Blood oozes from Draygar's wounds as I reach him.

"Vorathen. Protect me!" As if he doesn't have enough to worry about himself. Hopefully Vorathen can buy us more time.

Draygar begins to seize up further. The pain intensifies, bordering on paralysis.

"Finish them!" A commanding voice booms as their goal reshapes.

Vorathen's armour looks like it has weathered many years of bladed strikes. His sword and shield, bloodied. I can see his heaving, his arms dropping slightly.

Arrows thud against the steel of heavily armoured warriors as my archers try to halt their advance. One last swordsman rushes towards me and I let my hold on Draygar go as I roll away to dodge his advance. He then turns to Draygar, seizing upon an opportunity to attack the weakened beast.

Without even thinking, I just react. Draygar is but one strike away from death and I won't have that. I release an arrow through the swordsman's chest as he readies a strike, forcing his soul to depart in the direction of my companion. Draygar starts to gather energy as the last of my soldiers stand between us and the armoured brutes of the blue-sigillated enemy.

They stand there for a moment, pondering their next move as my archers fire another barrage from cover. Once again to no effect, the arrows deflect harmlessly off steel. I motion them to hold.

"Oh. What *glorious* battle!" Vorathen trudges up to join our forward line, looking like he's been wrestling with rose bushes. Blood streaks down his face. "Now you! Show me what you've got!"

Vorathen sets himself in front of the most formidable of the enemy. They stand firm, showing no sign of advancing.

Draygar takes to his feet slowly, calculating. I lead him over towards a mass of slain archers, keeping a watchful eye on our enemy's position. Within moments, the terrifying, morphed beast prowls by my side. *Painless.*

At that sight, the enemy soldiers exchange glances, then take a step back. "We do not wish to fight for Vilriyan." He is nothing but a brute. We did not choose this life."

Battle stops. Pointing toward the castle, I motion my archers to stay vigilant. Vorathen leers at me distastefully, waiting for an order. Nothing more than an exasperation of air leaves his mouth.

A plan concocts itself in my head. "Vilriyan trusts you, yes?

A nod is returned. "Yes."

"Put down your arms and lead us into Forvarr."

"He will have us killed!" Under all that armour are men who have no courage.

Vorathen steps forward, examining a twirling, blood-soaked greatsword. His words invoke the sternest of warnings. "I can see to that now if you like."

"No! No. We will obey!" The decision is made.

The men drop their weapons. Vorathen keeps an eye out for anything suspicious. We have lost a number of men, but our remaining force is enough to sway them.

They turn and we march … Then they stop at closed iron-embossed gates recessed in the cracked stone walls covered with moss. "They have shut us out!" We sneak closer through the cover of dense bush, surveying the walls for signs of lookouts.

Nothing. Just eerie quiet.

A small nook on the northern side of the castle wall catches my eye. Signs of damage, likely from a siege in years past. We take refuge inside, allowing me a moment to think.

Peering at the sigils etched upon the men who have unconvincingly defected, I point at one. "They will recognise you. They may just open the gate if you draw their attention."

Ordering one of my men to give him a sword, I compel him to make a move. We watch eagerly as he begins his attempt to make himself known. The sound of clanging steel pierces the eerie silence as blow after blow finds the weathered stone wall. He looks back toward us with a questioning glance, Vorathen urges him to continue.

"Stop that at once!" A strange husky voice from atop the wall calls out. I struggle to identify its source from where we hide.

"Open the gate. I must speak with Vilriyan."

"What of the boy and his dog?" The question cuts through me like a sharp blade and I bleed rage.

"We have him surrounded. Vorathen too."

"Ah, Vilriyan has plans for him." His raspy voice makes way for a chuckle.

Vorathen mutters under his breath. "Oh Lord. Give me strength."

"Would Vilriyan like to witness their deaths personally?"

I am impressed, although uncertain. *Is their act born out of fear or a confidence in finding a new allegiance?*

Time stands still as we await the verdict, then come the words that my ears are waiting to hear. "Open the gate!"

We steel ourselves as the sound of the opening gate reverberates across the ground. With the final clunk, we run with haste toward the opening.

Vorathen charges through the breach with the fury of a thousand lions. We halt suddenly as there is no one in sight. The gate slams shut behind us. A dainty figure disappears into the shadows behind the portcullis of a tower in the distance. The castle otherwise appears deserted.

We've walked right into a trap.

Beyond the courtyard, catching my attention is a pulsating blue glow that shines within a hall.

"Keep watch." My orders keep us from being ambushed, everyone stays behind except for Vorathen and the defectors.

Creeping closer, faint voices grow in the silence.

Fearing the worst to be caught off guard, we rush in.

"Alas ... We finally meet ... Young one," a low tone echoes throughout the hall as a dark figure turns towards me. I can make out nothing more than a silhouette.

"I ... have waited a very ... very ... long time ... for this moment ..."

At the sight of two dark entities, we stand perplexed. Hidden behind the bright glow of a blue sigil, a man kneels beside a crucible.

Hands reach for blades. "No … No … I would not … Advise such action. What … is your name … Young one?"

How do I respond? Expectation is grand.

"Arathyn …" My voice quivers.

"Ah yes … Arathyn… You have great … Power … Within you … Enmara chose you …"

"Enmara?"

"You have much … to learn … Fate … has chosen you …" The figure leans forward, pointing directly at me. "That sigil … you bear. That … is the marking … of Enmara herself. She has chosen you … to be her … Master …"

"Master?" My whole life is being re-created. A chuckle cracks apart the tension.

The same husky voice from atop the gate continues. "Oh, hurry up, Eldest One. I want to test my experiment."

"Enmara. Olynero. Vordera, Ixxenira and Kygeera. Ancient beasts. There we go. You'll *kill* each other or you'll *save* each other. Through your … ah … yes, spirit brands. See how quick that was, Eldest One?" If the figure that named me is capable of showing emotion, it doesn't appreciate being hurried. There is no response.

"Well, then, this here. What was his name? Ah, Vilriyan! Well, yes, throw him that vial of souls. Right over there, very fresh. That should get him started."

Souls. Vials. Started?

This is some kind of strange ritual.

"Best be off. Please welcome your Olyneran Spiritmaster, Vilriyan. Come on now, hurry. This will get messy!"

Ghostly draped figures hurry away through a doorway. An echoing boom thunders through the space as a door slams.

Vilriyan's body is empowered as wailing souls are absorbed into his figure. The *experiment* rises to its feet, turning to face us.

A chill sweeps through the hall as Vilriyan edges slowly toward us. *An absolute brute.* Footsteps leave a trail of frost in their wake. A body clad with steel from head to foot and surrounded by an aura of icy mist walks toward us. Armed with a large broadsword and a hefty steel gauntlet, his body continues enthusiastically. An Olyneran sigil beams blue light throughout the entire hall.

"Scurry, *vermin.* You would be a fool to face me now!" Our formidable enemy turns his head, cracking from sheer cold.

"Oh, Vorathen. I see that you have once again chosen to find what scant help you can get. This is what you chose? Have you returned for that daughter of yours?" Vilriyan speaks powerfully. The frost at his feet begins to spread across the stone floor.

Vorathen is undeterred. "Just when I thought you couldn't get any *colder*, here you stand! When I am done with you, I will rip your heart out if I can find it and feed it to the rats!"

All of a sudden, the Olyneran defectors surge in front of us and take a knee. "Empower us, Vilriyan. We will see to them!"

Their spiritmaster's power appears to sway them back to their former allegiance. "Approach … I will see to it."

Without a moment's notice, Vilriyan slashes at one, leaving a large gaping breach through the victim's plate which starts to crystallise and freeze. With a heavy hand, he swings around, buffeting the man with a powerful blow from his gauntlet that shatters his entire body.

"Whoo-ah. Feel my power!"

The other tries to retreat. Vilriyan lunges with his blade that pierces right through his next victim. His eyes freeze and his face hardens in fear before all signs of life appear to fade away. With one effortless movement, his body is violently tossed aside into a wall, shattering like glass.

Vorathen's face, for once, takes on a state of uncertainty.

Bewilderment runs rampant as I witness the extraordinary events unfolding right before us.

"I am not afraid of you! Let me bathe in your power!" A desperate plea sees Vilriyan hesitate momentarily as the last of the men pleads for his life.

"I am nothing if not curious." Vilriyan places his hand upon the shoulder of the last of the men. Just a touch.

Suddenly, the lesser sigil on the man's body becomes stronger and his armour glazes over in a frost. "Go forth!"

Vorathen steps forward to face his lesser icy assailant before charging at him as if his fear has taken leave. A savage strike impacts against a sturdy frozen shield, which barely gives way under the force.

He must be fuelled by the thoughts of his family. *Vengeance, liberation.* "Oh a test? About time for a challenge!"

A flurry of strikes ensues as the two men battle away. As stalwart as Vorathen is, he does not appear to be able to overwhelm his adversary.

Considering our position, I am not to be defeated without a fight either.

Vilriyan stands stoically front and centre, clearly impressed with his newfound power. Undisturbed urns and jars line the walls beyond the icy menace. *Maybe within myself is the only answer?* A plan is devised. *Maybe I will be able to do the same?*

A dash from my feet has me moving along the nearest wall. Draygar traces the furthest, as we loop around Vilriyan.

Suddenly, he turns and hurls his shield towards Draygar, who dodges it easily. Stone shears from the wall and crumbles to the floor. "Where are you off to, boy?!"

Vilriyan rips his aegis of frozen steel free, steel that has embedded itself into the masonry. Draygar slashes his way through ceramic urns while I shatter several jars upon the stone floor.

"Those souls are mine!" Vilriyan bellows, his voice morphing into a scream that begins to drown out his frantic voice. Souls circle around me. Closing my eyes, I let my body gather power.

This feels surreal.

Energy courses through every part of my being as I open my eyes to make out a crystalline sheen beginning to coalesce upon my armour. Turning to face Vilriyan, I gaze through a light, misty fog as if I'm at sea.

A glint of shining steel appears from the far reaches of my view, spinning, moving rapidly toward me. With extreme agility, I move as Vilriyan's sword shears the air beside me, through a white aura that encompasses my body. A sudden chill grasps my figure, followed by a sharp clang as his sword finds the wall behind me.

I am untouched.

"Impossible!" Vilriyan knows he has a fight on his hands.

Anger flashes across his face as he turns to face Vorathen. "Let me see you protect him!"

Drawing my bow effortlessly, I unleash a bolt which ricochets off Vilriyan's armour, exploding upon the wall instead. His subordinate is not so lucky. A bolt strikes his armour, nullifying the very power within him. His sigil darkens before the icy hue dissipates from sight. Vorathen shoves the drained man aside before delivering a fatal strike.

Vilriyan's onslaught is profound. Draygar roars furiously, which shakes the foundations of the entire castle. Vorathen covers his ears in an attempt to deaden the effect.

Vilriyan lunges as he pursues, a strike that falls agonisingly close to a direct hit.

"Still a bit slow, eh?" Vorathen somehow still finds humour.

Vilriyan turns his attention toward two of my soldiers who have stormed into the hall. They're no match.

A look of determination begins to grow upon their faces as I rush toward them. My soldiers raise their shields against the huge swing of Vilriyan's heavy gauntlet. Their defensive actions do very little to absorb his brutish power which knocks their flailing bodies to the ground.

Another forceful blow lands, mangling armour and weapons alike in their attempts to resist. One more menacing swing is readied. My men, exposed.

But they're spared.

Vilriyan is knocked off his feet by my lunging companion. Draygar leaps onto him before raking his stone-hardened claws along his armour. Sparks fly around the hall in every direction like fireflies. Draygar's rock-hardened legs begin to freeze atop the frozen menace and he struggles to break free.

A chill runs across my body. "I've got your pet now, Arathyn!" Vilriyan is boastful as he struggles under Draygar's weight.

With one swift move, sensing an opportunity, I throw myself onto Draygar's back just as Vilriyan lifts his gauntlet. Readying an arrow that crackles with pure-white energy before transforming, I draw the bow to its limits. Energy courses around me as I gather every remnant of my power. My diamond-enriched bow releases. Power swells before a concussive pulse is released. Vorathen throws himself to the ground, taking cover wherever he can.

Upon catching my drumming breath as the energy subsides, I throw down my bow. Vilriyan's sigil no longer shows any sign of light upon his wrist. The Olyneran Spiritmaster has been defeated.

His reign of tyranny is over.

Vorathen leans against a small blackened fireplace, breathing heavily. "Forgive me, Harriet."

A creak from high up penetrates the silent hall. A voice booms down.

"Arathyn … You … are the only hope … of … unifying … this land once more …

"Five beasts … ruled this land a long time ago … They remain among us … in *spirit* …

"Olynero… A Sapphire Goliath… Skulked high atop the Feygoran Mountains…

"Kygeera… A Crimson Leviathan… Fire and brimstone of the Askaren Wastelands…

"Vordera… The Tempest… A Storm Behemoth… Soared through the sky and over pinnacles to the East…

"Ixxenira… Nature's Hand… A Veridian Colossus… Raced through the forests of the South…

"Then, of course … Enmara … The Protector … Goddess of Arcura … a Diamondback Alpha …

"The Shattering … as it will be known … has plagued this land …

"Their spirits … have fractured … They seek … new hosts …

"Humanity … is in peril … You bear Goddess Enmara's Sigil … She … has chosen … you …

"Olynero … Vilriyan … There will be … others …"

Words trail off as the mysterious voice disappears before eerie silence sets in once more. A strange voice, yet somewhat familiar.

A well-earned reprieve is deserved.

⚜

My men stand at their posts in various positions as if they were completely oblivious to what transpired. I doubt that, however, given the emergence of two of them during. One thing is for certain. They followed orders and their loyalty is profound.

"It is done." The archers converge on my position without hesitation. I am joined by the two soldiers who were brave enough to step into the unknown.

Leading them into the hall, one trips on a chestplate which makes Vorathen jump from his slumber. "That was the best rest I have had in weeks. That bastard is dead!"

"What just happened?" one asks.

"I believe we are at the mercy of spirits. These sigils we bear are linked to the beasts that used to roam these lands. At the Ruins of Highgarde, something happened to me that changed our way of life. Mine in particular." I try my best to recollect what was said before.

One of my soldiers suddenly winces, he has a nasty cut on his shoulder. I grasp at an undisturbed urn, one of the last, shattering it on the floor. My sigil consumes the soul that escapes.

"Trust me." I place my hand on his injured shoulder.

A wisp of light binds us as his sigil illuminates further. Amazed looks peer on. My action saps the energy the soul provides. My sigil weakens.

Gratitude washes over his face. "Woah. The pain has gone!"

Vorathen doesn't seem surprised. "Lad. I knew you were something else from the moment you had me at the tip of your arrow."

I feel a profound allegiance, embracing the person, the leader I have become. It isn't a choice, however, the responsibility that now falls on my shoulders was given to me. "We are Enmarans. We fight to protect. We fight for peace!"

Cheers ring around the hall before the question is asked. "What about Vorathen?"

"I believe he bears a fragment of Ixxenira. We must not get too close to him. You have all seen what will happen." I beam in admiration of the man who stands before me. He agrees, raising an empty flagon that he has somehow obtained from the wreckage.

"We have a daughter of mine to find. She is hardy like myself. If there is any chance she is still alive, she will be." A heavy boot destroys a rotten door. Vorathen walks through the breach and down a set of stairs with his greatsword slung across his shoulder.

We descend into a labyrinth of damp corridors, the only sound coming from the shriek of vermin that scuttle away as our footsteps draw close. We search through the complex maze of tunnels, encountering haggard-looking dwellers who are unarmed. They hurry off as soon as they are spotted. The condition of these tunnels and the people within it don't fill one with any confidence.

Finally, we approach a heavy iron door that glows under the light of a kerosene torch to one side. The door, slightly ajar. Vorathen effortlessly pushes it open to a row of dilapidated cells. A young, malnourished woman lies within one. Skeletons sit among others.

The woman is dressed in white linen cloth. She lies upon a stone bench with only a small bowl of stagnant water offered at the base.

"My girl!" Vorathen shouts as he fixes swollen eyes upon his daughter. Running up to the cell door, he finds it locked. He pounds away furiously, but the resilient iron won't give. My eyes fall upon a row of rusted keys hanging on a wall by the entrance.

I point. "Vorathen."

"Oh, of course." His face turns red before emitting a laugh.

Gathering them with as much fervour as he fights with, he rushes back to his daughter's cell. After several attempts with different keys, the grinding sound of metal fills the room as the lock gives. Vorathen rushes in and picks up his limp daughter.

"No! You'll kill her!" My warning finds Vorathen immediately as a wisp of colour begins to coalesce. He nearly drops her to the ground as he hastily retreats from the cell. Tears run down his weathered face, but at least this means she is alive.

"What is she? Save her!" I can sense the wrenching of his heart.

Vorathen steps aside as I make my way into the cell, very cautiously lowering my hand toward her shoulder, pushing aside the linen. "She's Olyneran, but she is alive. It's the only reason why *The Shattering* didn't take her too."

Right at that moment, it hits.

Something has changed. Her soul does not wither at my touch.

The curse doesn't take hold.

"I can't thank you enough. How will I ever repay you?" Vorathen's expression of relief lifts the veil of anguish on his face.

Dodging the question, there are more important matters. "She needs sustenance. We will return to the village immediately. I fear she will not survive."

My arms carry her limp body. Groans echo throughout the tunnels as we make our way out.

Sunlight graces us. My men help me load her into Draygar's saddle quickly. It isn't perfect but it does the job. The situation is dire.

The gates are opened and we begin our descent. Offering clean water to her, she manages a sip or two. I rest my hand on her forehead, a fever is raging through her body. A day later and Vorathen would be burying her.

Time is running thin.

Beyond the fringe of palms, the sands of the Forvarran Coast greet us once more. The distant image of the village is in sight. A small crowd of men, women and children gathers as we return.

Mixed emotions are portrayed.

"Vilriyan is dead. May his demise let us live in peace for now."

My bed holds her body in comfort. She's burning up. I rifle through an assortment of supplies from the Inn.

"Seasnap. Hearthweed. Azurebloom." I find myself talking out loud.

I examine the room. I know enough about herbs to know what I'm looking for but my mind is clouded.

Then I laugh. *Silver Stars.* I still have one from earlier and it's sitting upon a bench like a beacon. It is a risk, but warranted. I slice it in half, halving the potency. This is no time for idiocy.

Her lips part and I press the berry into her mouth along with a cup of water.

I find myself unable to leave.

Eleven

VEXXYRA

My eyes open to the sight of oaken walls. A sea breeze whips through an open window. The distinct taste of a Silver Star in my mouth.

Where am I?

A young man peers at me with ocean-blue eyes. I check that I am covered in the linen sheets that I find myself lying upon. His long, streaky blond hair sits atop a lean and tall figure. A smile breaks upon his face.

My head is running hot, a bead of sweat trickles down my face. I have a fever.

A Silver Star. Thankfully, someone knows what they're doing.

"How are you feeling?" he asks.

"Where am I?"

"You're safe. We rescued you."

"We? What? Vilriyan?" My thoughts race faster than my fever. All I can remember is being thrown into a cell.

"Your father and I. Vilriyan is dead. You are from Coradal?"

Hesitation grips me as I try to comprehend his question. Words spill from my mouth as I attempt to recollect my most recent memories. "Yes … My mother was killed … I was … taken."

The lean figure walks over to the doorway and calls out my father's name. Before I can even take another breath, he storms in.

"Thank the gods. I couldn't bear to lose you too."

"Father, keep your distance." My warning baffles the young man, but he nods. He must understand what I do.

"I swear to you. I will never leave you again." My father's words are heartfelt, but he shouldn't blame himself. He couldn't do anything when I was dragged away.

"We should leave her to rest, Vorathen." My father agrees and they leave.

Yes. Rest.

⁕

Suddenly, my feet work. The fever is all but a mild inconvenience. Clothes are laid out over a chair by the bed, clearly the choice of a woman. A homespun skirt with a lovely leather tunic sits atop the pile.

An elderly woman appears in the doorway while I reach for the garments. "Oh. My apologies. I will leave you to dress."

"Did you choose these?" I ask.

She frowns. "Yes. Do you not like them?"

"I do. Thank you. What is your name?"

"Grelda. Caretaker. You can't lie around here all day. I will leave you to dress."

A warm smile grows on my face. She's very prompt, her dislike of tardiness is what I need.

After throwing on the clothes, I stride outside. Sunlight blinds me and I shield my eyes. It has been days since I've been exposed.

The young man is making a speech to the crowd on top of a black beast. I find myself blushing. "There is much that you will not understand. We carry the sigil of Enmara. We must protect each other but we work with anyone who is willing. This is our new way of life."

Then my father speaks. "Stay away from me and my daughter, Vexxyra. You know what will happen. If you do, it won't be the curse that kills you."

What is going on here? I understand the latter. Looking at my wrist, the symbol is still there, just as it was before I was taken prisoner. Blue, vibrant and simple. One line. Two circles. Within a diamond.

The young man spots me before riding over. I feel unworthy. He towers over me like I'm a peasant. "Vexxyra. I'm glad to finally meet."

Words don't even come to fruition. *Is he a king? How do I address him?*

His eyes bore right through me. "Do not be alarmed. Speak to me like you would anyone else."

"How did you defeat him?" It takes him a moment to discern my question.

"I am similar. But where he abused his power for tyrannical purposes, I will use mine for *peace*. On that note, may I test something that is on my mind?"

My eyebrows are raised so far they almost float above my head. "You're asking me for permission?"

"You're the experiment."

Shock washes over my face briefly. Conducting experiments is what I'm used to, just not with *myself*. However, I'm now at the height of curiosity.

Reservedly, I nod.

"With your permission, Vorathen. It will just be for a brief moment. If I am able to touch Olynerans, Grelda may be able to also as we share alignment," he says.

My father nods without the slightest sign of empathy.

"Grelda. Just for an instant, place your hand on her shoulder."

Time stands still as the elderly woman outstretches her arm at my blue sigil before it lingers above my shoulder. Every eye in the village is fixed upon Grelda's hand as I feel its touch. Gasps of disbelief catch the moment perfectly as there is no sign of the curse.

No wisp. No reaction.

The touch of my father's hand finds the young man's shoulder. A greenish-white wisp of light connects them which draws his subtle laugh. "You never know. I am sure it was on someone else's mind too."

His blue eyes pierce me again. His body cuts a look of pure satisfaction. "It is true. Whatever happened upon Vilriyan's death brought Enmarans and Olynerans together. Thank you, Vexxyra."

<hr>

A crisp seabreeze whips at my hair as I stare out into the abyss that is the North Arcuran Sea. Kerosene burns in a torch that illuminates me in the darkness. The moon is high, a beautiful reminder of how peaceful our home is. *If it still is.*

Numerous feet encroach from behind … I whip around, grabbing the torch in the process. It's him and his beast, hair gleaming in torchlight.

"Sorry. I didn't mean to startle you." His gentle voice is calming.

"That's my fault. After what I have been through."

"You can't blame yourself for that." *He's right.*

Guilt begins to creep in. "I never thanked you or my father. How did you meet?"

"I nearly killed him. He ransacked a town. Don't blame him for that either. Your father was desperate."

"Nearly?"

"The situation *forced* itself. Your father's life was spared. He mentioned that you were taken and here we are."

"One doesn't just *spare* his life. My father killed three bandits with nothing but a pitchfork." *I may have had a hand in that too.* He looks impressed.

"Your father and three others." Now he's gloating.

A warm smile almost makes me melt inside. "I'd better be careful then. Are you our leader?"

"Vilriyan was the Olyneran Spiritmaster. I'm the Enmaran. Call me Arathyn. This is Draygar. We're from Turinfall."

Turinfall. No wonder he's perched upon a beast. "I've heard stories of your kind."

Arathyn dismounts before reaching into a satchel conveniently placed along Draygar's side. "Please. Continue."

An outstretched hand holds a ration of dried meat. He sits as I accept his generosity.

Snapping easily as I twist it, I offer back half. "Is it true that you must live with a … *companion*?"

Arathyn presses his lips. "Yes. From the age of ten."

"I fear the worst for Oran and Arix."

His look turns puzzled before the meaning hits. "Oh, friends?"

Tears begin to well. "Yes. Dear ones. I have already lost Mira and my … mother."

He motions his wolf-like companion over and he leans against me. *I think it's a he?* Draygar's snout is at my hand, he sniffs … and then lowers his head. I brush my hand across his coat, it's thick, firm … but also soft. It's as if the beast senses my feelings. I don't budge. I let myself be vulnerable and bury myself in his warm coat. Arathyn lets out a weak smile. *Is Arathyn acting this way because of his status or is it purely out of kindness?* But it's heartfelt.

I just wish he were more mature. Sorry, Oran.

Twelve

ARATHYN

"Where is Arathyn? We are under attack on the western flank!"

My feet spring into action as I give Vexxyra a parting gesture. A sharp whistle leaves my mouth as I summon Draygar. The beast awakes and darts over. I quickly grace the saddle. Enmaran soldiers race to my side.

The western front. A fight between men is taking place in front of us, swords flurrying about.

"Stop!" Drawing my bow, I shift my balance on Draygar's back. Vorathen storms in from my right to aid us.

I raise my voice above the sound of clanging steel. "Stand down!"

Fighting ceases abruptly. There is no sign of the curse within the entanglement of bodies.

"Identify yourselves! Show me your arms!" One of the swordbearers throws his blade aside once he has noticed too.

An arm is raised, showing an Olyneran sigil as another runs towards me. "Have you stopped the curse? Oh, please have you stopped the curse?!"

"Fighting is not the answer, we will not harm you. You are Olyneran, we are Enmaran, the curse between our kind is gone. It still, however, lingers between others." A wisp of colourful light briefly emerges between my hand and Vorathen's shoulder.

I make my point.

Vorathen is used to being the example. "He gets his power from me," he says with a chuckle, trying to lighten the mood.

"Oh, Father, do not be so whimsical." Vexxyra's voice silences the masses. Dressed in leather from head to foot, her beauty stuns me. Her eyes narrow at the kneeling man, identifying a few vials tied around the Olyneran's waist.

"Mountainbloom, Draemar Thistle and Coradal Root. Very well prepared, I see."

Familiar names, these remedial plants are found around Turinfall. Perhaps she dabbles in medicine.

"Lower your weapons. Make yourselves at home." People go about their own business once more.

"Please. Help me." One of the swordbearers approaches Vexxyra, looking to benefit from her knowledge. Blood runs down his arm from a large gash.

"Of course. Let me see what your acquaintance has here." She glances back at me as if she needs my approval.

A warmth hits me, maybe she is just admiring our formidable presence. "Go on."

It dawns on me rather quickly that this place is not ideal to defend. Exposed from every direction. No cover. No vantage points.

A village that sits on level ground, as does most of the surrounding area. An easy target for a more powerful enemy. Given recent events, who knows what danger lurks out there.

Gathering Vorathen and my Enmaran Guards, a name I gave to honour the two surviving soldiers who fought with us, we draft a plan. "We are vulnerable here, this village is far too exposed."

"You are right. Any decent army would have no trouble overrunning this place," says Vorathen.

A guard shares his wisdom. "There are many of us. We cannot have uncertainty."

Uncertainty. I sense that will be around forever.

"We are but a small force for now. There will be more Enmarans out there and Olynerans seeking refuge. Danger can descend on us at any moment." An unspoken agreement is struck. "It is best we move as soon as possible while there is calm. We have the ability to protect these people."

The other guard breaks his silence. "Where do you suggest, Arathyn?"

Peering to the west, I point at mist-enshrouded peaks belonging to the Feygoran Mountains through the palms. "On the rise below the peaks. This will give us vantage, making it difficult to assail. Fresh water and an abundance of food, no doubt." Hunting and foraging experience come to the fore.

"An advantageous position, lad. Seems fitting." Vorathen gives his approval as do the others.

A plan approved. "Very well. We will prepare and leave upon nightfall."

⊰◈⊱

Horse-drawn carriages are prepared. Resources, abundant. Amazement grips me at how they all follow me blindly. Not a single person is left unprepared. *I'm the best hope they have.*

"We are ready." Vorathen's voice speaks for everyone. "A surprise waits for you too."

My interest is piqued as I follow Vorathen. Torchlight lights up the entire area.

"This man has crafted you a fine saddle." Vorathen points in the direction of an able craftsman who wears a belt around his waist upon which several tools hang. A face awash with nervousness locks on as he awaits my approval. The saddle lies prominently on the cobblestone path.

"No one wanted to … *saddle* … your beast." Vorathen adds his signature chuckle.

"Likely for the best. I admire everyone's intelligence on that matter."

Kneeling to inspect the fine piece of craftsmanship, my eyes make out its maple entirety. Excellent flexibility during sharp manoeuvres is what I need. Two seats made of hardwood, tough and smoothly edged, will bear my weight and provide a stable platform. My eyes drop to find cured-leather strapping with steel stirrups for footing, rounding off such a remarkable piece of equipment. If my contraption that I conjured up back at the fort had feelings, the sight of this would make the last of its mangled state crumble.

Overjoyed, I turn to the man responsible. "This is extremely well made, thank you. Your time is greatly appreciated. I will use it immediately."

"Will someone hand that man a mead!" Vorathen sees to it that he receives more than just a gesture of gratitude.

Draygar does not move a muscle as I bind the saddle to him. It fits very comfortably. Upon placing a foot on a stirrup, I spring up onto my companion's back. A cheer is triggered from the crowd, as well as Vexxyra of whom my eyes are focused on.

As comfortable as a bed, my body fits perfectly into every recess. Nothing more than a slight jolt tickles my frame as Draygar strides forward.

"Our journey begins." We march out, leaving the village in our wake.

Torchlight leads us forward through darkness as we make our way along the coast. Our path, a westward direction. Ears attuned to crashing waves upon the coastline nearby so as to not lose our way.

I lead from the front with Vorathen by my side. The two Enmaran Guards hold the flanks while a band of light swordsmen guards the rear. Jepp walks with Grelda and Vexxyra carries a torch.

Sounds from small creatures are persistent as they dart away from us. Every so often, I keep the newfound Olynerans in check. I can't afford to take any chances. Their attempt to fight us holds my interest, although I believe they are just lost and misguided like most of us.

A marshland is nearby, the sounds of a vast array of insect inhabitants drown out the sea. "We will rest here for the night."

Vexxyra hastily runs off with a flame. Marshes provide an abundance of enriched plant life. Following her curiously, I grab a spare torch.

Darkness grasps at me, a single flame does little to keep it at bay. A moon hiding behind thick cloud offers no light. The torch that Vexxyra holds is my only sense of direction, a torch that waves back and forth above half-submerged reeds as she focuses intently. Numerous glass vials hang off a coiled rope, belted around her waist.

"Would you like some of this?" A resistant coil of Marshvine lies in my hand as I slice through it with the other.

"Oh. Yes. Do you know what this is?"

"Marshvine. Most of my childhood was spent hunting animals, gathering all sorts of plants with my parents in Turinfall. That was our way of life. I do not know the properties of most, but I am sure I could identify them."

"You hunt ... *animals?*" Perplexed eyes find Draygar before resting on me.

"Only *rabid* ones. We need food to survive, just like everyone else."

She laughs. "*Was?* Where are your parents?"

I take a moment to consider my answer. *What point is there in being dishonest?* Never have I been so smitten. "I was exiled."

"Oh. Now you *must* tell me."

"That is for another time."

A look of disappointment flashes across her face before she smiles. "Marshvine is excellent for construction, it can hold an entire house together. My father and I used much of it on our farm, it still stands strong today."

"Do you have much knowledge in the profession?"

She chuckles. "Too much."

"I'm guessing you are an apothecary?"

"You're speaking with the newest member of the Coradal Apothecary's Guild. Now, maybe the *only* member."

I'm taken aback. That is a remarkable achievement. "Congratulations." Now I'm the one feeling unworthy.

We both devour a Silver Star, which litter the reaches of the marshland. After several trips back and forth with a few extra hands gathering reagents, we are done.

Energy is sapped. Weary faces ask for respite. After a day on foot, we rest.

⁕

The dawning sun begins to uncover our surroundings. Mist is chased away. It is my time to take watch. Palms that line the distant village are now all but small figures behind us. The marsh is vast. Rivers that feed down from the mountains reach a delta on the coastline.

A small forested area on the lower rise of the mountains draws my eyes. A perfect location. An ample supply of herbs and lumber awaits. Pure water from the river at a short reach. Not to mention wartime advantages.

"That will do it!" Vorathen wakes to a chilling wind that whips up. His hands find a fur coat before it's thrown over his shoulders. He is the last to rise.

"Let us continue. Warm yourselves. We will have to endure the cold from here on." People hurry about searching for warmer garments.

"We have sight of our new homeland!" Pointing in the direction of the forest beyond, we begin to move as one.

"Hold!" Movement in the distance. People look around frantically.

"What do you think, lad?" Vorathen spots it also.

"I am not sure. It looks fast." Readying my bow, I advance before motioning others to follow.

"Beasts?" Vorathen says.

I cannot make it out. Flat and open landscape spreads vast. Discretion is an afterthought as I sense no immediate threat. Confronting an ambush from further off is better than being caught by surprise at close range.

Continuing toward the mountains cautiously, my eyes survey a thick cluster of trees that line a river. Nothing stirs in sight. It would not be safe to explore further, so we keep ourselves near the coast.

Drawing further away from the source of previous movement, our direction becomes exact. The marsh has almost been entirely circumnavigated.

"Arathyn! Something is coming!" One of the rear swordbearers bellows a warning.

Draygar's bounding strides have us in motion, we're at the rear in no time. Vorathen follows behind. Large, unknown beasts bear down on us.

"Positions!" A barrier is formed of guards and swordbearers, several men draw bows behind me.

"What ravenous animals are these?" Vorathen prepares himself.

"I have never seen anything like these before. Ready yourselves!" Drawing within range, they show no sign of slowing. People huddle over. Grelda's voice sings songs of harmony to worried children.

"Fire!" A volley of arrows leaves our line before whistling down around the beasts. One is struck on its back, it loses balance and falls to the ground before regaining its feet.

"Nice shot! Stay in rank!" Vorathen draws forward in a line with our infantry, instilling heart into the group. We prepare a second barrage as the beasts close in.

"Fire!" Maintaining my balance upon Draygar, I aim carefully before releasing an arrow into the body of the foremost. All but my arrow miss their intended targets.

Vorathen surges forward before suddenly stopping. The beast misjudges his movement and lunges right by him. A heavy swing of his shield knocks it aside.

Draygar quickens in an instant. A saddle so smooth, I can easily return fire.

Our forward line holds firm, protecting our people behind. Lunging jaws strike directly upon steel, knocking one swordsman back. The impact of such an attack is underestimated, but the beast is stunned long enough for a guard to surge in to make quick work of its weakened state.

Draygar leaves the ground with such rabid movements, lashing at one of the beasts which narrowly misses.

A lunge is parried by Vorathen's greatsword before the beast trips him up from behind. Menacing fangs are exposed right before his eyes. An arrow embeds into the beast. Mine. Shrieks cry out before the beast drops.

"I owe you one!" His gratitude is short-lived. Another targets him, only to be pinned down by his bladed shield. His thrusting blade sees to its end.

The remaining one flees.

"That was … *different.*" Vorathen gathers himself before checking over the others.

Examining the mass of huddled bodies, no one has been injured. Vexxyra holds Jepp in her arms. People begin to find their feet, peering at Vorathen with admiration. The way he fights with such confidence does wonders for morale.

Beasts draped in haggard grey fur, they look weak and gaunt. Their lean bodies indicate starvation. In their eyes, we were no doubt a huge feast to a desperate pack. Possibly their last chance given their state. There isn't much, what meat to take is taken as well as the fur.

Pressing on toward the mountains once more, conversation stirs behind me. Whispers of joy, but their words I cannot make out. A feeling of satisfaction hits me knowing that we are able to bestow hope within our ranks.

⚬

Our footsteps grace the forest on the eastern side of the rise. "Heed caution. There may be danger at every turn."

A deciduous landscape welcomes us. Green canopies cover high above. Large trees of mostly cedar carve a path toward land that takes a sharp incline. The ambience of wildlife intensifies as we venture further into the forest before mountainous terrain is underfoot.

A rock face. Our westernmost point is reached. My eyes scour the unassailable wall, they make out a snow-capped peak that looms above. We have arrived.

A flatter recess in the slope is surveyed. Enthusiasm is rife in a man who speeds past me in a hurry with a banner.

Oak, in the form of a large spire, laced with hide etched with Enmara's sigil, is driven into the ground. Vorathen and I can't help but cheer.

The foundation is set.

Supplies lie everywhere, it is nothing but a mess. People are hard at work, beginning to build. There is an advantageous mix of professional ability within them. I look around, everyone has a hand in something of use. *Beginning to build.* A new purpose I wear with such responsibility. People to lead, lives to protect. It no longer feels surreal.

Vorathen walks with me as I survey the location of our establishment, gathering intelligence of the immediate area. Our forces stay behind. Vexxyra has made her way down to the marsh once more, darting through the trees, gathering what she can. *She never stops.*

This is the first time I have ever left Draygar alone, hoping that he's more of a use as transportation rather than wandering aimlessly. Nevertheless, I have the next best thing with me.

Heading south, we traverse the slopes beneath the Feygoran Mountains. A picturesque view of forests below welcomes our searching eyes as we make our journey.

An unnatural row of stone lies ahead, carved from a much larger body of rock. A weathered and disjointed path curves its way up the rise from the land below that appears to lead inside the mountain.

We approach cautiously, turning around the wall as the sun begins to recede over the ridgeline.

Eeriness sets in as we fix our gaze upon huge stone walls. Ramps and parapets. A dark abode that appears long abandoned, much like Forvarr was. Moss reaches over the entire floor before rising up the walls. A forge, accompanied by its large anvil, lies in decay towards the rear. Loose stone lies scattered amongst the surroundings, broken away from dilapidated constructions. A vital resource, no doubt.

"Careful, lad." Vorathen's warning brings about caution as my steps stutter. Others would know of this desolate place, it must have been here for centuries. Convincing myself that I want Draygar with me to explore further, we decide to return. My mother would never forgive me if I fell without my companion. A strange energy feels present in the shadows. Sunlight will provide necessary exposure as will additional sets of eyes.

Retreating out into the open, I quickly throw myself into cover behind a rocky outcrop, as does Vorathen.

"Look. Below." Men stride confidently up the winding trail. Their alignment I cannot make out, they are too far off.

"Plan?" Vorathen knows I am quick on my feet to think of something.

"We need to know who and *what* they are, they are far too close to remain unknown." Fearing not to be discovered, we carefully make our way into a better scouting position.

Their approach continues, unhindered by the steep incline that the path takes in several places. The company of a woman is discovered as we peer through gaps in the stone barrier. Vorathen stands ready at the opening, just out of sight.

"Do we really need to be here?" A sharp tone splits the silence.

"Of course we do. Souls of the dead linger here." A chill runs down my spine as footfalls add to the suspense as they draw near.

For the first time, I see a sigil with one more additional circle than the Olyneran. It has a yellow hue, exactly like the rune I have previously seen at Highgarde.

They pass right by us, completely oblivious to our presence before heading down a darkened hallway under torchlight, taking a turn out of sight.

"We need to inform the others. We have seen enough."

—◆—

Braziers light up our camp, the progress is astounding. Tents are propped up in recesses in the mountainside, sheltered from a chilling breeze that races across the slope. Incredibly, a small house is almost completed, it's just missing a roof.

Distress is present. I worry, considering morale was high earlier. Making my way over to a guard, I ask, "Did something happen?"

"Rumours have it that the curse has returned. An Olyneran and an Enmaran. The rumour spread quickly, but they soon confessed that they must have been mistaken."

My gaze finds a gathering of people with split alignments that are finishing work for the day. Nothing, as proven earlier.

"Carry on. Stay vigilant. As will I." A nod is given before he sets off on a routine patrol.

Thirteen

VEXXYRA

A chilling breeze tugs at my hair. I find myself still questioning our choice of location. Houses are erected, a palisade wall protects us. *What an effort that was.* I have never used so much Marshvine in my life.

Jepp is extremely useful, his unlimited energy is extraordinary. He returns from a forest run, hands full of flowers and vine. "Here. This one's for you."

My heart melts as the young boy hands me a stem with a rose upon it. Such a beautiful smell. "Be careful of those thorns. Thank you, Jepp."

"I have a great teacher." *Oh, please stop or I'm going to faint on the spot.*

Imagine if I had my own apothecary hall.

No. I couldn't ask. That would be extremely selfish.

Arathyn is training our archers. Arrows find makeshift targets. My father is swinging away at our infantry in a flurry of steel.

I have a great teacher. So do they.

I raise my eyes to find watchtowers, nearly finished. Bowmen stand on raised, makeshift platforms, surveying the land beyond the walls.

Arathyn gathers everyone's attention. We walk toward our modest leader, waiting for him to speak. "Our home shall be known as Enmara's Vigil. Everyone will take a day of rest, you have earned it."

We have. I glance around, and there is nothing but admiration everywhere I look.

Something is on Arathyn's mind. He gathers my father and one of the Enmaran Guards. Draygar rushes over to him. I find myself staring. *How I wish Mira were here.*

Then I overhear conversation.

"The Vorderans must be up to something. Knowledge of whom we do not have." *Has he found others nearby?*

My father speaks boldly and then predictably. "I'll gather my weapon. Shall we head out? It has been days without real battle."

Arathyn returns to the crowd. "We will be back before too long." He leaps onto Draygar. I notice the empty seat behind him.

"Wait!" *What am I doing?* He stops and looks over his shoulder. "May I join you?"

He looks at my father for approval, his decision rides on that glance.

"Bring that blade with you." My father points toward a rack of assorted weaponry, his response does not baffle me at all.

"You may ride with me." Arathyn's offer has me dumbstruck. *I did ask, didn't I?*

Murmurs are on the wind as our people look on. Once again, I'm the centre of attention.

"Be careful though. Draygar can be ferocious." Arathyn gestures at the vacant seat behind him. Not to be perceived as wanting, I stride over with a determination, grasping a dagger before calmly climbing upon his beast.

Walking out through a gate in the wall, my father joins Arathyn and I. "Careful, lad. My sword may seek you if she comes to harm." The threat is there despite a hint of a joke.

Arathyn gives him a wry smile in response. No one wants to be at my father's mercy, there is *no* mercy.

Rings of clinking glass pass through the air as I bounce about, vials holding various concoctions jangle around my waist. I consider putting my hands on his lean body to stabilise myself.

No. I couldn't. I grasp the handle instead. "This is very comfortable."

Adventure. Great. I can use the distraction, but my eyes make out reagents everywhere.

Frostbane. Eldermoss. I'm not going to ask him to stop.

Turning south, a bend in the rock formation leaves our home hidden from prying eyes. Draygar seems to make light work of transporting the two of us. A decrepit stone fortress ahead grabs my interest.

"Be on your guard. The Vorderans must be up to something." Arathyn brings about caution as we approach. Enormous moss-gripped walls tower above us as we make our way toward the gaping entrance of a place of great mystery. A torch is pulled from Draygar and set alight.

A short hallway leads to a sharp descending turn. We dismount as it is easier to navigate on foot. The air grows colder. An eerie sound of dripping water echoes throughout. I gulp.

Curiosity heightens. "What would they be doing here?"

Arathyn straightens. "I have no idea. It is as dark as the night sky." Walls of a narrow corridor give way to a large open chamber. Torchlight reaches out into the distance, exposing further hallways that lead in every direction. Rows upon rows of stone caskets line the floor.

"This is a tomb." My father speaks the words of an exact thought in my mind.

Suddenly, Arathyn's sigil starts to brighten as an almost opaque aura surrounds him. "Arathyn, look at you." My delight captures the attention of others.

"There must be some kind of dormant energy. Lost souls, perhaps. Spirits that linger here." His words are a pathway for the dread that grips me.

"They are empowering you, lad." My father's observations are true.

Arathyn examines Draygar. His beast's eyes begin to change as his fur starts to glaze over.

Draygar can be ferocious. His beast is certainly starting to show it.

Suddenly, a worrying thought plants itself in my mind. *The Vorderan Spiritmaster is here somewhere.* Possibly just as menacing as Vilriyan was.

Continuing our search, we step past rows of dilapidated caskets. Arathyn's aura now provides a secondary source of luminance.

A scream echoes throughout the tomb like a crack of thunder that catches us all by surprise.

"Down there," my father mutters, his voice carrying easily in the dead silence. A gesture is thrown in the direction where the sound resonated from. Cautiously, we descend the hallway. The flame upon our torch is extinguished.

Dim light cast by Arathyn's aura is enough to find our footing. Ahead, numerous torches dance about in the darkness as the odd silhouette passes by. A large gathering is present.

"They must be twenty strong," my father says, trying to make out their numbers as we hide from sight behind a large casket. Judging by the height of immediate objects around, it's what our newfound acquaintances lack.

"Youths?" Arathyn utters by way of an answer. I nod.

They stand upon a raised altar at the centre of a large open chamber. Worry creeps in. They may discover us. Arathyn's aura might ruin our concealment, although it is very faint.

"You are a fool, Kira. What do you expect?" A voice echoes around the walls. A cover on a casket has been pried open.

"It is just a skeleton. Are you scared?" A male voice continues sarcastically, confirming what has become increasingly apparent that this is a place for the dead.

"Look!" Another shouts, grabbing the attention of those gathered. Wisps of light dance around the faint glow of a yellow sigil on a wrist, a spirit that hovers above the sigil, circling in the air.

My father rubs at his jaw. "They do not seem to be able to consume that spirit."

For once, I find myself unable to explain something. "Consume?"

Arathyn explains. "Yes. Your father is right. I believe only a spiritmaster is able to."

What is Arathyn capable of?

One by one, the figures grasp at the wisp of energy. *Consumption,* none succeed.

"Are we not able to grow stronger? You said that we could!"

"Yes. I saw a woman. Her name was, uhh … Thiedra, I believe. She just transformed … into this … storm-like person … She left us behind and that is when we found you." This information goes completely over my head.

Arathyn explains further. "Thiedra must be their spiritmaster, which means she is not here."

"She sounds interesting," my father jokes, before a swift kick of my boot pulls him into line. A wisp of light rises from the contact.

One cries out, looking in this direction. "What is that?!"

Arathyn looks at me with a furrowed brow. "We have been spotted."

I shouldn't have asked to come.

"There is someone over there!" Torches begin to encroach on our position.

"Vorathen. Stall them." Thoughts must be racing through Arathyn's mind. "Stay here."

And he's gone, through the maze of caskets.

Youths full of anticipation leave the altar and flock over towards us.

"You will go no further!" My father's voice ripples through the silence as he jumps from cover. Torchlight encapsulates the warrior-like figure as a torchbearer stumbles backwards into his companions.

"Who are you?"

My father thrusts his sword towards the face of one of the boys, piercing the thick air before it. "Your worst nightmare!"

He wields his greatsword before them, chuckling as he realises the group is harmless.

"He's green!" Further backsteps are taken.

"Fear not. I will not harm you." My father's words predictably do not relieve the tension. Fear stops me from making a decision. *Where is Arathyn off to?*

"What is going on here?!" An older voice takes its turn as a second group appears from the hallway with torches ablaze. "Get away from him! What did I tell you about Hammerknell? This place is cursed!"

Blades are drawn. Tension turns into hostility.

"Hah! You want to fight me?!" My father counters with the utmost confidence as he wields his sword effortlessly in front of his adversaries. Even though he is outnumbered, he appears fully in control.

"This soul will find peace within me," Arathyn's voice announces euphorically, capturing everyone's attention, including my own.

"Look! On the altar!" In one synchronised movement, all eyes divert.

More light emits as Arathyn's sigil strengthens. Gliding souls shine above like stars in a picturesque sky.

Arathyn opens his arms in acceptance. Souls begin to orbit around him, drifting ever closer as they descend from the highest reaches of the tomb. As they draw closer, they shoot into him emphatically, unable to resist.

My hand covers a gaping jaw. I gasp. My eyes are locked on, everyone's are.

Fourteen

Arathyn

The last of the lingering souls, like shooting stars, surge into me from afar. Transformation beckons.

My entire body glistens in a diamond glaze. Hair like crystal strands drop alongside my body. Limbs bulge with muscle. Tranquil, pearlescent light illuminates the entire chamber, cast from a mesmerising aura of white energy.

A silent voice reaches my ears effortlessly by inhuman means. "Do we run now? Has it come for us?" My senses heighten. Heartbeats thrum in my ears.

My voice crackles with energy as I step forward. "I only seek peace and unity."

"Enmara's will. My duty. Together, I will bring us all." My words resonate within them. Fear dissipates immediately. *Draygar hasn't moved an inch.* His mind, blank.

Sigils of all colours respond as I approach. This is uncharted territory. I do not wish to harm them.

A frightened voice speaks up. "How can you help us? We've seen … your type … That sigil! Lives were taken from that very mark that you bear!"

Racking my brain for a way to convince them, it strikes. "Vexxyra. Will you do me the honour?"

Fifteen

VEXXYRA

Unable to believe my eyes, Arathyn is standing like a god before me.

How can I refuse? What if I do refuse?

"Are you sure?" my father interjects.

"Yes." Arathyn's voice is so alluring, energetic.

My heart is enamoured. I follow it.

Time freezes as footfalls echo softly upon my approach. Each step adds to the suspense as Arathyn shines brightly before me.

Everyone has retreated to the walls, but they look on. Draygar stands obediently nearby.

Blue light begins to gleam from my Olyneran sigil as Arathyn extends his hand. Drawn closer, a blue hue sharpens before brightening further. My wishful fingers touch his outstretched arm before me. Upon that touch, energy flows between our sigils.

Energy courses through me. My body lurches as it rips through. All control is lost but for a moment, a blue glow weaves around my body, forming into a mist as delicate as the ocean fog. Crystallised sapphire becomes my armour. My Olyneran sigil gleams.

Lost for words, I catch the sight of a tear running down my father's astonished face.

Beauty. Arathyn knows it too, lust embedded in his eyes.

Words snap me out of my dream-like state. "How did you do that?"

I can't answer.

Arathyn's god-like voice relieves me of that burden. "She is Olyneran. Her spiritmaster was defeated. Her kind and we Enmarans have escaped the curse that divided our alignments. Help does not elude you. Vordera's time will come."

"Come on. We have seen enough." The Vorderans retreat after being ushered away.

Nothing but sorrow clenches at me. *I hope their time will come.*

⚜

Our Soulforms begin to wane. *No! Why do I have to lose it?* A feeling so empowering yet limited. *Oh, how I wish I could do something about that.*

My silence is broken. "Arathyn. That was amazing."

"It was my pleasure." *We're back to normal. I think?*

My father speaks up. "Lad, I must tell you …" We stop to hear him out. "I feel an urge to travel south as if something is waiting for me. A tick within the mind."

Did Arathyn's presence in Spiritkind bring this about?

"Spirits are likely drawn to their masters." Arathyn's conclusion makes sense, the energy must be messing with his mind. A strange summoning, perhaps.

Upon our return to the first chamber, souls begin to drift around us once more. Hovering above my sigil, they do not absorb, much like the Vorderan youths before.

Astounding.

My waistline is the target of hurried hands. I grab an empty vial before holding it above the sigil on my palm. Like a moth to a flame, one enters and I slam in a stopper.

Optimism comes to the fore. "You never know."

Light from the eastern sun blinds us momentarily as we leave the tomb. Not being exposed to natural light for quite some time, my eyes take a moment to regain focus.

Hammerknell, we leave behind. Our vision true.

Sixteen

ARATHYN

Dawning sunlight splits the horizon as I stand watch above the Vigil. An ever-present mountain breeze licks at my hair. Thoughts flood my mind as I ponder our recent encounter with the Vorderans. Youths, just confused and on edge. No doubt that my appearance in Spiritkind will not go untold. They need guidance, trouble will find them eventually. I feel it's my responsibility to protect them.

Thiedra. The name on my mind. *Where is she?* She sounds like the one I'll need to encounter.

Making my way up to the top of the southern watchtower, I cast my glance over the half-lit landscape to the southeast. The Vorderans are most likely taking refuge further south, below the peaks.

Vorathen and other keen swordsmen are slashing away at dummies that already need restorative work. He never misses a moment to hone his skills. His example gives others courage and determination, the virtues of a warrior.

The guards join him at the targets. A commander is what I need, someone to assume responsibility for the Vigil while we are away. These two have risked their lives for us countless times. I cannot think of better men to put in charge.

Calling the two over, I ask, "What are your names?" *My mind has been so encumbered by my own matters that I've never thought to ask.*

"Bernard and Henry. We are brothers," Bernard replies, gesturing respectively.

"Brothers?" I'm surprised. *What luck to have family aligned.*

Henry answers, glancing at his sigil. "Indeed. We lived in Elmgrove, before everyone fled as our way of life was torn asunder. We watched in disbelief as our bodies were emboldened with this *strange* white marking. Little did we know at the time how lucky we were, that our fates would be aligned. Honoured we are to serve you for what you have done for us."

A warmth grows inside. "You both aided us with Vilriyan and his cohort. You are both very able men. Which of you will do me the honour of commanding our Vigil while we are away?"

Both sets of eyebrows are raised. A moment later, Henry speaks. "It is an honour to fight with you, Arathyn. Leave it to me, I will see to the Vigil's safeguarding. I will swear an oath to protect our people with my life."

Henry kneels before me, gesturing with his sword. *Never have I seen an act like this before in Turinfall.*

Vorathen laughs. "Are you going to leave him kneeling all day? Accept his oath, lad."

Vexxyra chuckles, covering her mouth.

"Or decline it." Bernard sees the irony in it too. Embarrassment creeps in.

"My apologies. Very well, Henry. Command the infantry and our people. Bernard, you will accompany me on our travels."

An agreement is reached. The brothers exchange an embrace before heading off for further training.

"Lad, you show the leadership of someone twice your age." I'm glad Vorathen thinks so, perhaps he's just saving me from further embarrassment.

"Are we leaving, Arathyn?" Vexxyra is full of excitement.

She is excitement.

"We will leave once prepared. Our path will be true to the south. I suggest that you pack some extra warmth." I soon realise that I'm the only one unprepared. Vexxyra has enough glass fixed to her in various places that she could bottle herself.

Vorathen trudges up beside me. "Everything I need is within my hands."

"Bernard! We will leave momentarily!" My shout climbs above the clanging of steel to get his attention. He stops for an instant to acknowledge me before parrying a swift blow from one of our ever-improving swordsmen. I race off to grab my belongings.

We depart on our search for the Vorderans. They may have given up hope at Hammerknell as their quest to morph went awry.

Heading along the range, my eyes scour every inch of forest near and far. Hammerknell passes us by, not likely to encounter any more of the living for a substantial period of time. Only a short distance ahead, what must be the highest peak in the Feygoran Mountains, shoots into the clouds. Not sheer but it dwarfs other peaks around it.

Thick forest obscures the sight of much of the nearby land below. My feet find a path that snakes its way high up into the snow-capped mountains. Wind whips up as we begin our climb, packing extra warmth was a smart idea. I have no doubt that we will have the best view of Arcura, you can see the summit of these great mountains from Turinfall. Our path will be a cold, treacherous one, warmed by our companionship.

My feet are misguided as the path disappears under a layer of snow. The dream that I would one day get to visit such a place has now come to fruition. *What a beautiful sight to behold.* Draygar's paws imprint the soft white cover for the first time.

Vexxyra's admiration is shared among us. "Such a beautiful place, Arathyn."

Anxious thoughts burrow in. "Beautiful, but no doubt perilous."

Our way suddenly becomes very difficult to navigate, the landscape rises or dips in every direction. We stand upon a crest that drops away to the west.

Pressing on toward the base of the highest peak, our progress is halted, it is far too steep to climb further. A gradual slope curves around it, and we divert.

Snow cover gives way. Our feet find solid ground once more.

Up ahead stands a strange object, unnatural and foreboding.

A strange monument lies on an overhanging shelf above a large precipice. An icy cave tunnels inside the peak nearby.

Vorathen stumbles on an object as we move forward. Large bones are littered across the shelf around us.

"I do not have a good feeling about this." Vexxyra's caution hits harder than a hammer. Danger grows heavy amongst us.

We creep closer towards the ledge ahead. We will be rewarded with an outlook over the entire southern region of Arcura.

Between howls of wind, the faint sound of grunting reaches my ears.

Draygar. It's not him. "Do you hear that?"

"I wish I did not," Bernard says. His gaze burrows into the cave.

"Look." A mangy white beast strides out of the cave onto the rock shelf.

"Ah. That is no challenge." Vorathen's voice is enough to spook it back into the darkness.

My nerves calm once more; however, I am not certain that such a small beast was the source of the sound.

A high-pitched roar cuts right through us like a sharpened cleaver. Ground trembles below our feet after a large thudding crash. Snow falls around us, cascading down from above.

An enormous beast with four horns, a gnarly grey hide and limbs as bulky as a tree trunk, sniffs at the air, taking in the smell of its next meal. *Us.* Embedded with shards of ice that cover most of its back, the beast drops its jaw, spilling out half-digested carcasses of wolf-like origin.

Pinned between a sheer drop and a rampaging behemoth, Vorathen speaks. "What in all things mighty is that?"

There is no time to reply. Firing my bow at its massive skull, the arrow deflects harmlessly aside. All I've achieved is enraging the beast further.

Beastly strides don't hesitate as it leaves the ground. We're a whole buffet.

Bernard is the unfortunate one, its first target, who musters the courage to stand before it. Raising a swift shield, he ducks under a heavy swipe. Claws of solid ice and bone rake across the steel, emitting an ear-splitting shriek. Bernard circles back to Vorathen and the pair stand stoically before me.

Charging again, it swings its massive paw into Bernard's shield once more. Splinters of ice explode upon impact. Force unimaginable throws my guard against the rock wall.

Vorathen rushes in, sensing opportunity as the beast recovers. Slicing at a hind leg, he forces a sharp cry.

There is no retreat. Fighting for our lives is the only option. The cave provides no escape, snowfall blocks its entrance in its entirety.

Furious stomps question Vorathen's footwork as he weaves below it. Taking an opportune moment, I loose another arrow into its exposed flesh as it turns slightly. Anguished cries ripple my eardrums. Jerking rapidly, the behemoth slings its crystalline tail with vigour, spearing shards of ice in our direction that fall agonisingly close.

Vorathen slashes at another leg. Finding it extremely hard to locate him due to its massive size, the beast slams the ground further, causing rock to split. Each one would crush him, but he's too agile. Until he's too slow. Narrowly dodging a vicious swipe, he fails to avoid a subsequent headbutt that launches him far in the air before landing softly in heavy snow.

Exposing its gigantic teeth, the behemoth lumbers towards us, wounded.

My best men dazed and swept aside.

Vexxyra is no match, nor are we.

Rearing up the yeti-like figure bellows out a roar that shoots right through me. My flesh clings to bones. Arrows simply aren't enough to stop it.

Draygar races off at my command, lunging at a bleeding leg, previously sliced open from Vorathen's blade. Teeth rip and shred as he hangs on for his life.

Wounded, though far from mortally, it stomps furiously once more, trying to shake Draygar loose.

Draygar is finally thrown aside by sheer strength. Vexxyra and I find ourselves as the last of its targets. Narrowly avoiding its lunging mass as it races past, we find ourselves with our backs to a freezing rock wall. Approaching us slowly, snorting, the behemoth calculates a final strike.

Death is imminent.

A clinking of glass catches my ear as the beast drags a fur-laced hoof across the shelf. Vexxyra's vials ring alarmingly across rock as she moves to brace herself. Turning my gaze away from menacing jaws, our eyes meet. A trust blossoms that we share the same idea. Glass is shattered upon jagged stone.

Souls wail in the air as they escape their confinement before redirecting suddenly as my sigil draws them in. The beast leaps back, startled.

I morph into Enmaran Spiritkind.

The behemoth's meal is further delayed.

Reaching for Vexxyra's hand, we glisten in the western sun as she transforms into her sapphire beauty. No longer does the sound of the behemoth ring in my ears, sensations of peace and serenity are all I hear.

Slamming into me, the behemoth pounds away blow after blow, yet I feel nothing.

I am a fortress.

Turning its attention to Vexxyra, realising I'm now the insurmountable one, the beast backs up as she runs some distance. *Smart. It can't face us both at once.* A newfound courage fills my body and I fire a bolt into its hind leg as it speeds towards her, which knocks it off balance. The behemoth swipes at Vexxyra, catching her as it falls. Ice shards spear in every direction off her crystalline body as she is driven back by a somewhat resisted blow.

Draygar beckons as the behemoth wearily begins to stand. But before I reach him, an unusual movement before me catches my attention. Ancient, weathered bones start to circle around me. Similar and distinct bones are drawn together, moving toward me. Searching, seeking.

Cries of wounded beasts fall upon my ears. Reaching down to touch the amalgamation of bones, in a flash, a white energy as pure as snow traces a skeleton as they form together. One by one, bones come to life, forming skeletal entities.

My mind is one with these spirit beasts and their aggressive nature. Focusing back on the task at hand, the behemoth stands weak, afar. Reincarnated beasts surge ahead with extraordinary velocity, springing onto and climbing all over the wounded beast, gnashing with vicious jaws. On the brink of defeat, the monstrosity staggers backwards onto the edge of a precipice.

Firing one last time at the dominated goliath, the savage beast disappears.

Draygar shuffles his way back over to me. I sense pain within him. Peering around at the mass of bones, there is no more response. The revival of these ancient beasts has sapped almost all of my power. A power that isn't limitless, every action that requires it contributes to its depletion.

Vexxyra makes her way over to Bernard. He sits up against the wall looking aimlessly into the sky. Vorathen sits half-covered in snow, breathless. My men are very fortunate that they wear armour, especially in this climate.

"You are full of surprises, lad!" Vorathen's voice carries effortlessly from afar across the rock shelf. He regains his feet after wrestling for a sturdy grip amongst the white cover.

Bernard's mangled shield shows the indentation of a massive paw upon its face. "Now that is a great souvenir, Bernard. You should jump into the abyss and thank it." Vorathen's lighthearted humour is music to my ears.

Bernard's earthy eyes find me and he laughs. "They'd have to believe me now."

"Your daughter saved us all." My eyes find Vexxyra, she's human once more. Vorathen shares my gaze as he makes his way over to us, almost showing a hint of jealousy.

Vexxyra examines them both. "They will be fine. Just a good bruising."

"Well, I'm sure I speak for everyone when I say I was not expecting that." Bernard checks over his bulky, tall frame, brushing snow from his slicked-back brown hair.

We cast our eyes over southern Arcura. I can just make out the sea far to the south. Smaller peaks stand below us, leading down towards a lush forest. A castle, although appearing miniature from here, sits elegantly to the southeast.

To the west, expansive rolling grasslands stretch on forever, dotted here and there with pockets of trees. Peaks far in the distance to the northwest rise prominently above a desolate tundra, mostly hidden by a looming haze. The view is stunning.

I return to examine the monument: markings are bevelled into a rounded stone dial on top. Markings that match the runes at Highgarde and the sigils we wear upon us.

There is a sixth marking here, one I have not encountered.

"Arathyn." Bernard grabs my attention back from wandering thoughts. "Southeast. Smoke."

Faint plumes rise high in the air above a wooden structure nestled within a forest on the nearest side of the Whistling Plains.

"The Vorderans?" Vexxyra's thoughts align with my own. There is no other sign that hints of their whereabouts.

"We have a target. Let's move before another one of these things appears." Our battered bodies begin to move as one.

⟡

The forest below sweats in humidity. We strip off our warmth.

Bernard shakes his head, sporting a grin. "I would have never believed in a thousand years I would be walking with spirits."

"I have no idea what to believe anymore. I have my daughter back. Whatever life lies ahead of us, I feel that I have put my trust in the right place." Vorathen's ability to grow morale is just as strong as his words.

"Absolutely." Vexxyra's eyes lock onto mine. Her look is calming and assured.

I find myself overwhelmed by their words. *Whatever life lies ahead of us. I know a lot of that depends on me.*

We continue along the fringe of the forest. Plumes of smoke rise high above the canopy; however, it is much harder to pinpoint than from the mountain. We are closing in.

Moving as silently as possible through a thicker area of forest, I spot a group of youths moving towards a path that is heading in the direction of the smoke. They disappear from sight.

"They look familiar," says Vexxyra.

"No doubt." Our pursuit continues.

A row of small timber structures lay beyond a path that weaves its way through a final barrier of tall oaks. A village that stands completely defenceless.

"How is this place still standing?" Vorathen notices the obvious lack of security.

I scratch at my head. "I do not sense any hostility. It appears that's mutual. Keep your wits about you."

Approaching the structures on the northern side, they look as if they have been abandoned for some time. A fire rages inside a large brazier in the centre of the village compound, around which a few sit. We are almost right on top of them before they notice us.

One jumps up. "Who are you? What are you doing here? You are not yellow."

Others start to gather around. Vorathen remains vigilant as he examines each new acquaintance.

"I am Arathyn. The yellow you speak of. Vorderans, Vordera's kind. I am not here to—"

"Are you here to harm us?" says a woman. "Was that you at Hammerknell?"

"Indeed. Enmara chose me to bring peace upon Arcura." I point at her wrist. "These sigils that you bear. Do you understand?"

"Enmara? Vordera?" Her puzzled look proves otherwise.

"The spirit of Vordera is in each and every one of you. That sigil harnesses a fragment of its spirit. I will find a way to bring everyone together. To rid the curse, that I assure you."

Some look excited, others not so.

"You … changed."

Pointing at my more luminous sigil, I explain, "I only know of my ability to empower myself and others. Why, I do not know. I was chosen as Enmara's spiritmaster."

A questioning face peers back. "By whom?"

I rack my brain, thinking of the dark figure at Forvarr.

What I remember of the explosion at Highgarde.

I don't have an answer.

Vorathen sees me struggling and interjects. "Are you leaving?" He glances towards belongings that are bound to a cart, ready for transportation.

"Yes, we are to head east along the river."

"Where to?" My interest peaks along with my eyebrows.

Another man joins the conversation. "A woman. Thiedra. She was very inviting. Told us she could provide a better life."

"This Thiedra that you speak of, was her sigil as bright as mine?"

"Brighter than ours. She was quite abrupt and we have almost run out of supplies here. What choice do we have? We have seen the … curse. She is yellow … Sorry … Vorderan too."

Seeking more information on her whereabouts, I pry. "Did she describe the place where you were to travel?"

"There is a village there with large waterfalls. We will just follow the rivers."

My feet respond before I can think.

I step back, Vorathen and Vexxyra are both none the wiser at his answer. I draw my bow instinctively. My thoughts shift protective.

"Woah, lad!" Vorathen draws his sword in a rapid blur. "I thought we were just going to talk."

From the description given, I immediately know of the location.

Turinfall.

Even though I have been exiled, I cannot stand for it to be attacked. "They speak of Turinfall. It will not be invaded on my watch!"

Vorathen rubs his jaw and chuckles. "Ah, this is quite the predicament."

A moment passes as I take a moment to think. *I know what I'm going to do.*

"Do not dare!" Vorathen's booming voice scatters wildlife from nearby trees. Trembling hands retreat from hilts.

The situation is tense. Vorderans are too frightened to make a move. My arms drop, lowering my bow. A deep breath is taken that instills calm amongst us.

My bow finds its place upon my shoulder once more. "My apologies. How long ago did Thiedra ask this of you?"

A quivering voice dares to speak. "Two … days …"

"Head to the north, there is a place known as Enmara's Vigil. Follow the mountainside beyond Hammerknell. When you find it, tell my people that Arathyn sent you. Do not follow us. If you do, the next time we meet, I will not be so hospitable." All I receive is the nod of a few heads. "Will you be needing those horses?" Heads shake.

"I've never ridden." Vorathen's statement catches me cold. *Of all the things he could say.*

My words spill confusion. "Really?"

Then he's off on horseback.

Seventeen

ARATHYN

Past the Whistling Plains. Past the bazaar. I find myself parched. Animal transportation, spent. *What a ride.* Fuelled on by the likely assault on my childhood home, we now find ourselves sitting under the gloom of night at the base of the Grand Turinaar Pinnacles.

I hope that Thiedra will take a diplomatic approach. Although I know that Argora would provide a determined resistance to any form of invasion.

If Turinfall still exists.

The Shattering has taken its toll everywhere; nowhere has been spared.

We set up camp in a secluded nook nearby. Rest is of the utmost importance. I have never travelled so far, so fast. Preparedness for what tomorrow will offer is paramount. Fidgeting around, my mind is absent in thought.

"Get some rest. I'll take the watch." Vorathen knows what I need. The others are already in a slumber.

Worrying thoughts force themselves out. "My mother. Argora. Our village."

"All the more reason to rest." His words are stern.

"Will they welcome me back?"

"Family is family. Argora did what she had to do in order to protect her people. Now it's your turn." His words quell my anxiety at the expense of heightening the importance.

"Have you really *never* ridden?"

"I have now."

———✦———

The call of roaming striders fills the air. We're close.

"We approach from the northwest. The falls there rise above the village. We will be hidden." Knowing the area very well, confidence is on my side.

A storm brews overhead as we make our final approach through the rugged landscape. We relieve the steeds of their duty before continuing. Unmistakable sounds of plunging water fill the air. Rivers roar over the edge of falls. Approaching the edge cautiously, it is not the time to make a false step.

"As I suspected …"

Not rangers, but several bands of armed men and women patrol around Turinfall. The village itself appears largely undisturbed. Villagers go about their daily work as if nothing has changed.

"We have the advantage of a surprise attack. It appears, however, that we are well outnumbered." Vorathen is right, that would be foolish. Not even knowing where my mother is, let alone Argora, is dangerous. *They could be hostages or worse.*

Turinfall is well guarded. Any hostile action could bring about mass suffering. "We will approach Turinfall in peace, we need to know what we are dealing with."

The need to leave Draygar behind is of grand importance, I cannot risk them knowing I have a companion. Only one outcome will be the result of that being known. Peering back at him, my companion sits barely visible against a shrouded backdrop.

Our feet find one of the wooden bridges. The same one I traversed when I ran for my life. *From … nothing?* Outskirts appear lightly guarded beyond Turinfall's exterior pathways.

Traversing the bridge over the pearlescent lake below, Vorathen and Bernard walk on opposite sides, unarmoured. Vexxyra, behind.

One of the armed warbands notices us. A man from within approaches, dressed in mail. "Stop! What business do you have here?"

If only he knew.

I eye his sigil, then my gaze lifts to unwavering eyes. "We seek Thiedra."

Eyebrows are raised. "None of you show Vordera's alignment. She will not bother herself with the likes of you."

Batting away his negativity, I continue. "All that we ask is that we speak with her."

"As I said, she does not take well to outsiders. It is likely in your best interest."

Tension grows as they reject our proposal. Vorathen clenches his fists.

"Look here, lovely. How do you know she will not speak with us? Do we look like your average *outsiders?*" Vexxyra's statement is bold, her confidence takes me by surprise. *Our constant pestering might alarm them.*

A questioning glance is thrown back at his accompaniment. No attempt is made at swaying a decision. They stand ready for action. "Drop your weapons. We will escort you."

Another band is called to assist. Nothing is left to chance.

"Very well." My acceptance is given.

Vorathen whispers softly. "I hope you know what you're doing."

I don't. But that wasn't going anywhere positive.

Vorathen throws down his greatsword and shield. Curious eyes study me as I place my bow upon the damp earth. Bernard follows.

"This way." Walking towards the centre square, now surrounded by a dozen armed men and women, we are led on like a group of prisoners. Stinging memories of my father's last moments rush back.

Be strong, my son. My eyes draw courage from my father's bracelet. *That's why I'm here.*

Signs of battle appear as we are ushered further toward the mahogany buildings. Shops have been torched, others damaged.

Grounds are clear of bodies, it feels as if I am looking at a mirage. Ashed wood lies at the base of the bonfire pit with human bones scattered throughout. *This is for you, my son. Revel in what is to come. Believe me, Father. I will.* Two women walk off towards Argora's stead.

The Turin's grand buildings are untouched, no one would dare destroy such beautiful homes.

Fists beat away on the mahogany door. The skull turns and within a moment, the door is thrown wide open. A woman appears, standing in light chainmail. A head encased within a helmet drapes blonde hair that escapes through gaps. My eyes trace her hair down to her arms to find a bow, none other than Argora's, at her fingertips.

"Why do you disturb me?" A light but firm tone carries the question. *What of Argora and my mother?* Surely means that they are in danger, if not *dead.*

If adrenaline could make me morph, I'd be standing here in Spiritkind right this instant.

How could they be bested? Turinfall's Rangers are very well trained and these people with their mismatched weapons and armour look nothing more than mere conscripts.

An unsteady voice speaks up. "These people asked for you by name."

"Oh. Did they?" Thiedra grins, gracing us with her presence as she strides over confidently.

The sight of my Enmaran sigil is taken in. "You have some nerve, young man. What brings you here?" Her voice is so calm, but no doubt dangerous.

Batting away her threat, I answer, "Seeking peace."

Intrigue flashes across her face. "Peace? You're the one stepping into Vordera's domain. You are the only ones here that do not share the gracious alignment of Vordera. This is our home. Vordera ruled over this area and now its kind, us, will reclaim its homeland. It is our birthright."

"Nice place you lived in, lad. I am certain it would have been beautiful before all this mess." Vorathen is right, it was beautiful.

Thiedra's face distorts with anger. "Tell your lackey to shut his mouth!"

Vexxyra rolls her eyes before chuckling. "Good luck with that."

"Escort them out immediately, I will not have the *unaligned* here." Thiedra hastily retreats, slamming the door behind her.

A large group of nearly a dozen accompany us as we're led on uphill towards the huts.

To my surprise, some of the huts have been cleared out and makeshift gallows have been erected in their place. *There's a body dangling.*

Rage overcomes me. It's Auriella.

Peace? *No.* Thiedra deserves to die.

My old bow and hunting knife. *Are they still there?* Huts have likely been ransacked. Just as I have that thought, I see Vexxyra slip the blade she took from the Vigil into her father's hand. No one notices.

Vorathen looks at me. I know that *look*.

What am I about to start? I can hear my father's voice in my head. *What are you doing? Do you even know where your mother is?!*

He made his decision. He died for me.

Now it's your turn.

I dart through the shawl, anger and intent flood my body.

"Come back here at once!" Yelling voices start to pursue me. A thud reaches my ears as someone is knocked to the ground, followed by the cringeworthy sound of flesh being pierced.

I'm in luck. The chest is untouched.

Vexxyra rushes in behind me and my hands gift the hunting knife. "You don't have to use it."

A Vorderan swordsman appears through the shawl before he's met by a knife in the back. *Who am I trying to persuade?*

"I have now." *I've heard those words before recently.*

Another crashes in. I draw my old bow, which snaps in half under the tension. *Great.* But I still have a weapon. Dodging his flailing strike, I pierce him with the arrow in hand.

Oh, how I wish Draygar were here.

Preparing myself for the worst, Vexxyra and I emerge frantically from the hut. Vorderan bodies lie amassed in front of me. Bernard is kneeling down to one side, breathing heavily with cuts on his arms. Depleted, he is. Vorathen is nowhere to be seen.

Two men wielding crossbows appear in view from behind. Weapons click before being raised at us. *This is it.*

Vorathen darts out of a nearby hut but he's not close enough.

A crossbow fires and the bolt grazes my arm. Pain is intense but ignored as I tackle Vexxyra out of the way of a second that whizzes past us, embedding into a wall.

Bloodcurdling cries ring out as flesh is pierced. My weary eyes peer up at stormy clouds as rain begins to fall on my face. Vexxyra is already working on my arm as if it is the only thing that matters.

Vorathen checks me over, he's largely untouched. "Thank you, lad."

If it wasn't for my intervention, I wouldn't have a beautiful young woman attending to my wound.

Just as I wished, Draygar bolts over and within an instant, he becomes a living terror once more. There are slain bodies everywhere, fuel aplenty for his deathly form.

"You'll live." My arm is heavily wrapped in cloth. She then races over to Bernard.

Refocusing on the task before us, I leap to my feet. "No time to waste, we have a spiritmaster to attend to."

Power courses through me as I mount Draygar, pain is an afterthought. My human senses are left behind. Our resurgence on Turinfall has begun.

Descending back toward the square, the crashing sounds of waterfalls are drowned out by the cries of a magnificent beast. My ears are attuned to Enmara's call. Groups of Vorderans scuttle away into hiding as they see me. Vorathen and the others keep a close watch.

Stopping in front of the courtyard with a bow drawn, I notice it does not transform with Enmara's energy. *There's no diamond?*

Taking a steady aim, I embed an arrow deep into Argora's door. Within a moment, Thiedra appears once more in the doorway, clearly unimpressed.

Thiedra stares at Draygar and me before something clicks inside her mind. A laugh ensues.

"Oh, of course. You've come home to roost, have you? That I cannot allow. As I said before, this is our home now."

"How much Turin blood have you and your barbaric minions spilt?" My voice is euphoric, but my words aren't. It is taking every ounce of restraint not to unleash on her.

Completely dodging the question, she studies my inhuman form. "Such power, Arathyn. I knew there would be others."

This is not the time for pleasantries. "Where are Argora and the other villagers?!"

"Oh. I didn't ask who they were, I just took what I wanted. This sacred place ... Vordera is here with us now."

"I will not ask again!" Nocking another arrow, I aim it dead at her.

Thiedra sighs heavily. "So, it has come to this?"

Releasing the arrow, it deflects harmlessly off an invisible barrier in front of her, a barrier that momentarily crackles and surges in yellow light before being absorbed by her body. "The storm shall rage inside me!"

Bright yellow tendrils with razor-like barbs grow out of Thiedra's body that crackle with energy. A beaming aura encompasses her energetic body. Laughter emits in cacophony as she embraces her new form. Spiritual eyes flick back to me.

"Thank you, Arathyn, for this moment. I am a thing of beauty. Did you really think that I would be bested so easily? How do you think I conquered this place? With a sword and shield?"

My immediate thought is that my mother is dead. *They're all dead.*

Releasing another arrow that whistles through the air, a defensive barrier of multiple flailing appendages blocks its advance.

Vorathen and Bernard don't move. Steel isn't the answer.

"My turn!" Thiedra runs like the wind, twisting and turning as bolts of lightning are hurled towards us. Raising my arm as they hurtle into me, nothing but a strange sensation is all I feel as the energy discharges upon my aura.

Another bolt strikes Bernard which forces him to the ground. His entire body spasms as the energy singes his arm.

Leaping off Draygar as we dart towards Thiedra, his rage-fuelled figure slams into her. Her body bounces off the beast like he's made of rubber. Appendages lash at him ricochet harmlessly off his stone-embossed hide.

Bernard is the target of my grasp, his body feeds on Enmara's energy. Half-morphed and diamond-encrusted, my guard leaps to his feet. Smirking, anger takes over. Rushing into the fray, he moves as if he weren't just disabled.

"Oh boys!" A metallic shriek pierces the pristine air. Numerous men race over to her, answering her call. A well-placed arrow strikes one as they rush in.

They morph right in front of us as they bathe in Thiedra's power. They too grow sparking tendrils, but to a lesser extent.

Vexxyra suddenly grabs my arm and my body obliges. My human senses are returning.

Crystalline armour glistens in the sun as she sprints in. Her body is caught by a slicing tendril that shatters fragments of her icy form. The Vorderan half-morphs swarm in, circling her until there is no chance of escape.

My power is sapped. *I don't have my bow.* For once, I struggle to find any way to assist. If I do something rash, Vorathen would too to aid me.

Sparks fly in every direction as Vexxyra bears the brunt of multiple strikes. Strikes that tangle them together.

Energy courses through linked limbs. They start to spark profusely, overcharging. The Vorderans seize up. A paralysis takes hold before a discharge emits a shockwave that knocks Vorathen off his feet.

Sapped of all power, they stand.

"Oops. Did I do that?" Vexxyra is gleaming with confidence.

Vorathen and Bernard take the opportunity to overpower the now vulnerable men. But one runs off. Icy hands grab him by the throat. An icy breath exhales from his mouth as his movements grow sluggish until he's practically frozen. Vexxyra's grip loosens and he falls to the ground.

Vorathen stares at his daughter. *We both are.* I worry that this power may get the best of her. Then I wonder why I ever doubted bringing her along in the first place.

Thiedra is growing increasingly frustrated at her inability to best Draygar. "Get them! I'll deal with this thing myself!" Her repertoire of lightning abilities doesn't appear to have any effect on the stone-scaled beast.

But no one answers her call. Frantic eyes look around alarmingly, realising there is no one left to aid her.

A crazed flurry lashes aimlessly. I fear to be anywhere near her empowered self, as does everyone else.

Appendages are coiled around Draygar's legs, forcing the beast off his feet. Jaws hold them before she can withdraw.

A new wave of strength shoots through his body as he violently lurches, ripping the tendrils from her body.

Thiedra is stunned temporarily. Draygar's energy wanes.

Souls do not escape the bodies of the fallen Vorderans; the once-morphed versions of them seemingly retain them. *Or lose them completely.*

Thiedra is waning. So are we. This may be settled as humans.

Out of nowhere, a familiar face appears from my left, a High Ranger I know personally with a red marking upon her arm. A distinct bow is raised at Thiedra. A bow belonging to none other than Turinfall's Rangers. "Leave our home, vile woman!"

There may be hope after all. If she is alive, then there must be others.

After her statement receives no reply, the bow is released. Thiedra's form has regenerated. The High Ranger's arrow has the same effect as mine. *Useless.* Thiedra dashes over to the woman whose face depicts fear. Several razor-tipped tendrils puncture through the High Ranger's body.

The Vorderan Spiritmaster grabs her limp figure and raises it in the air, cursing at the slain woman in a rage.

I do not wish to believe as Thiedra's energy gathers and seeps into the woman.

She is reborn. Her sigil realigned Vorderan.

Thiedra's power completely diminishes, entirely spent in the process of reviving the Ranger.

"No … No!" The Ranger just stands confused, looking around as if she were previously blind, having just had her sight restored.

In one final act of determination, Thiedra rushes towards us, nothing more than a human. She barely makes it ten steps before an arrow impales her and she drops to her knees. "I have failed you, Vordera."

She gasps as a second arrow strikes her heart.

Looking over my shoulder, my eyes grow large with amazement. Upon the hill is Argora herself. She lowers a bow, leering back at me.

A smile grows upon her face, as does mine.

Retribution. Finally.

Then an arrow.

"No!" Argora clutches at her chest and drops to the ground. The newborn Vorderan Ranger has carried out one last favour to her slain master. My mind descends into rage and Draygar carries out my wishes.

We run.

Vexxyra and I reach Argora just as she is fading away.

"Arathyn … is that you?" Delirium. A tear runs down her face. Ixxenira's sigil upon her wrist, fading slowly.

"I … am sorry … I left you … all by yourself …" Anguished eyes flicker as pain strikes further, forcing yet another gasp.

"I hoped … Find … your… moth—" Death takes her before she can finish.

Find your mother.

Vexxyra looks at me with determination. "You have got to try, Arathyn."

I still have limited energy. Vexxyra is right.

Ripping the arrow from Argora's chest, I grab her lifeless body with both hands. Driving out all else, I focus on Enmara's cry in my ears as my eyes stare up at the moon above. *Please bring her back.*

My power diminishes, my body is sapped of every ounce of energy that still remains. My hands are a vessel in which the light travels towards Argora's body.

Closing my eyes for a moment, I focus my mind on Morathaen's pendant until the very last remnant of my empowered state dissipates. Vexxyra's warm embrace surrounds my chest.

After what seems like an eternity, the sigil on Argora's wrist is renewed white and begins to brighten. An aura envelopes her briefly, then disappears.

Argora's eyes open once more to Arcura.

Eighteen

ARATHYN

The afternoon light streaks through the edges of the shawl. I awake in the comfort of my former hut. My sudden desire to rest has been fulfilled.

I falter to remember how I made my way here, every emotion is racing through my head.

Argora's revival.

Find your mother.

Draygar lies at the foot of my bed. There is no time to waste, Turinfall must be liberated. Gathering myself together, I grace the ground outside. Vorathen is sitting on the highest point nearby, staring at me before he wanders off.

The village is badly damaged. Majestic views of the surrounding nature do little to hide the destruction that is now clearly evident.

Upon making my way down to the courtyard, I notice that our weapons and armour have been collected. They lie in a pile next to an open campfire. Draygar wanders over before sitting calmly in front of Argora.

I still can't believe she's here. Vexxyra sits by her side, engaging in conversation.

Swinging open the mahogany door of the huntsmaster's building, I find shattered remnants of ceramic urns in their hundreds that litter the floor. Thiedra's power explained.

"Nice of you to join us, lad." Vorathen is the first to address me as I exit.

Vexxyra's caring words follow. "Did you rest well?"

All I manage is a nod in reply. My gaze shifts to Argora and she notices, her eyes find Morathaen's pendant around my neck. "I knew that one day you would return, Arathyn. But not like this." Argora raises her newly aligned Enmaran sigil to her face.

"This … tore us apart. Our village. I have never seen such fear and dismay." She shakes her head. "Not even in your last moments here."

Swollen eyes shift to my companion. "Poor Draygar. I remember when you two were very young. Innocent. A sense of dread runs within him."

If there is one person who knows Draygar better than me, it's her.

"Thank you for driving that cruel woman away. Whatever you are. Whatever you have become. Your bond with Draygar is unlike anything I've ever seen." Argora is completely puzzled. *I know that feeling.*

My thoughts flash to my mother and my voice suddenly returns. "Did anyone else survive?"

"Yes. We were taken and held inside Dweller's Run. We fought our way out when some were recalled."

Dweller's Run. A maze of caves. A gauntlet to master, requiring speed and teamwork. A training ground for Rangers and their beasts.

My heart sinks in anticipation of the worst news. "What of my mother?"

"She and Delbura are safe. It was terrible, most of our companions were lost. My dear Miratharl also. Loyally, they tried their best to protect us but that cursed woman was too strong." Argora is heartbroken, but my worries lift quicker than a blast of steam at the news that my mother is still alive.

My father's bracelet is the focus of relieved eyes, his delight I can imagine. "I must see her."

Argora leads us towards a storehouse on the edge of the village. "We moved them in here once it was safe to do so. They are weak."

Argora pushes open a creaking door. Four survivors take up the space within the building, ragged and in pain. *I hope there are others.*

"My … boy!" My mother's voice calls out with so much relief riding in it.

"Mother!" A large smile grows on my face as tears well up and gather around my eyes. All my worries are whisked away.

I can only look on helplessly as I find a dim green Ixxeniran sigil upon her.

Helplessly. Not forever.

It doesn't stop her from mustering every morsel of what little strength she has left to run towards me. As I fight my feet to backtrack, Vorathen runs in, catching her in his arms.

"Thank you, Vorathen."

"I will see to her. You have my word."

—◆—

The crackling of a bonfire is just cozy enough to wash my worries away. A small number of additional survivors have made their way here, albeit not enough to outweigh the loss. Most of them are familiar faces and each one fills me with a growing satisfaction as I identify them.

Alignments are scattered amongst our larger group. Sigils have been the new normal for some time now, everyone knows of the dangers and acts accordingly.

The storehouse is still well-stocked. Never is there a shortage of food and beasts roam everywhere nearby. Sinking my teeth into a haunch of Reygyre meat, my tongue dances about the delicacy, juicy and tender.

Vorathen is already in conversation with my mother and they're sharing a laugh.

Stories of my childhood?

Embarrassing moments?

I'm not sure I want him to know any of that, even though he probably already knows me better than myself.

Vexxyra's hand encloses mine as we make to the top of the falls that overlook most of the village. Sitting upon a large, rounded stone, I peer down at the survivors below, dwarfed by the raging bonfire.

My eyes catch hers. "Do you think this will ever end?"

"You have gotten yourself this far, Arathyn. The Vigil. You have freed many that would have failed otherwise."

"I hope that my choices do not put our people through harm. However, I feel that is unavoidable."

Vexxyra's arms wrap around my body as warmth starts to burn inside. *Vulnerability. Now it's my turn to feel it.* "They follow you blindly, the *end* is what we make of it. You've rid Arcura of Vilriyan. You've bested Thiedra, brought your ruler back from death. Saved your old home and your mother. What more can you really do?" She speaks the truth, I certainly have succeeded in many aspects thus far.

Then I frown. "Something doesn't seem right. My *destiny*, it is unclear."

"None of this is right, Arathyn, but you seem to have a good understanding of what is happening." Her enthusiasm is contagious and it brings me back to reality.

"That is what worries me, my *understanding*. Peace doesn't seem to be the outcome, only death. Look below, this is not peace."

A gentle hand falls upon my cheek as a lock of brown hair plays with my skin. "You will find peace, Arathyn."

"I will lead us back to Enmara's Vigil, it is not safe here." There is only one place I know that offers us the chance.

"Here, I want to give you this." Eyes widen as I reach for the gold-chained sapphire in my pocket. Thoughts of what Vorathen will think make me feel uneasy. Nevertheless, it gives me great pleasure.

"Oh. This is beautiful. Thank you!" I place it around her neck below two blushing cheeks, then she kisses mine. Fingers toy with the pendant before the gleaming sapphire comes to rest upon her smooth skin.

As expected, Vorathen is staring at me but my mother is smiling. Vexxyra's face, a picture of gleaming beauty. Her fingers are willed upon the gemstone, unable to keep from fidgeting with the fine piece of jewellery.

"It was as clear as day, lad. From the moment you first laid eyes on my daughter." I am a fool to think that he hadn't already picked up on my fondness for her.

"My loyalty to you does not outweigh the protection of my family." Vorathen's words are stern as he raises his greatsword for inspection, a thinly veiled warning. I smile back at him before he chomps down on likely his fifth serving.

Buzzing. Energy.

My ears prick up, followed shortly by the interest of others.

"Do you hear that?" Vexxyra's words need no answer.

"Look!" It's Arkryn. He's pointing at a large, mostly opaque yellow spirit drifting above the village.

Looking like a mythical creature, I find it somewhat similar to the one I've seen in my dreams. The head of a beast with a wing-like structure stretching from its body. A long tail with splines weaves through the air behind.

Stopping directly above us, it lets forth a sharp cry as it floats effortlessly. Its gaze turns on me.

Bernard asks the question on everyone's mind. "Vordera?"

"I believe so." I'm filled with uncertainty as I ponder what to do next.

"It seems lost. It's crying for help, Arathyn." Argora and I have the same thought.

Suddenly, I remember what the husky voice mentioned at Forvarr. Enmara was the Peacekeeper. *Has Vordera's spirit left Thiedra? Is it now lost, searching for me?*

I call Draygar over and climb on his back. The spirit-like figure follows our every move like it's attached to a string.

We stop. The spirit begins to descend. Others look on in anticipation as it draws within arm's reach.

There it is, on its underbelly: Vordera's marking. After a short moment, the spirit curls up, looking all but defeated before dropping down onto Draygar and I.

Vordera's spirit resists momentarily before it is entirely consumed. A bright flash, accompanied by a powerful blast of energy, is expelled across the vicinity. Feet stumble. The fire, extinguished.

I feel nothing. *Is Enmara protecting me also?*

My mother stands shocked. "My son … What has happened to you?"

Vorathen scratches at his head. "I am still trying to figure that out and I have fought alongside your boy numerous times."

I am glad Vorathen deflects the question, I'm unsure how to answer.

My mother gives Vorathen a look of gratitude for his service. "Thank you for looking after my son."

He laughs. "Believe me. He is looking out for us, I just keep him true."

I pull Argora aside. "We must leave Turinfall, we cannot care for them amidst this damage. We have an establishment, they'll be safe there."

"*Safe?* Where is such a place?" Argora is completely dejected, but it fills me with desire. "Arathyn, I always knew in one way or another you would amount to something. It feels like years ago that you were last here. Everyone here speaks so highly of you, Morathaen had the same qualities. It makes me so proud that you still wear his necklace, after everything that has happened."

Grasping the onyx stone in my hand, I return a look of certainty. "I would never part with it."

A smile grows and it brings about a warmth. "Very well, let me pay my respects."

"We have all suffered greatly here. I anticipate that we will be safe for the night. Gather your strength and rest, I will take the watch. We leave at sunrise, we are heading home."

Nineteen

VEXXYRA

It must have been difficult for Arathyn to return here, let alone see Turinfall in this state.

We leave it all behind, finding a lush grass beneath our feet and a sweet aroma in the air.

"How far is our new home?" Elraetha looks much better now, Arathyn has his mother back. That thought burrows right down into my soul. *How I wish I could rescue mine too.*

"A couple of days," Arathyn says.

"If anyone would like to rest their feet, Delbura will welcome you." Arathyn's mother is a lovely woman, although I doubt Delbura can bear any more weight. The beast is heavily laden with resources.

There is no chance that I will take that offer. I'm sitting behind the man that Arcura depends on and I still can't take my fingers off this gold. "I love the way that you find yourselves as one with your companions. It's beautiful."

Finally, I feel a sense of fitting in. *My name amongst others in Coradal.* No longer do I question it in my company.

"It is a very special bond we share, Vexxyra. It is our way of life." Argora's face is covered in a look of sorrow, she has lost hers.

"I would love to have my own." I brim with excitement.

"Do you propose a visit to the Proving Grounds?" Argora's offer is very intriguing.

Not surprisingly, my father's curiosity is piqued. "Now that sounds interesting."

"The Proving Grounds?" I ask.

"It is a place where I tested would-be Rangers to prove that they have the courage and ability to tame an elder beast. A test of their being, in preparation to ward off any threat to Turinfall. If successful, their current companions were offered to the villagers who were in need of one, or they would serve as a domestic companion. When on duty, the Ranger always had their Proving Beast with them."

Before I even have the chance to acknowledge how interesting that is, my father jumps in. "Sign me up! I would love to give these withering boots a break."

"Vorathen, it is very unusual for a non-Turin to take part in this challenge, it will be more difficult to win over the heart of a beast. However, with my guidance, it is possible. My dear Morathaen managed to accomplish such a feat."

I rub at my forehead. "What would you have us do?"

"Within the pinnacles, a short distance to the northeast, beasts roam. Some quite savage. It is at your discretion which to choose."

"Savage will do." I roll my eyes at my father.

"Vorathen. It is just one part to show strength, you must also understand and connect with the beast. It will either kill you or succumb to you, depending on your approach." Argora's words carry a warning.

"You make it sound more appealing with every word! I understand."

"Arathyn, will you allow us the chance?" I address the body in front of me, or more so his long hair, seeking approval for a diversion.

"Of course, I am very intrigued. Argora, would you be kind enough to lead the way?"

Travelling will be much quicker if we aren't on foot. Bernard keeps watch over the survivors as they stay behind.

Argora leads us over a sharp rise between two towering rock formations. Our path dips down into a valley of lush greenery. Crags line the edges of the jagged landscape above the treeline. Therein lie several caves, likely holding some of the strongest beasts.

"Beyond us you will find a vast variety of beasts, everything from common Featherkin to a vicious Moltecern." Argora looks at Arathyn when mentioning the latter. "This curse does not seem to affect beasts, as such, so this sacred place should be undisturbed."

"May I?" I ask.

"Of course. We will observe." Argora gestures out into the unknown wilderness before me.

Followed by my usual company, I speed off into the unknown.

Excited beyond words, feet full of eagerness bring me to a small lake in the centre of the valley. Beautiful white-feathered, cat-like animals roam around me elegantly, each augmented slightly in different shades. Approaching them, they bound into stride and move away.

"Vexxyra, they will respond to you if you show them *fight*." Argora is likely the best mentor I could possibly find. Pricked ears listen intently.

My eyes make out a larger one with a bluish hue. "This one is exquisite."

"My girl, do not hold back now." My father's words ring in my ears.

Drawing a dagger from its sheath, creeping feet close the distance. Caution instills on a fur-laced face. A cry is let forth as the beast studies me. Aggressive, no. But something tells me it is ready to defend against any advance.

Lurching forward, my hands thrust forward the dagger which misses intentionally. Beastly eyes keep their focus.

"Stare into its eyes. Show it no fear!"

Circling around the beast, I gaze into its eyes. A hefty paw beats against my tunic in an effort to warn.

"I do not wish to hurt it." *Am I really doing this?*

"Command it! Control it!" Argora's words echo across the valley.

Timing an advance perfectly, my quick feet guide my body under a swipe before propelling my figure onto its back. Violent shakes throw me off before snarls are returned in my direction. *Hopeless.*

"Better!" The remark injects a second wind.

Rising to my feet with anger and determination, my thoughts redirect to the Apothecary's Guild and how I rose to that challenge. *My mother would be cheering me on.* A tear sparks a newfound courage.

Don't hold back. Weaving around wandering eyes, the beast almost lets me mount it. *Connect with the beast.* Right. Arms grip on for dear life as the beast thrashes about but it cannot shake me off this time.

"Now, comfort the beast!"

"Harriet would have loved you," I mumble. My hands stroke upon a smooth mane.

Argora is convinced. "Dismount! Return!"

Within a few moments, the beast relaxes and stands at my side. Heading back, I keep a keen eye on it as it follows me. Confusion sets in. *Now what do I do?*

"Hold out your hand. Call the Elder Featherkin."

Elder Featherkin. Amazing.

After a moment of hesitation, the beast strolls up to me. A majestic blue-hued head rubs against my side. I can't help but smile.

"Beautiful," says Argora.

She is certainly right, it is. I am congratulated.

"Vorathen, let that be a lesson to you. I have no doubt that the beast that you seek will attempt to destroy you."

"I would not have it any other way!"

"Lead the way, Vorathen. Vexxyra, now is the time to nurture your companion. You may have it tamed, but now you must earn its keep."

I'm already smitten, cuddling and playing. I wonder how many tinctures I can carry on this. *Stop. I need to earn its keep first.*

Moving through dense forest toward the crag, numerous beasts look on as we pass by, none of which are deemed worthy of my father's challenge. Arathyn keeps glancing at me. *Maybe he's worried? Jealous? No, surely not.* He is of Turin blood, sitting on one of the most formidable beasts I've ever seen.

Trees thin as our feet fall upon barren ground. Land rises sharply out of the valley. The ominous sight of darkened caves ahead draws a feeling of discomfort. My father keeps his path true before kneeling down to examine the lay of the land before him. Lesser rock-infused beasts with exoskeletons prowl around him, taking an interest. *Oh my.*

Sunbalm Root graces my fingers as I pluck it from a crack upon the jagged surface. My eyes don't miss a thing. If we stay out here much longer, I might have to concoct something with it to negate the strong sunlight.

Standing watch at a distance, he ponders what to do next. Anyone else would be showing interest.

"Only the best will suffice. I just hope he is ready." *I don't know why I'm doubting him.*

"Only half the test is strength, he will still need to connect with the beast." Argora repeats herself, clearly worried about the latter.

The Proving Grounds look fairly scarce, there isn't much movement across the barren rise. A suitable challenge he may not find. Continuing to swat away the interest of smaller beasts, my father searches near and far, occasionally disappearing inside a dark opening only to emerge later unconvinced.

Argora points to the group of beasts grazing near my father. "Granite Horrors."

Like the name, they look like their hide is made of stone. Most of them look small. Argora has such profound knowledge, she is a walking bestiary.

Horrors nip at my father as he walks by. A swift boot quickly pushes them away. Cries travel afar as he begins to show some fight. Lunges are met by his bladed shield and blocked. These small beasts show such ferocity for their size. However, they cannot breach his plated armour.

Hefty slashes from his greatsword ricochet off the bone exterior of another. Identifying a weak spot on the beast's neck, it scuttles away into a recess on the side of a cliff.

As if the vulnerable was the leader. Horrors follow the disoriented beast in a stampede.

My father turns towards us, his quest seemingly a failure before the echo of heavy thuds grabs our attention.

Something is looming.

His body whips back around before his eager eyes gaze into one of the caves. A large silhouette in a horrifying shape stands at the opening.

A much larger, unique Horror storms out with haste, shrieking. Gasps emanate around at its unfathomable look. Numerous boulders are amalgamated together between thick bone. A head of stone opens in the form of a gaping maw, a thing of nightmares. It stands before my father, swaying back and forth, examining him.

"The Horrors of the depths, never have I seen one above the surface until now. A band of us encountered one of these a long time ago when we first discovered the caves. We ran at the sight of it." *That's a big statement coming from Argora.*

My father slams his greatsword into the ground before extricating it, waving it before the Horror. Vines begin to protrude from within its bone structure and lash about.

"Oh my goodness." Stress takes a grip on my body.

Arathyn smirks, knowing that this will definitely be a *challenge.* "If there is a man for the task, it's Vorathen."

I don't see how he can. "How is he going to defeat that?!"

"You do not need to defeat the beast; however, I am unsure of whether or not this creature can be reasoned with."

Without a moment of hesitation and with a will of determination, a smile grows upon my father's weathered face as he charges in. Unexpected agility on the Horror's part catches him off guard. A heavy swing of its rock-hardened head hurtles his figure to the dirt. Rearing up, the Horror pummels the ground with enormous stone legs, narrowly missing its target, who rolls away.

Vines with barbed mouths lash at my father, but they only find his chestplate as he leaps to his feet and steadies himself once more. *What else is this abomination capable of? Death, surely.*

My father grasps at a vine, managing to take hold as he is flung around effortlessly by the monstrosity.

Argora does not take her eyes off my father. "Not even Morathaen, bless his soul, had the courage of this man. Fear does not exist within him."

Additional vines begin to entangle him as he beats away at its stone core. With his shield before him, my father finds himself completely bound around the chest and unable to move. Not since our encounter with the yeti-like behemoth upon Mount Moradar have I actually feared for his life until this moment.

My father writhes about as vines struggle to contain his muscular body. Opening its maw, the Horror looks set to devour him until he manages to wedge his greatsword between its jaws. Jaws that grind against the large blade. A downward slash of his bladed shield through vines sees to his release as the beast retreats with a blood-curdling shriek.

Huge stone feet drag across the ground, kicking up dust before it surges forward faster than I thought possible. At the final moment, my father ducks under its lashing bite and with all his strength, protected behind his sturdy shield, he impacts its forward legs.

Its momentum is its downfall: it stumbles, careering down the steep incline to the forest below.

"That is probably enough for one day, follow me!"

We follow.

Coming to rest against a tall tree that has split apart upon impact, the Horror lies immobile. My father stands over it with a look of pure satisfaction. Struggling to lift its head, a low-pitched rumbling cry is all the beast manages to emit.

My father looks at Argora whose expression is already an answer. "Any ideas?"

After a moment of hesitation, I offer a suggestion. "Water?"

My father isn't convinced but he clearly doesn't have a better idea. Turning his back on the Horror, he strides towards the lake.

All of a sudden, in what seems to be a feigned state of weakness, the Horror regains its feet and charges at him.

"Watch out!"

My father spins around, raising his blade to the onrushing monstrosity and with one wild swing of its granite-like skull, his blade is bashed out of his grip, landing with a splash some distance away. Gazes target each other for what seems like an eternity as if to see who will falter first. There is almost a mutual respect.

The Horror takes a step back, picking up a large rock before hurling it at my father's feet, an action that lacks hostile intent.

"Well. My sword could use some extra edge if I can retrieve it."

Argora shakes her head. "Unbelievable!"

"Care to lend some expertise?"

"The Horror has responded to your courage, Vorathen. Anything would. This is uncharted territory, do what you think is right."

Right. Just don't make a wrong decision.

My father stares down the Horror, if that's even possible. "I could use those vines now."

Approaching cautiously, the Horror watches his every move. A hand finds its stone exterior. *My eyes, I can't believe.* With not even a flinch, an exoskeleton that doesn't move aids my father's effort to climb atop. And once he's up there, he looks like a god: unassailable.

The Horror looks parched, weakened. My apothecary mind sets in.

The Horrors of the depths, never have I seen such creatures above the surface until now. It is now exposed to dry conditions, unadapted to natural light.

Right on cue, it begins to pant heavily before rushing off and, in an instant, leaps into the spring with my father only just about holding on.

"Oh dear."

Arathyn is all but enjoying the entertainment at my father's expense. "This will be interesting. Maybe it'll best him now."

What am I thinking? They both are.

"Perfect! While I'm here, I believe I have something to find!" My father gives the monstrosity a damning look.

These are the men I wish to follow? I give myself a *damning* look.

My father is completely soaked but at least he's standing. With all of that armour on, if it were deeper, he would be sinking to an underwater grave. That doesn't stop him, however, he dives under the surface of the water beyond the Horror that has almost completely submerged itself nearby.

Argora wanders off into the vicinity of a large cluster of oaks, searching for a beast. Very few Featherkin remain near the spring, most have fled in fear.

Carefully examining the beasts within the grove, she must be searching for a specific type. Some frolic about her presence, others seem uninterested. Her eyes find one that lies on a low-hanging branch and she whistles a beautiful melodic tune which grabs the beast's attention instantly.

Then, in a dramatic change of emotion, she takes a blade and slices open her palm. I wince, but she doesn't show the slightest bit of discomfort as blood runs down her hand. I'm thankful I got away with not having to spill my own blood. Even Arathyn looks surprised. Argora's methods are extreme.

A slightly darker-coloured Featherkin reacts immediately, leaping down to the ground to approach her. Argora gracefully poses before the beast as she runs a smear of blood across her forehead, whistling the tune once more. The beast only shows a slight hesitation upon its approach, it is like she has it under a spell.

At arm's reach, she runs a bloodied finger down its nose and around its mouth. The Featherkin licks its lips before accepting Argora's hand which runs along its mane.

"What a woman, that was effortless." I stroke my own companion's mane, feeling extremely lucky.

"I expected as much." Arathyn's accurate words bring about jealousy but I soon shrug that off.

"Now, let us see if Vorathen is still alive." Argora brings me back to reality. Being so impressed with her methods of taming, I forgot about my father.

We lead our companions back toward the lake, Draygar is showing signs of cautiousness with our new beastly following. My father has escaped his armour, looking nothing more than a drenched commoner. The Horror is still partly submerged, looking much more comfortable, but no less petrifying.

"Enmara's Vigil awaits, we are done here. Bernard is probably wondering what is taking so long." *Right. We're rescuing survivors.* I need to get my mind back on track.

"Ah. The unmistakable glint of steel! I am reborn!" My father booms in the wake of retrieving his blade. "How do you suppose I get this thing out of there?"

"Vorathen, no matter how unnerving it may be, all creatures have heart. What does your instinct tell you?"

"A rock!" I thought it was obvious, this whole situation has numbed everyone's mind.

My father peers around and sets his hand upon a loose stone, running it along his sword before throwing it at the Horror. Its jaws crush it with ease. The Horror leaves the lake, its vines have mysteriously regrown. Huge stone feet imprint into long grass once more which its mouthed vines unearth and devour.

Arathyn chuckles. "Progress."

Twenty

Arathyn

"What in all things mighty is that?! Never mind, nothing surprises me any longer." Bernard's face is one of bewilderment while he examines Vorathen's Horror, thrice-sized compared to Draygar.

"Anything to report?" I ask.

"Nothing. I assume we are off to the Vigil?"

Bernard and the others have set up a campfire. Our travels are done for the day. "Let us rest the night, this locale will do us well."

Vexxyra shows signs of riding prowess, unlike her father. Argora, as expected, rides upon her beast like she has had it for years. Vorathen walks ahead of his Horror, of which everyone keeps their distance. Given its presence within a totally unnatural habitat, it is no doubt unpredictable.

My mind wanders as we take up a steady pace with Turinfall's refugees in tow. We aren't all that far from Highgarde as we track westward. So much has changed since my last visit there.

We are stronger. We have some form of knowledge.

Feeling a sense of duty to return, there is a need to explain to the others how this all began. "I need you all to understand what happened to me, to us. We will divert and follow the path to the Ruins of Highgarde."

We divert. Everyone wants to know. *Or do they?*

The sun has reached its apex in the sky as we are reunited with the path that leads to the Forvarran Coast.

"The curse was a result of your actions?" Argora studies me, but there is a look that she already knows.

"I believe so. I do not know what happened, but I understand the consequences and my path forward."

Small peaks come into view once more on our approach to Highgarde. The path inclines, revealing the sight of the ruins dead ahead. "Watch your step, this place is unforgiving."

We approach cautiously, scouring the ruins from afar and it's as if time has forgotten this desolate place. Unchanged, *The Shattering* had left its mark, but nothing further has been disturbed.

Vorathen peers around as if this place doesn't warrant the significance to destroy everyone's lives. "You were led here, lad?"

"Yes. To this very place."

Approaching the dais, a hum grows as specific runes start to brighten on the stone floor. The Enmaran, Vorderan and Olyneran runes begin to emit light. My hand stops the progress of others.

Drawing closer, the runes continue to react until I am right at the base of the structure. Encased in bright light, each rune shines in its own unique hue.

Looking over my shoulder, I see sets of eyes gazing fixedly.

Vexxyra is frozen in awe.

As if a voice was waiting for its turn to speak, it addresses me. "You have returned, Arathyn. Olynero … Vordera … Welcome us once more."

"I can feel their … presence. Within this forsaken place."

"The curse … its hold has weakened. Other spirits remain … The less … fortunate. The curse will linger …"

"Enmara chose wisely … As did I …"

As did I?

Frantically, I try to place the source. Nothing. "As did I?"

"Do you not … recognise … my voice, Arathyn? I … led … you here … Your body was … able."

Suddenly, my brain draws a link between the present and my last days at Turinfall. A voice none other.

The Eldest One.

I shout out into the unknown. "How!? Why!?" My *understanding* has just fallen off the highest pinnacle. "I was exiled from my home! My father was killed!"

Anger begins to draw tears. "Unfortunate … events. Do you not … revel in your newfound power?

"Your mind … I could sense … *Ambition.* An insatiable hunger … when you were only but a … child.

"The spirit of … Enmara … grew within you … for years. Right from that very moment you first set foot here …"

My mind jumbles with pieces of information it just can't resolve. I want to understand. I *need* to understand. "Why do I not feel your presence any longer?"

"Unfortunate … events … Arathyn …

"You … are … following Enmara's will …

"The spirits … have found peace … Your path … remains true … Arcura needs you …"

Then, I spot it. In a flash, a familiar figure within the shadows of a toppled building moves with inhuman speed, sensing its discovery.

Then, it's gone.

Vexxyra's warming hands drop on my shoulder. "Are you alright?"

"I thought I understood, but I am no longer certain."

Vorathen is looking at me, trying to keep me from breaking. "Do I really need to give you my praise again?"

No, he doesn't. None of them would be standing here if it weren't for me and I now have some form of an answer.

"There is definitely more to that thing, that is for certain." Vexxyra's thoughts mirror my own.

The spirits of Vordera and Olynero react with the runes on the dais as I suspected they would. Something doesn't sit right with me though. *Why did the Eldest One insist on leading me back here?*

Enmara's spirit grew within me for years? The Shattering happened after.

What of my childhood curse? A memory of the Eldest One's grip on my mind comes rushing back, I struggle to find any reason within it.

My newly found purpose is to bring peace to Arcura, to unite a land divided. People … families … spirits released here were the birthplace of the sigils, the curse, upon humanity.

The birthplace of the curse upon humans. Not mine.

Argora notices the thoughts flashing across my face like the wind. "You will find the answer, Arathyn."

"Lead us home, lad. We are done here."

I retreat from the dais, the light on the runes subsides as I move away. What I thought I knew is once again shrouded in mystery. There are surely people out there within Arcura that still need my help.

Home. It has been too long. Diversions. No more.

⊰•—◦⊰❖⊱◦—•⊱

The path home does little to straighten my wayward thoughts. Turinfall. Myself. I can hear faint murmurs among our following.

Vorathen and Bernard stride beside me, the former keeping his beast in check, of which its thundering footfalls keep me alert. My mother, Argora and Vexxyra ride together at the rear just behind the remainder of the group, forever chatting away.

Palms thin to the north as we continue west to the mountains, a journey all too familiar.

"Do you hear that, Arathyn?" Bernard's tone brings us to an abrupt halt.

A crackling drowns out the sound of insects. My eyes find a clear night sky. Stars gaze down on us.

Purple light pulsates from within a forested area nearby, which brightens with each crack of energy. Argora wanders closer. "What do you feel, Arathyn?"

"Strangely, nothing. Bernard, keep watch. Vexxyra, come with us." Having her save us on more than one occasion, I'm not going to take anything to chance.

Riding toward the anomaly, Argora readies her bow as Vorathen runs his blade along his beast's body. "Keep your wits about you."

Our foursome clears through an opening in thick vegetation. My eyes set upon a large circular field of energy.

Nearby trees, withered. Grass, dead. Air, distorted.

A sense of dread washes over my mind. A dread of which my own mind evades. *Draygar's.*

Beasts coalesce in the confines of the field before shooting out toward us. As dark as the night, blood-curdling shrieks rip through my head.

"Fire!" Argora releases an arrow that flies harmlessly by its intended target. Beasts of extreme agility dodge with ease. One diverts, tracking towards Argora, bounding at her with rending claws as long as my fingers. Upon dodging, the sprawling creature flips past her head, leaving a trail of white light in its wake. Further shrieks ring out as white energy scalds its fragile frame.

Leering at Draygar, the creatures emit otherworldly cries. All I sense is confusion within his mind. My companion stands frozen in paralysis as if his soul has departed.

Jumping off, I feel in control and vulnerable at the same time. Ravenous beasts circle around us. It dawns on me that blade and bow will not suffice. *Too small. Too nimble.* One look at these creatures indicates they're bent on pain and suffering.

More emerge.

A great risk of being overrun has me concerned. Frantic looks gaze on as doubt ripples among our following.

Vorathen lurches towards one, but it's of no use as it lunges onto him quicker than he can comprehend. Slashes scrape against his armour as other beings join its assault. His only saving grace is an earthshaking pound from his Horror that forces the creatures back momentarily.

"Give me strength!" Vorathen manages to shake off the more persistent ones.

"Vial! Now!" My arm is thrown toward Vexxyra without a thought. Hands rummage about her waist before grasping a small vial of wispy nature.

Souls come to my aid once more as the sigil on my palm glistens upon their escape.

Am I always going to rely on a glass vial?

Within moments, I am encapsulated in Enmara's aura. Unwavering attention fixates upon me. In one ear-piercing cacophony, drawing hands to ears, they speed towards me. Hundreds of limbs, claws and sharp incisors lash at me until there is no more.

A disintegrating death upon the touch of her power.

Spawns of death. Soulless ravagers. Husks of an evil scourge.

There is nothing of the living to consume.

"Come with me!" No time is spared.

Our legs propel us towards the anomaly. A large circle stands before us, encased in deathly-weaving of sinew that crackles and hums, expelling energy out into the air around us.

A rift.

"Stay back!" Approaching the construct, I raise my arms as energy flows towards the rift. Cackling laughs and demise-ridden thoughts tap into my mind before the rift burns. Silence ensues.

My eyes find Draygar. My mind picks out dread and suffering within his heart.

Death.

Just like the beast that left the cave before this all began.

"Do you think this is to do with the Eldest One, Arathyn?" Argora puts my thoughts into words.

"Yes. The way they were drawn to me. Not a moment of hesitation as they rushed to their death. Why me?"

I stare inquisitively at my sigil. "Why Enmara?"

⸺⸻⸺

The sun begins to set over the Feygoran Mountains as our second day of travel comes to an end. Steel glistens in the abating light. Steel upon the Vigil. I wonder at the sight of towering fortifications that come into view.

"Feast your eyes upon your new home!" It's untouched, from a combat point of view.

I lead us toward a portcullis lined with steel, set inside a border of stone. A burgeoning figure accompanied by two Rangers appears atop the rampart, watched on by marksmen manning the watchtowers.

"Arathyn! You have returned!" Henry's voice booms from within a plate helmet.

"Remarkable, Commander. Your work will not go unnoticed." Admiration is all I feel as we walk through the opening, surrounded by a fortress of stone and timber. Noticing an etching of Enmara's sigil on Henry's shoulderguard, it draws a smile on my face.

Henry takes in my company. "Come one, come all. Enmara's Vigil welcomes you."

The portcullis is closed behind as the last of us make our way inside. Enmara's Vigil is barely recognisable from when I last stood here. People put down tools and watch as I sit upon Draygar examining the fortification, waiting for my approval.

Eight watchtowers, all manned.

Living quarters, featuring beautifully constructed small timber houses.

A blacksmith. A fletcher. All spread loosely around training grounds filled with weapon and armour racks.

My nose leads me behind the combat quarters. The aroma of cooked meat draws my attention to a kitchen beside a leatherworker who hastily works with hides.

My approval? How could I not? I'm ecstatic.

Gathering every last one of our people, I try to make myself look as formidable as possible on Draygar. "Henry, you have outdone yourself. Every single one of you has my gratitude."

Once again, I glance at the sigil on my wrist. "You may all feel that your life has been ripped from within. Many of you have seen death and suffered a great loss. However, the curse will never take hold within these walls! With the Spirit of Enmara, through me, your lives will flourish and prosper."

Drinks are raised before cheers fill the air as Enmarans and Olynerans embrace each other. My mother and Vorathen, they are the Ixxeniran "outcasts" here, but no less loved.

"Come on. Have a drink." I toss a mead in Henry's direction which is caught in his gauntlet. After raising it to me, the beverage is heavily chugged.

"Mother. You need rest." All she can do is smile and blow me a kiss and it tears us both up inside. *I just want to throw my arms around her, maybe one day I could again.* She's safe at last, holding knowledge of what the curse will do to her. Knowledge that many others would have loved to have, but didn't get the chance.

"I will see to her, lad." I offer Vorathen a quick nod, then I'm off to join the festivities. Festivities that were quite obviously planned for my return.

—◆—

It's the dead of the night, I didn't drink as much as I thought I would. My sense of duty overshadows the urge to be reckless.

I haven't seen Vexxyra all night, she's probably out in the wilderness picking every piece of luminous flora there is under the moonlight. The thought of which is appealing but it's far too dangerous out there. *I hope she knows that.*

Draygar is gnawing on a boar's leg within the close confines of the dying bonfire. He gives me a look as I start the short climb to the rampart, then his hungering impulse turns his attention straight back.

Vorathen's Horror is half-submerged in a stream running down from the mountains above. It looks content, I wonder if it has caught anyone's attention yet.

Footfalls echo upon stone behind me, I turn my head to see Henry making his way over.

"Assaults on the Vigil?" My thoughts immediately return to the deathly creatures.

Henry seems surprised. "Not even a sighting, Arathyn."

"I offered a group of Vorderan youths safe passage, I was hoping that they made the journey here."

"Nothing at all."

I scratch at my head. "What of the curse?"

"Ever-present. Without your presence, it lingers. We must adapt." Henry says it without a touch of concern.

Without my presence. This needs to stop, I can't be everywhere in Arcura at once. Everyone has to relive the pain over and over again.

"Arcura is a deadly place, it's changing rapidly. There are still others like myself out there who seek the power that I have. We are lucky to be alive; however, we can't sit back and let that unfold. The curse needs to be stopped."

Henry grows puzzled. "How?"

"Steel and arrows will offer little protection from what is out there. The Eldest One and his dark secrets continue to plague my mind."

"The Eldest One?"

"It appeared again at Highgarde. The same being we met at Forvarr. It has another purpose, I was under its control until this happened to all of us." I point at Henry's Enmaran sigil by way of explanation. "We defeated Thiedra at Turinfall. The Turin have suffered a great loss. A rift has opened, pouring forth beings of death. There will be more, I am certain."

"We are all at your side, Arathyn. We've been through much together already. You didn't raise a force to sit here and be dictated."

Dictated. The Eldest One certainly can't be trusted. Death must be after me for a reason. I only have one path to follow.

Narrowing my eyes, a determination grows. "We need you and your brother, Vorathen and Vexxyra. We will seek out Ixxenira, it exists somewhere, Vorathen is proof of that."

"I certainly am." Vorathen's voice falls from the watchtower above. Forever vigilant, I am not at all surprised by his presence.

Henry chuckles. "You do not miss a thing, do you?"

"No. I prefer to stay alive." Vorathen's boots thud as he descends the stairs.

"I have a matter to attend to. Then we will seek out your spiritmaster."

"You would relieve Henry of his duties, lad?" Vorathen's concern is appreciated, but there is one person who is a perfect fit.

"The Vigil is built for ranged defence, I am sure Argora will be able. Ruling over our people effortlessly in Turinfall, she needs this. Shattered at Turinfall, defenceless in her home, she couldn't possibly have beaten Vordera's Spiritkind. Yet many were saved in the face of certain death."

"Your trust sounds well placed, Arathyn. Are you sure she is ready?" Henry is as loyal as a Turin's companion.

"I will need to speak with her."

"It has been too long without a real battle. I will retire, then it's swordplay in the morning." Vorathen's bulky figure descends the rampart and disappears into the night.

⊰•⊱

Clanging steel rings throughout the Vigil as soldiers improve under Vorathen's tutelage. Argora walks around aimlessly like she's a completely different person. *I did bring her back from death.*

Grabbing her attention, my proposal starts. "Do you feel at home here?"

"Turinfall. I can't escape the thoughts." Her words are heavy, I place my hand on her shoulder in an attempt to comfort her.

"Will you ever forgive me, Arathyn? I took your father away from you. Perhaps I should have been the one was was taken." A tear streams down her face as guilt sets in.

"Are you forgetting that you died in Turinfall? I feel his presence with me every day. You were protecting your people." I smile and it draws one from her. Argora needed to hear that.

I sense that now is as good as ever. "Nothing would give me greater pleasure, would you take command of Enmara's Vigil? Henry and Bernard will accompany us south. If you accept, you will take command of our men, just as you once did for Rangers."

"Thank you, Arathyn, one needs a purpose. I will continue Henry's work and see to the safety of your home."

"*Our home.*" Arms are thrown around in a mutual embrace. I have to pinch myself. *Did I just give Argora an order?* Of all people.

Twenty-One

VEXXYRA

Sophia? Esther? Oh, I am hopeless at this. Monthera? No. Ah, Moncera.

I reach down and stroke the mane of my reagent-laden beast. "Moncera. Sorry that took so long."

Why am I so bad at naming things? It's a good thing all the herbs have already been named. Or have they?

I ride on Moncera's back towards the Vigil, draining a glass of crystal clear spring water. It certainly beats the algae-tainted water Coradal offered. Elraetha is racing about foraging. She is a different woman, committed. *Safe.* It is uplifting seeing her full of energy. Arathyn must be relieved.

Delbura doesn't look all that different from mine, except she is burdened with numerous baskets of berries.

"Looking for something?" Arathyn's voice makes me jump as I scour the edge of the marsh.

"Just missing one last ingredient for a lethal poison." A ghost plays with his face.

"Here, Moncera." I rip a grub from the earth and throw it towards her. Moncera's elegance fails momentarily as a rabid bite snatches it from the air.

"Lovely name."

"It only took me a whole day to decide. The herbs here are excellent, much better than useless weeds that grew near Coradal.

Do you know what this does if mixed perfectly with Snapseed and filtered water?" A five-petaled crimson flower twirls in my fingers.

He chuckles. "Are you sure I want to know?"

"Our enemies won't want to find out." I yearn for further knowledge, also I need to replenish my soul vials. "Are we heading to Hammerknell again?"

I feel as if I have fallen into the perfect situation. *I can actually make a difference.* This is all so new. So much to learn, far beyond the realm of herbalism.

"You're after spirits? A good plan, I am glad you asked. Henry, Bernard and your father will accompany me south in search of the Ixxenirans. Argora will command the Vigil and the Rangers. Will you accompany us too?"

I expected as much. It is delightful to be important enough to be asked. "Are we leaving now?"

"Momentarily."

"Then I have much to prepare." A determination finds my feet as I rush off.

⚊⊰❖⊱⚊

A crudely organised table lies before me. *Organised.* There are glass bottles everywhere, each with a ground powder inside missing vital ingredients. I stare at a barrel of fresh water. *What am I missing?*

"Vexxyra, Arathyn requests your presence. We are leaving." Henry has come to collect me, I thought I had more time.

Do I have everything? My mind wanders as I join our travelling party. Henry and Bernard are dressed in crested Enmaran armour. Such a beautiful crest upon gleaming steel.

"As per your request, we will head to Hammerknell first." I have already prepared in expectation of Arathyn's approval.

Then, Arathyn and I are whisked away. Henry is up to something. "Follow me."

At the highest point of the Vigil stands a larger wooden structure with Enmara's mark etched within the frame in numerous places. "I saw to the construction of this one myself, Arathyn. It was completed only this morning." Henry marvels at the beautiful timber home, as does Arathyn.

"I'll leave you be. My brother wants a word." Henry departs.

Arathyn enters the two-storey dwelling with a balcony overlooking the majority of the grounds.

I just stand before the door, stunned.

"Are you coming?"

Arathyn pushes open the door. My nose finds the smell of freshly cut timber that lingers heavy in the air. It is bare, as expected. Climbing the stairs, we exit onto the balcony, watching contentedly over his people.

"Why did you bring me here?"

Arathyn draws his bow before unleashing an arrow that thuds into the ground a few paces behind Argora, who is patrolling the grounds below. The action draws the attention of a few swordsmen and the gaze of Argora herself.

"Up here!" Arathyn raises his bow.

Argora rips the arrow from the earth before making her way toward us. "Keeping me on my toes, Arathyn?"

Argora wears a grin. They certainly have an interesting relationship.

Not wanting to sound rude, I ask the question again. *Maybe he missed it.* "Why did Henry bring us to this beautiful home?" *Perhaps he doesn't know?*

"Per my request." Argora appears behind us at the top of the stairs.

Oh. *Where were my thoughts heading?*

"You've given me a newfound sense of pride," Argora says to Arathyn. "This house. The balcony. Brings back lovely memories."

"You'd best get comfortable then, I would like you to call it your home, Commander."

Argora's eyes widen. "Commander?"

"As per our previous discussion. You will be known as Enmaran Commander Argora, charged with the safekeeping of Enmara's Vigil. Will you accept this honour?"

The tip of Argora's head signifies her acceptance which is now just a formality.

Confusion hasn't left yet. *Why did Argora request me to be here?* I feel like a ghost eavesdropping on a private conversation.

"The *Commander* might like to hear what I have to say." Arathyn is playing with my thoughts and it's working. "I mentioned that you may like a hall to help with your … *profession.*"

Why does he say it like that? Well, I guess dabbling with spirits of the dead isn't exactly apothecary work.

They are both looking at me, expecting a response. I couldn't. But my brain is going into overdrive.

"It would be better than a crude workstation beside the cows." An imaginary hand whacks my face at such a statement.

"Excellent. Argora, see to its construction while we are away. There should be many hands available as the workload has lightened."

Argora sees something in me, so did Sophia. This isn't just an act of kindness on Arathyn's part, it feels more like an act of *necessity.*

My own apothecary hall. If only days could pass instantly.

Bodies upon beasts we march, Henry is riding upon Delbura which Elraetha offered. We swallow up ground effortlessly as we glide along the mountainside.

I nod at my father's beast. "Do you have a name for it yet?"

"That is too cute for me, my girl. As long as it crushes our enemies, that will suffice." My eyes roll but I know he's right. *Who knows what our next encounter might be?*

Hammerknell, dark and foreboding, graces us once more as we round the slope. *We're back here already.* My eyes make out the towering stone entrance. We dismount before descending into the dark hallway. Bernard and Henry see to torches and we proceed under firelight.

I need to be quick, we are here because of me.

"This place chills me to the core." Henry's first visit has his face wearing uncertainty.

"Stay vigilant." Arathyn cautions.

The hallway opens up into the first chamber, the place we had initially overheard the Vorderans.

"Souls, come to me." My voice is so whimsical. Raising my arm, I expose my sigil to the eerie chamber. Just as I beckon, spirits glow near and far, floating around almost waiting to be trapped. Creeping around, I swat at them with empty vials as they turn into faint wisps of light, drifting towards my marking.

Broken glass reverberates throughout the chamber, amplified in the dead silence. I've dropped one. Every set of eyes pierces me like ravenous wolves stalking their prey in a firelit den.

"We are done here." Nervous, stocked, we need to leave. The last of my intact vials finds a place upon my glowing sash.

As we turn to begin our exit, a dull crackling catches our attention, emanating from a lower hallway. Our heads turn in unison.

Suddenly, I'm drenched in guilt. *What have I done?*

"Another rift?" Bernard says.

"Whatever it is. It is far too close to home to ignore." Arathyn is right.

Great. I don't want to spend another moment here, but my clumsiness does.

Sounds of further crackling grow louder as we descend. My father draws his blade. The now-abandoned altar rises above before us.

Swirls of dark energy pattern the cold stone walls. Souls glisten above like stars as Arathyn approaches the altar. Without hesitation, he raises his arms in acceptance before morphing as they speed into him.

A terrifying cackle cuts through the room as if the voice is right at my ear.

Then, it stops abruptly.

It is a trap. After a moment of eerie silence, dark, bulky appendages shoot out of the swirls on the walls before lashing at Arathyn.

Distracted by his surge into Spiritkind, tendrils catch him across his chest that shear through his aura. White plasma sprays outwards as he cries in pain. He keeps his balance and the tendrils retreat, burning at the tips upon touching his form.

Arathyn dodges several more strikes, leaving a trail of white substance in his wake as he retreats. Then, he collapses.

"Arathyn!" Henry is in disbelief. Shocked eyes look on his blade which is covered in Arathyn's … *blood?*

A blade that illuminates brightly. The substance expands, oozing up Henry's arm to his chest.

"Arggggh! By the light!" Henry's body is encompassed in a white aura. "What is happening to me?!"

Arathyn's wavering voice travels from somewhere within the maze of tombstones. "Go forth, Champion!"

Henry's face is suddenly awash with determination. Rushing toward the tendrils that writhe and wait above the altar, a bolt of vaporising energy flies over his head and explodes upon the purple energy source on the far side. Disintegrating instantly on impact, its spawned tendril falls limp.

Weaving my way through the array of tombstones, I know where Arathyn is. A near-opaque illumination of light in front of me guides my steps. *Please save him.*

Arathyn's gleaming bow lies on stone by his side, not in hand. A large gash reaches across his morphed body, of which its seemingly untouchable form did nothing to counter the strike. *A yeti couldn't breach it? Perhaps his body was still under transformation.* My questioning mind wanders, I need an answer for everything.

Bernard creeps over. "With permission?"

"No!" *I can still save him!*

Bernard turns his gaze, looking at me like I'm a peasant before I realise he's after what's left of Arathyn's power.

"Yes …" Words under pain leave Arathyn's mouth as he gives his blessing.

"At your side, brother!" Bernard joins his kin in a similar form.

Appendages lash at the brothers in futile attempts, striking shields traced with energy that burns them at every touch.

Should I? My father is stranded by himself, itching for action. He can't join the brothers, that would surely spell his death.

Tendrils are undergoing constant regeneration, the Enmaran brothers' attacks are useless. Every time they cleave off a segment of its writhing flesh, it just grows back.

Should I drain the last of Arathyn's power? Will it completely drain? It might kill him. Time is of the essence, he needs urgent care of which I am certain I can't provide that here.

Eyes stare at me like he knows what's coming, that's enough of a cue. Upon touching rescinding strands of diamond-laced hair, energy shoots through my entire body. *This time I'm ready for it.*

"Alright, you two. Let the Sapphiress take it from here." My voice turns the air into a cool mist before me. *I just sound silly.*

Joining the brothers with a frozen blade in hand, my crystalline body stands upon the altar surrounded by an icy-blue aura. Vials upon my waist glow brighter. Cold eludes me.

Tendrils squirm around, studying me as if they have eyes. After coiling, like a whip they strike at me. Spinning around effortlessly, frozen shards spear in every direction. Frozen shards that pummel into the guard's shields. Frostbite takes a hold of the deathly appendages before they begin to freeze.

"Over to you, boys."

Bernard and Henry are astonished, they look at me as if I'm a strange woman made of ice. A quick flurry of plasma-charged steel shatters frozen flesh. The last of the energetic swirls disintegrate. Crackling stops.

Arathyn cries out in pain. As suspected, his power has waned. Pain strikes at his human body.

"We must get him back to the Vigil immediately! I can't treat him here."

"It's … watching us …" Arathyn is delirious. "Ever since my return to Highgarde … The forest … Hammerknell … It can't be a coincidence."

"You'll be fine lad, it's just a flesh wound." My father is just trying to be supportive. *But he won't.* The wound is deep and will require significant stitching. Arathyn is going to hate me for what I'm about to do.

Bernard looks worried. "This terrain is no good to walk an injured man. Can you manage on Draygar?" The brothers' power wanes as they carry Arathyn over their shoulders.

"I'll … need a hand …"

Arathyn's words are an understatement.

The wound is weeping. My makeshift mesclun wrapping is failing, there is too much blood.

"Open the gate!" Henry's request brings about an immediate gathering of Rangers. Argora appears beyond, gasping as she identifies bloodstained cloth around Arathyn's chest.

"We were ambushed at Hammerknell, by … *Death*," Henry explains to Argora whose look alone is asking for answers.

"Take him to my room!" I find myself demanding of our leader, but I don't care. He won't be alive for long if I don't take control of the situation.

It's not much, but I have a bed and dresser. The brothers drag Arathyn in and place him upon the soft blanket. I'm going to need a new one. Blood instantly finds a path within the threads.

"Just a moment." I rack my brain until I remember where I put it. The workbench near the kitchen, hopefully a drunk hasn't made off with it.

It's still there, bottled and ready.

Arathyn's eyes flicker as I reach his side, he's barely conscious. Never have I used Gloomroot Acid before. Extremely potent in the right consistency, it is excellent for concocting heavier doses of medicine.

A glass is slammed down on the dresser, my hands pour a mixture of Azurebloom and Gloomroot.

An audience I have. Within the small room, my father is barely far enough away from the others. Anxious they all are as they wait for me to do something, but there is patience.

A flame is lit upon a bundle of Silverwisp. Grasping a set of tongs, they hold the tincture over the heat until it boils.

The mixture bubbles. It is time.

My throat gulps as I remove the bloodstained mesclun. His flesh is turning black within a strange taint. Arathyn looks at me.

Oh, please don't look at me with those eyes.

"Don't hate me."

A hand crosses his heart as a smile emerges. I hesitate. *How can I do this to him? A life without him, I can't imagine.* That thought alone causes my trembling hands to tip the vial, the mixture finds the wound in its entirety. Gasps ricochet around the room as his flesh convulses at the touch of the liquid. Arathyn doesn't even make a sound, likely because his body has just gone into shock.

I grab a needle and thread from my kit and get to work. Most have left, it's not what eyes want to see, but I have the stomach for it. Arathyn can consider himself lucky the burn finally knocked him out. This would be worse.

Over and under until the wound is stitched. This time I can dress the wound properly and within a moment I am done.

Twenty-Two

ARATHYN

Sounds of rampant sniffing wake me from my slumber. Draygar sits right beside the bed, studying me intently. I'm wrapped heavily in cloth. There is a burning sensation on my chest. A dull pain.

I can smell acid? This isn't my room. My curiosity peaks. I begin to run my hand under the wrapping.

"You don't want to do that." I know that voice. Vexxyra is standing in the doorway looking as beautiful as ever.

"What did you do to me?" My eyes check over the rest of my body.

"Burned you alive."

I gulp. "Thank you."

I look at Draygar whose mind is full of compassion. "I will be alright."

"Can I walk?" She looks at me with a questioning glance while fiddling about her apothecary kit.

Her feet find a stride. A gentle hand examines my forehead before resting on my shoulder. "Your legs are fine."

That's all I needed to hear, I refuse to be bedridden forever.

Upon finding determination, I attempt to climb out of bed. The wound is still tender. My eyes peer at Vexxyra once more, seeing if she thinks I'm crazy, but she just smiles.

There are small chests everywhere, filled with every leaf, stem or root you can imagine. *This is her room.*

"He's alive!" The voice of a commoner rings out across the training grounds. A voice that fixes all eyes on me.

Vorathen momentarily turns his attention away from the infantry. "Do you think it wise to be on your feet so soon?"

Vexxyra scoffs behind me. "Of course, Father, are you discrediting my work?" Vorathen laughs before turning to strike a target.

"Arathyn, the sight of you has just lifted a pain from within these walls," says Argora. "I have never seen the likes of one man have such an impact on his people. Something I was never able to match. I hope this comes as a warning to the challenges you will surely face." Argora's words hit me like a stiff winter's gale. Arcura is unpredictable, dangerous. And there is still the matter of the Eldest One.

⁕

I have taken up residence near Argora's quarters. My coat hangs upon the timber wall, sewn back to its original state. I dress myself for an appearance. Whatever Vexxyra did to me only hinders my movements slightly. *What did I do to deserve all of these incredible people?*

As I push open the door, my appearance draws cheers from those nearby.

I descend the slope towards the training grounds. "Vorathen, do you still sense that compelling draw? It is time we seek out your master."

Vorathen looks bewildered. "My master? You are standing right there!" Then, he leers at his daughter. "You haven't messed with his mind, have you?"

A leer that is returned with even greater intent. "Your wrist, you daft fool."

Vorathen's face is one of embarrassment. "South. For certain."
"We need to end this. Gather the Champions."
"No".
Everyone turns their attention to Vexxyra. She looks like she wants to hide in a dark corner for eternity at such a statement. "You can't go out saving everyone yet. You can walk but you need a few more days."
So we wait.

⸻❖⸻

The castle. It's all that now occupies my thoughts. If Vilriyan chose an abandoned one to do his bidding, then it's likely that one appearing in better condition will be harbouring people.
My heartfelt look finds Vexxyra. "Thank you for bringing me back to reality."
Reality. Is any of this real? Here I am walking around with a beastly spirit empowering me with soul energy.
"Who else would lead us on such an exciting adventure?" She is growing fond of me.
Vorathen gives me a look before addressing his daughter. "As long as your excitement doesn't get us killed, I'll be a happy man."
I'm not sure if Henry or Bernard enjoy our conversation, but it does not seem to bother them at all. One thing I certainly know, they are extremely loyal to me.
We reach rolling foothills before climbing to the highest point. Darkness sets in, revealing torchlight to the south.
"We're close."
Vorathen makes sense of my statement. "The castle?"
I nod. "Let's make camp here."
Vexxyra checks my dressing that she has now changed several times. *I yearn for her further touch.* There is no longer any blood, the wound only shoots a very slight pain as I move.

"Eat well. Tomorrow will hold more answers."

A grand castle stands tall to the southeast beyond a thick, entangling jungle. A large prairie to the west. The Feygoran Mountains are no longer a barrier to visibility.

"The sensation grows stronger, lad. No doubt they are holed up in there."

Henry pries at a plan. "Seems like an obvious choice, what do you suggest, Arathyn?"

I agree with Vorathen. "We know nothing about this area or its people, it would be unwise to approach without scouting ahead first. We will take to the glade, it will conceal us well."

Air grows humid as we make our way into dense foliage. Buzzing from insects dominates the area. I have to wipe my brow every so often to keep the sweat out of my eyes.

"Duskshrooms, Crimson Bells; a moment." The herbalist in Vexxyra emerges yet again. *She probably has a recipe to make one live forever.*

As she plucks the flower from the plant, a vine reaches out and coils around her arm, dragging her in. With a swift draw from her free hand, the razor-sharp blade of her dagger slices right through it. Vine uncoils and drops to the ground.

Henry chuckles. "And here I thought the only danger was from humans. Boy, was I wrong."

"If there is one thing she knows, it's plants."

Vexxyra gives her father a scornful look.

A glimmering pool catches sunlight that shines through gaps in the canopy. Our companions drink profusely. Environmental effects sap their energy as does the burden they have in carrying us.

"Quick. Cover." We hide at Bernard's warning. A small band of soldiers makes their way along a cobblestone path. They wear armour with a crest which I haven't seen.

"Sylvora will be ours. That idiot is wasteful with the power he has. Send word to Rogar, preparations are nearly complete." The group splits. Half of them head south across a field while the rest continue their march.

Sylvora. Llorelth mentioned the castle earlier in my travels.

Henry is alarmed. "They're preparing a coup."

Immediately, I feel it my responsibility to prevent this. *Peace.* This couldn't be further from it.

As the path crests ahead, they disappear from sight, meandering over a hill.

Prevention is of the utmost importance. "We must follow the others."

Cautiously crossing the path, we keep to what little cover there is. A field that is vast and flat lies before us. A small village on the far side holds several people who welcome the party we are following. An inn stands behind the group engaging in some form of conversation.

"They must be Ixxenirans, there are a large number of them," says Bernard.

"Then we are where we need to be."

A loud shout echoes across the field, breaking the calm of a windless day. I cannot make out the words. A man is dragged out of the building by a soldier, a medallion on his armour. Probably higher than a squad leader. He raises his arms, begging for mercy before a sword is run through his chest. The bloodstained weapon is then turned on others while its wielder stands over the corpse.

Another tyrant. *Hopefully, he ends up like the last one.*

"No wisp?"

Vexxyra is right.

"Keen eyes, Vexxyra. He has slain an aligned. It would appear we have arrived at the right time. Mount up, we're going in."

Riding across the field in formation, we are undeterred. It won't take long to be spotted. Just laying eyes on us should quell the unrest. Vorathen to my right, the brothers on my left, and Vexxyra behind with her arms locked around me.

Heads turn. Bodies scatter. Others watch in anticipation. A soldier points in our direction, and the murderer spins around in disgust.

"And who might you be? Here to fight Rogar too, eh?" His words carry a profound confidence and I realise he is speaking about himself.

"Why did you kill that man?"

He counts. "Do you really think you can intimidate me with a few ... animals?" He does a double take at Vorathen's choice companion. "Five strong? I have an army at my disposal!"

His eyes once again fix on Vorathen. "Ah, you're one of us. Why are you with these outcasts? Once I take that deer-loving Gelreid's power, I could make you a god."

Vorathen is considering his proposal, imagining himself as the aforementioned.

It seems as if the land in which Rogar walks is just an afterthought. "If only you had any idea."

"I wasn't talking to you. I've had about enough of Enmarans."

Rogar's threat infuriates me and I narrow my eyes. "I'll ask again, why did you slay that man?"

"It was one of Gelreid's cohorts. A spy, no doubt."

"Do you think murdering your own people will make you a leader?"

Rogar raises a hand to silence me. "Enough. I see that I need some extra ... persuasion... To me, men!"

Nearly a hundred militiamen emerge from various parts of the village and congregate behind Rogar. *He isn't bluffing.*

"Feast your eyes upon Rogar's Assault. We will take back Sylvora and kill anyone who stands in our way!" Loud cheers follow his words.

I see that I need further persuasion. "Allow me to introduce myself. I am Arathyn, Spiritkind of the Peacekeeper Enmara. I cannot allow this!"

"Ah, I have heard of you. Causing trouble in the north and here you stand before me."

"Then you will know that your efforts will be futile."

Vexxyra's words aren't well calculated. *They aren't dead yet and I don't think we have enough souls at our disposal.* But there is discomfort on Rogar's face as he takes a moment to contemplate the situation.

Then some context. "We've waited far too long living in this quaint place. That castle is our home!" They've been forced out, I still think Rogar's methods are bordering on the extreme.

"Have you knocked on the gate and asked?"

Vorathen's sarcasm is met abruptly. "Gelreid will not have it. His hatred toward me forced us out."

I dig deeper. "What brought that about?"

Rogar sighs. "It is his family. They've always looked down on us like peasants. Ever since this damn curse came to the fore, it has driven everyone insane. It's his birthright, so he says, to command Sylvora. I've spent god knows how long assembling this resistance, we've fought off countless others. What else do we have? Hope? The power has gone to his head!"

Am I actually feeling remorse?

"Who commands Sylvora?" asks Henry. I think he is onto something.

"Iravelle Evermoon, Gelreid's grandmother."

Henry's hand finds his jaw before his eyes examine us. "Then it is his birthright, no?"

"Enough!" Rogar grows discomforted.

There is definitely more to this. "Deer-loving?" I say.

"He strides around the Evermoon Swamp on his *sacred* beast while his Royal Guard defend the castle. Sylvora is barricaded heavily." His words carry a touch of jealousy. "He seems to have some kind of connection to it. His beast glows with him, that swamp is a mysterious place."

I need to meet Gelreid. "Your spiritmaster, no doubt. Would you be kind enough to escort us?"

"I care enough for these people not to throw their life away. If you insist, but be warned, he will not appreciate the sight of me." *Likely for good reason.*

A ruse I wish to aid. *For now.* "Bring your following, it may just persuade him enough with our presence."

Rogar addresses the masses. "You heard him, gather your things. Vari, bring me my steed."

I find myself relieved. We've dodged a battle in the name of questionable diplomacy.

Vorathen points at the man's corpse from atop his Granite Horror. "A word of warning. I have been bereft of battle for some time, let's not do anything silly. Will someone show that man some respect and give him a proper burial. He was probably just as confused as you are." No one dares to speak back.

We journey eastward with a hundred strong Ixxinerans following behind. The path forks. Sylvora stands in grandeur at the end of the southern heading, barricaded heavily behind its huge iron gate.

From atop a rampart, we are being watched. A rampart that seems to kiss the clouds. Guards join the scouts above before we are concealed behind thick forest.

"No turning back now." Rogar is sitting comfortably on his chestnut mare. Gelreid will surely be informed of our sighting.

"Onward to the Evermoon Swamp. Champion Henry, take the rear. Make sure we are not followed." Once again, I'm leaving nothing to chance.

Henry diverts upon Delbura and races to the back, heads turn as he glides by. We continue ahead. Vorathen keeps his eyes trained on Rogar, as do I. He is certainly capable of betrayal.

Swamplands, a stickiness sets in, the Coramine Sea on the horizon. Vexxyra's eyes are peering everywhere, but we are not here to pick at flora.

Rogar stops us. "Here we are. Not much to see."

A small town stands far off on the coast to the north, I am certain it is that of Mistral Grove. Thoughts of the Moltecern come flooding back and the lady who kindly helped me transport it. A different life, left behind.

A strange swirling pool captures my interest not far off into the lake. A lake encompassed by dead trees that somehow find the strength to stay upright within the surrounding muck.

The pool continues to swirl around water that sits stagnant.

Vexxyra follows my eyes. "Strange. I have never seen anything like that before."

Rogar notices it also. "Like I said: mysterious."

"There!" Bernard is the first one to notice. A figure emerges on the southern end of the marshland, riding over the central lake as if it is solid ground.

Rogar confirms my thoughts. "That's Gelreid, alright."

Gelreid races across the water. His stag glows green. As he turns abruptly to our general direction, I can make out an aura that encompasses him. Stopping suddenly as he notices our gathering, he takes a moment before charging toward us at incredible speed. The stag leaps high in the air before crashing down into the swamp before us, showering us in a deluge of water. Half-soaked, I wipe at my eyes to regain my vision. Gelreid moves toward a swirling pool, empowering himself further.

"What an audience! To what do I owe the pleasure?" Gelreid's voice is an energetic crackle.

"Our spiritmaster is quite the sight." Vorathen's words force a kind gesture from Gelreid.

"Is that you, Arathyn? The one from my dreams?"

I find myself unable to answer.

"None other," says Vexxyra.

"Thank you, milady. I see you've brought a familiar face. I can only guess why." I'm sure he's talking about Rogar and his tone changes at the last.

Regaining my stature, I put forward a proposal. "These people seek a home within Sylvora. Would you grant them the honour?"

"They are free to come and go at will, I have always been inviting. All except one. However, while they remain loyal to that barbaric animal, I will not grant that of which you ask."

Rogar moves further back into the ranks of his followers. A blade unsheathes. A man cries out as he is grabbed unsuspectingly, the tip of a dagger against his throat.

"Do I have your attention now! One false move and he will choke on his own blood."

My fear has now come to fruition, the act of defiance in front of Spiritkind is a foolish ploy. Rogar's victim resists, but every move has that blade drawing more blood.

"Durrand! Oh, how I've searched for you for so long. How did you end up in this mess?"

It's personal.

"That's right! Let us in or your brother is drawing his last breaths." Rogar's following recedes and he is soon only standing with Durrand.

"Us? It looks to me that your people are abandoning you as we speak. It is over."

Vorathen dismounts, edging towards Rogar with his sword drawn. "Let him go! No more blood will be spilled!"

Rogar drags Durrand back by his neck. "Not another step!"

"Are you underestimating who I am? What makes you think I won't be able to bring him back?" Gelreid's words are tense. Without Enmara's touch, I'm unsure if that is even possible. *Thiedra was able, although that seemed to have a different effect.*

Impatience festers on Gelreid's face. "Put down your blade. These people may call Sylvora home. The dungeon below, yours. That is what you wanted? No?"

Sensing his defeat and his defiance proving a failure, Rogar rips the blade across the exposed flesh of Durrand's neck before throwing him to the ground. In a crazed rage, he charges at Gelreid.

"Durrand! You will pay for this!"

Vorathen steps in front of an advancing Rogar. Gelreid raises his staff before unleashing a bolt of energy into Vorathen. Beginning to bulge into a green-hued, stone-hardened warrior, he wrestles with energy coursing through his veins. His blade drips with a venom that makes the grass congeal at its touch. Warboots draw roots from the ground that unearth with every step. Eyes pulsating in a green serpentine glare behind numerous eyelids.

"Father!" Vexxyra's look is one of shock.

"Oh, that is gorgeous. Slay him!"

Rogar reaches Vorathen in a frenzy, but hopelessly outmatched. Thrust with fury, the reptilian warrior's blade pierces right through flesh and bone with ease. Rogar's body darkens, twitching as venom travels through him. Nothing more than withered flesh and bone on the ground is the result of such acidic toxicity. Roots exude from the immediate ground around

Rogar's corpse and pull him into the earth before grass emerges in its place.

"Great! Now you've turned him into a real animal." Vexxyra says exactly what's on my mind.

Gelreid approaches the body of his fallen brother. "Forgive me brother, may your misguided soul rest for eternity." A hand is laid on Durrand's body while eyes within a shaking head look at me. A wrapping of roots encases the body which is then fastened to Gelreid's stag.

"What do you think, lad?"

Please don't kill us all. How does he even speak like that?

"Can you control *it*?" A part of me is unsure if Vorathen is under Gelreid's control.

"Yes. It gave me great pleasure! I never put my trust in Rogar."

Gelreid and Vorathen's power wanes, their bodies returning to human forms. Rogar's former following are anxiously awaiting a decision.

"As I said before, Sylvora welcomes you!" Gelreid heads off toward the castle. Conversation stirs within the crowd before a collective decision is made to follow him.

"Of course, you are most welcome too." After throwing an invitation our way, his voice begins to trail off.

Just as we begin our return to Sylvora, the ground jolts violently, throwing Draygar and I to the ground. Trees as stiff as statues suddenly shake as if a gale is roaring across the marsh. "Get down!"

A loud drone reverberates throughout the lush landscape, almost as if it is some kind of strange voice, completely unintelligible.

There are a hundred eyes peering in every direction. A few anxious moments later, the sound stops abruptly like a door slamming shut, silencing the area beyond.

"Is anyone injured?" I ask.

Silence is all that ensues.

"Are you feeling alright, Arathyn?" Vexxyra's gravely concerned look has me aghast. She bounds over toward me. Within dozens of darkened looks, she is but a light within.

As if I need to mention it, I ask, "The earthquake?!"

Vorathen is dumbfounded at my statement much like everyone else. "An earthquake?"

No one else felt that? Everyone is just staring at me as if they're questioning my sanity.

Gelreid brings back reality. "You are troubled, Arathyn. Make haste for Sylvora. Be on your guard, Arcura is unpredictable at best."

⸺⟡⸺

We're dwarfed as we walk under Sylvora's arched gateway. The grand stone castle is unlike anything I have ever seen.

People rejoice as they are reunited with familiar faces. Others grow grim as the fate of loved ones seems all but decided.

Durrand's body is removed from the steed and taken away hastily before Gelreid turns and approaches us. "Join me, Arathyn. This is a cause for celebration and a chance to mourn my brother. You may stable your beasts over there."

We are led into a grand banquet hall. Firelight, dancing inside iron chandeliers, fills the room with a warm, embracing aura. A huge granite table lined with mahogany chairs sits in the centre as butlers race to and fro.

Gelreid gestures over the table and we sit. Eyes peer around, awestruck by the grand setting. Vexxyra places her hand on mine as she sits next to me with a worried look on her face. Vorathen checks me over with prying eyes.

"Nice of you to join us, dear Iravelle. There is plenty to go around. My apologies that we met on such mundane terms, Arathyn. To what do I owe the pleasure of your journey south?" Gelreid chomps down on a haunch of meat as an elderly lady dressed in pure white sits beside him.

"The Eldest One."

I'm here for Ixxenira's spirit and Vorathen but he doesn't need to know that yet.

"And who might that be? Hopefully not another hallucination."

I press on, ignoring the latter. "Have you not encountered forces of death?"

He wipes over his mouth with a silken cloth before returning his fork to the cool stone surface.

"I have lived here for twenty-five years. My mother and father, bless their souls, were taken when all this began. Iravelle and I are lucky to be the *same*." He places a hand on Iravelle's dainty arm. "We've had bouts of aggression from others, much like Rogar. But nothing of what you speak. You sound troubled."

"And what of the Kygeerans?"

"I suppose you mean the reds? I believe Rogar and his cohort had encounters with them over on the western edge. They have not troubled us here. Well, apart from the few that were branded as such on that fateful day."

Obviously, he hasn't seen much outside the walls of Sylvora. It seems death is only interested in me.

All of a sudden, screams from outside pierce at the hall doors. Throwing them open, we race outside. Scores of ghoulish fiends litter the area. Dread upon Draygar's mind pulsates within my head like a migraine. Doors slam shut, the joyous atmosphere abates. Not a single sound remains but a horrific chittering of teeth and legs.

"There are too many!" Gelreid is right, they are as far as the eye can see.

"They are here for me." Creatures of death scuttle about, taking no further advance. Horrifying screeches and rampant cackling grow above the chittering as they lie in wait expecting a response.

Acting on impulse, I summon Draygar over, carefully watching the immediate area before me. Creatures gaze at him as he moves toward me. Dread dissipates immediately as I mount my beast. My mind suddenly clears.

"Arathyn?" Vexxyra questions my actions as I raise my hand to acknowledge her.

Receding in a circular pattern as we reach the front ranks, the creatures scuttle back almost as if a force is pushing them. Others watch on with looks of confusion as we stride around unhindered. Something isn't sitting right with Gelreid.

"You? Did you … *summon* them here?"

Henry immediately discards that thought. "No, Arathyn is Enmaran. How could you possibly draw that conclusion?"

But Henry's words fail to sway.

"Look at him upon that beast. He is one with them!"

Vorathen carefully studies the situation. "They're afraid of him."

Vexxyra draws her own conclusion. "Yes. But the rift after Highgarde. Why is it different now?"

Gelreid has seen enough. "I will not have this pestilence here!"

A sharp laugh diverts our attention high upon a towering spire. A booming voice of death cascades down. "Fool! Ixxenira … Why did you seek … such filth … The darkness … comes …"

"Why are you here?!" My yell is so loud that the sky feels my wrath.

"Peace … is not in the hands of many … but only one … Is it no longer … what you seek?"

"Gelreid is not my enemy!"

"You … must destroy him … Only you … have the power to stop … the hordes …"

Destroy him?

"Your hordes?!"

A terrifying laugh splits the air once more. "Arcura … is twisted … The very reality … has been torn. There … will only be more … Look around you …"

Gelreid runs toward his stag and leaps upon it before racing toward a makeshift pool nearby. Not a single creature takes their gaze off me.

Until he morphs.

"Begone! Scourge!"

"Death … has a taste … for the special ones …"

Within an instant, the shadowy gaze of a thousand eyes fix on Gelreid as if I have just disappeared from existence. A cacophony of shrieks rings out, ricocheting off stone walls.

Gelreid remains confident. "Do your worst!"

It dawns on me that he is soon going to regret his actions having seen it firsthand before.

Lurching forward in droves, the creatures leap upon and rip at the Ixxineran Spiritmaster. Gelreid screams in pain as blasts of green light displace several rabid fiends.

Vastly overwhelmed, assaulted by the hundreds, the light subsides. Being in Spiritkind is detrimental here, yet that same power within me can subdue them. Enmara is indeed the only true protector.

Henry slams the grand doors of the banquet hall shut. Creatures scour the walls, skittering around in every direction, hungering for more. After a short moment of my ears enduring the terrifying sound of nothingness, the spirit of Ixxenira rises from Gelreid's body.

And I am ready.

Draygar and I dash forward just as the horde takes a significant interest in the spirit. Hovering in the air in front of us, it waits. Wanting. Our bodies impact into the reptilian haze moments before the horde does. An energetic release sends forth a shockwave that obliterates the deathly creatures around it. A blast that blows doors off hinges and shakes the castle's foundations.

"We must find Kygeera and bring an end to this."

The Eldest One is long gone. I have to heed its warning, these assaults have to stop for there to ever be a chance at peace. The fall of Gelreid, I am certain it is all a part of its plan.

People begin to grace the grounds once more sensing that all may now be safe, but most eyes stare through windows.

One looks at me hysterically. "Have mercy!"

My presence needs convincing. "You are safe, for now."

I feel the need to shout to reach the ears of even the most cowered. "Do not let fear control your lives. As you all look upon me, I can see the fear in your eyes. I am not your enemy."

I then turn to Iravelle. "Milady, be brave. These people need leadership and they will look to you. A safety I cannot guarantee while I am here. Gelreid gave his life, one that will ultimately lead to the safeguarding of Sylvora for years to come. Be proud." She has seen much loss in her time, now more. Gratitude is offered before she slips away into her chambers.

"You are a true inspiration to the human race, Arathyn." Henry speaks proudly, others agree with his sentiment.

"Arcura needs me in its darkest days, I was given the responsibility and I will see it through."

Kygeera. Where is it?

Right on cue, Bernard is curious. "Where do you propose we travel? We've never encountered the reds."

"Sylvora's people have. West. We will take the path beyond the village and be ready for anything. We must leave immediately, these people have suffered enough. I'd hate to draw further death upon Sylvora. Bernard, take Rogar's steed. He will not be needing it."

For the first time, the five of us have our own companion or some form of transport. Our journey west lies ahead. Bernard dresses his mare in armour generously given by Sylvora's blacksmith.

I now have the ability to empower Ixxenirans. The ability to empower our entire party. Wherever the Kygeerans are, hostile or not, we are a force to be reckoned with.

Twenty-Three

VEXXYRA

I am so far from home. Everywhere my eyes look is grassland as far as the eye can see. The peaks of Mount Moradar are so prominent to the northeast in comparison.

Arathyn stops us as he runs a hand through his hair. "Does anyone have knowledge of the west?"

"No, lad. Farmers from a forgotten coast. We were lucky to even travel as far as the mountains. I likely speak for everyone in that regard."

My father is right, most of us thought the mountains were as far as one could travel west.

We reach a crest, exposing a little more of the mystery ahead of us. Jagged mountains rise in the distance across vast swathes of flat land at half the height of the Feygoran Mountains. Small settlements lie on wind-torn plains. Nothing more than a place of temporary respite.

I instinctively duck as we spot movement far off to the southwest, a band of ten or so. They head toward a coastline holding pockets of trees.

"We have to assume they're all aligned. No doubt by now, the curse has lured people to where their masters are," says Arathyn.

"They're hopelessly exposed out there."

"One thing is for certain, Henry. If they feel comfortable enough to do so, this entire domain must feel safe."

"We have our heading. Let's see what they're up to."

Upon my father's words, we begin tracking them down.

⸻ ❈ ⸻

Following the ridgeline, we near the coast. The group, unbeknownst to our constant monitoring, turns behind a large mass of rock. Finally, they disappear. We slalom through an ever-increasing barrier of birch trees as we head away from grassland. Waves lap against the rocky shore as a coastal breeze grips my hair.

A cave. Gloomy. Eerie. I already know the answer.

Bernard rubs a hand over the back of his neck. "In there?"

"I do not see anything else of interest, nor them." Arathyn begins to descend.

A large opening in the earth swallows us, leading into a spacious cave system wide enough so that we may continue on mount. The air dampens, a chill grips my skin. We descend into the abyss. Unintelligible voices echo throughout, clear enough to gather a sense of direction. A small amount of light penetrates through from above, enough to mar the use of a torch.

My curiosity gets the better of me. "What in the world would they be doing down here?"

Henry swiftly answers before we are hushed. "A possible hideout."

My father's Horror appears much more invigorated in its natural setting. Foreboding. It moves quicker and sharper at the expense of more noise. Giving away our location is the least of my worries.

Voices become louder, so much so that I expect to see someone every turn we make. A warmth hits us square in the face, the air dries. Light hits us as if the sun is beaming down in a clear sky.

We have caught up to them.

Ten Kygeerans, dressed in strange stone-etched apparel, stand above a volcanic vent that lights up the entire cavern. Two men wheeling a cart laden with bones, suddenly stop and tip the contents to the ground.

A young female voice full of glee chimes in. "Can I keep one this time?"

"As you wish," a male voice answers.

"Alright then. A leg. Another leg … Oh! *A skull.*"

My father whispers. "What are they doing? Putting a skeleton together?"

"I think I have everything ready." Bones are stacked in the young woman's hand.

"Go on then."

The woman's skinny arms toss the selected assortment of bones into the chasm. After a moment of examination as they all peer into the gap, they step back. "Here it comes!"

A small magma-infused beast peeks its head over the edge and gazes around.

"Oh, It's beautiful! I'll name it Blaze."

Once again, Henry is astonished. "Well I'll be—"

My father smirks. "She's going to get quite the shock when they turn around and I tell her I'm taking it."

One by one, old bones ignite into fiery beasts as the Kygeerans continue their work. Brighter and brighter, the cavern glows with each new lava-infused addition. *Are they under total domination of their masters?*

"That'll do nicely, the Alphas in Skalgard will be most impressed."

What we're witnessing feels like only a small demonstration of what they are actually capable of. My mind is racing. *Necromancy. Summoning.* This is far, far greater than what I ever expected possible. *I must study this further.*

"What are you doing?" An answer, I don't receive. Arathyn dismounts, moving Draygar into position. Glistening in firelight, Draygar's eyes show intent. *I trust he knows what he's doing. We have made it this far.*

"What … is … that? That's not ours!" Draygar is spotted and the mood shifts abruptly, a roar so loud the sound rages around my head. Lava-infused beasts flee into recesses as the Kygeerans brace themselves.

"Do we … catch it? Why does it have a saddle?" A trembling hand reaches for a heavy netting draped over a cart. It dawns on me what they are tasked to do.

Arathyn motions for my father to dismount and move into position.

An older, commanding voice refocuses the group. "We will surround it. Ready the net!"

Creeping closer in formation, it's obvious the Kygeeran's have done this before. My father is just a few steps away from Draygar, peeking beyond nothing more than a thin outcrop of rock concealing him from their view. Arathyn gives him a nod.

Sailing through the air, the net is let fly. A heavy slash of my father's sword slices through the rope with ease. Arathyn rushes out, throwing himself onto Draygar's back.

I guess it's my turn to make an appearance. I wish I were more formidable. We're discovered. "Bandits!"

"Oh. Give me more credit!" My father is front and foremost once more.

Maces are drawn as backward steps are taken. "How long have you been there?"

Arathyn takes control of the situation. "Long enough. This can go two ways: we seek your spiritmaster—"

"You are not Kygeeran, she has no time for you. Ask the last non-aligned she met. You'd have to dredge their body from the chasm." A jaw is rubbed before eyes stare death back at Arathyn.

"What is the other way?"

"We'll leave that to your imagination." My father swings his greatsword about, heeding a warning.

"There are ten of us. What do you think you're going to achieve?"

My father only moves forward. "Unfortunately, you won't be alive to find out."

A heavy tension fills the air as fiery beasts are called to their side. "We are not afraid of you, I think you underestimate us."

A woman takes a charred wand to hand, and Arathyn reaches for his bow. Henry and Bernard draw their swords before raising crested shields. My hand unsheathes a dagger, gripping it as tight as possible until my knuckles go white. The other pours a pestilent glaze over it from a tincture on my waist. Doubting my actions at first, the growing realisation of the situation we find ourselves in quickly quells that.

"I am Enmaran Spiritmaster Arathyn, let this be your final warning."

We're ready.

One observant man steps forward. "Your alignments are split, how are you …?"

A question that brings about indecision on the faces of others. All except for one. Nothing but determination on the face of a woman who twitches at her wand. My eyes do not leave her.

"Burn!" A barrage of firebolts is unleashed. An arrow from Arathyn's bow strikes her immediately as if he noticed her twitching too. One bolt catches Draygar on the side of his head that singes his fur. Another crashes into Henry's shield. Others fly harmlessly by, exploding on the wall behind us.

Beasts of lava charge and jump upon Arathyn. His coat starts to smoulder as he struggles to throw them off. My father rushes to his aid, tackling him with so much force that the beasts are thrown off. His Horror bashes its way through their small skeletal frames with repeated swings of its head while devouring another whole. Flames simply douse upon wet stone, rendering the spawns completely useless against his beast.

Arathyn's look is one of bewilderment but my father's act of intervention certainly worked. Bewilderment expires as he throws himself onto Draygar before flanking around, dodging arrays of firebolts that explode in his wake.

Fidgeting at my waist, a misty blue vial finds my grasp. *Perfect.* A potent concoction of Winter's Bite Drapeweed and Vilevine. Shaking the glass violently until I feel the energy testing the limits of its containment, I hurl at the men who are advancing. Glass shatters as it strikes solid ground. An icy blast is the result, spreading a slick entanglement of roots and barbs before them, hindering their advance.

"A witch!"

Is that what I've become? It was nothing more than a mere experiment.

Bernard stops his advance before looking at me in surprise. One of the Kygeerans attempts to walk over the aftermath. Ice grips at his boots, rendering him immobile. Flailing around, he tries to stay on his feet.

Then I realise it's spreading. Fast. And not toward us. Pinned between a deadly pool of frost and a fiery chasm, the Kygeeran's find themselves. Desperation grows as ice forces back weathered boots.

Frost begins to rise, taking a path up the legs of the man stuck inside the slick. Thorns grow from frosted roots, digging into him, drawing blood.

Oh no. What have I done?!

Spell after spell of a flaming repertoire does little to hinder the advance of my experiment. "Our spiritmaster believes the ultimate sacrifice will empower the rest of us! If we can't stop you, then we will aid her!"

Arathyn turns his gaze back to the Kygeerans. "You would sacrifice your lives? I can rid you of the curse!"

A choice they don't seem to have. *I surely wouldn't want to be over that side.*

"You are the curse!" A woman cries as they all jump toward a fiery death. Plummeting screams echo from deep below until an ominous silence sets in once more.

Looking back at the now deceased within the frozen entanglement, frosted roots and thorns have grown over his entire body. A statue of frozen torment.

A statue of witchcraft. My craft.

I sit there with my head in my hands. They're all dead because of me. *Peace. Arathyn is trying so hard to protect everyone.*

A warm hand falls on my shoulder and I grab it. "I don't know what I was thinking."

"That was amazing. You didn't force them to jump." Arathyn's voice is nurturing.

I look up and point at the deceased who is now beginning to thaw. "Or be frozen, pummelled by thorns and strangled to death."

"At the risk of sounding insensitive," says Bernard, "they did try to kill us and what you've conjured up is incredible. I guess I'd better thank you for not throwing that slightly closer to me."

I laugh. Bernard's words do ease the burden of guilt. *They instigated it and it is incredible.*

"We can't save everyone," says Arathyn. "Who knows, you may have just saved us all once more. Let's get out of here, we have a spiritmaster to find."

Sunlight graces us once more, the sound of lapping waves upon the shore eases my mind somewhat. Guilt is still festering at the back of it though. *Taking lives doesn't get any easier.*

Once more, we reach the treeline only to be met with the vast expanse before us. Peering around gives us only one answer.

"We must cross even though we will be hopelessly exposed," says Henry.

"We hide no longer. Enmarans are a beacon of hope, not a sight to be feared." Arathyn is steadfast. "No doubt we will meet our darkest hour. There can be no telling of what she is up to."

The Kygeeran Spiritmaster. Those youths sacrificed themselves for her cause. *What sort of deranged following does she have?*

— ◈ —

We speed across the barren land before us. The openness brings about feelings of excitement and freedom. Exhilaration grips my body. I grip tight of Moncera as her blue-tinged fur waves in the breeze our bounding strides create.

I feel unstoppable.

"No turning back now!" Arathyn's voice carries back to me as he leads the line.

Barren land starts to decline in front of us, exposing a large circular crater. A single figure stands in the centre, rustling back and forth through a tome.

The head lifts. "Ah! You've come!"

"If it isn't the Enmaran himself … Perfect." A man dressed in a red robe, lined with orange trim speaks gracefully. Throwing his head to one side, his jet-black shoulder-length hair whips around.

"Let me introduce myself. I am Ganharen, one of the Kygeeran Alphas. You have set foot upon the Skalgard Boneyard. If you wish to proceed further, you must go through me."

Henry scoffs. "You are just one man."

"Indeed. Indeed. How very observant of you. A long time ago, the beasts of Kygeera's brood were destroyed. Their bones were scattered, left to gather dust right in this very place. Now, they will have their time again!"

If there is one thing Arcura has taught me. Beasts and lots of them. He may only be one man, but I fear what we witnessed earlier was just the beginning.

"Arcura will burn brightly once more. Kygeera's flames shall engulf you!" Ganharen starts chanting a strange dialect from the ancient tome in his hand.

Arathyn steadies himself and takes aim, firing an arrow, only for it to be met by a blast of flame from a fiery ward that appears to encapsulate Ganharen.

"Believe me, Enmaran. I am the least of your problems."

Bones are upheaved and swirled around in a vortex above Ganharen. Crashing to the ground, they ignite in the form of a crimson goliath. Ablaze and thrice the Horror's size, plumes of smoke burst from its body. Eyes stare a fiery death.

"The Magmascythe. Kygeera's Beta. Incinerator of Worlds. Let's see how you handle this! Destroy them!"

Ganharen has it under a spell, this is beyond my expertise. *A summoner, perhaps.* Craning my neck up nearly to the sky, I make out its steaming head.

"Fan out!" Without even a thought, Arathyn's command has me running. Steps that don't seem to be giving me any further distance.

The Magmascythe charges at Arathyn with bounding leaps, leaving scorched earth in its wake. Draygar darts to the left, narrowly avoiding a direct hit. It turns, unleashing an infernal breath which singes Draygar's body. An arrow is fired, embedding into its fiery husk with almost no effect.

Bernard is thrown to the ground as his horse bolts. Sensing a weakness, the colossal beast whips around and bounds toward him hurling embers through the air.

"Oh no, you don't!" My father charges in to intercept the goliath that shows no sign of stopping. His Horror shrieks as it barrels into its side with its stone skull, causing the goliath to stagger briefly.

The Magmascythe shrieks with such volume that I grab at my ears. Slamming the ground with such ferocity, it creates waves of flame that shoot outward. Henry and Bernard are hit behind shields and knocked to the ground. Evasion on my part requires a different strategy. Moncera leaps over them with perfectly timed jumps.

I'm getting better at this. I need to be better at this.

"Amusing! Siphon the life from these weak mortals! Burn in fiery wrath!"

No human can defeat this, we must target its source.

Arathyn's voice powers through the dust. "Vexxyra. Come with me!"

Moncera bounds over. Luck has it that I picked the right companion. I'm amazed she hasn't bolted too.

Meeting up with Arathyn, we flank around towards Ganharen who turns to face us.

"I will burn you to ashes!" A volley of flame is thrown towards us. Draygar leaps over it with ease as does Moncera. A smile is shared as my eyes find Arathyn gripped upon Draygar's saddle.

A forceful blast hits us, cannoning us backwards forty feet. Landing in a heap, my body throws up a cloud of dust. My weary eyes peer around as the dust settles. Glass vials are strewn about.

Why does he have to be so easy on the eyes?

"Pathetic." Ganharen finds our resistance unworthy.

Moncera runs off in the distance. *Typical, as soon as I think of how lucky I am.*

Getting on my knees, I peer over at Arathyn who has made his way back to Draygar. The others are attempting to keep the Magmascythe at bay. It is futile, they can't defeat something they can barely reach.

Examining the dusty vials on the ground, defeat finds me. Souls from Hammerknell, they've all escaped.

I was so sure of my ability.

Sunlight catches on a vial that draws my eyes. A tincture of blue nature. The glass is cracked but it is still intact.

Silverfrost. Made from Winter's Bite, Silverwisp and Palm Oil.

I know what I need to do, but I can't do it alone.

I'm still sure.

Regaining my feet, I swipe at the rectangular-shaped vial before ripping the laces from my boots. "Arathyn!"

He runs over to me.

"An arrow. Now!"

He doesn't hesitate. I fix the concoction to the arrowhead as best I can. *I hope it holds.*

"Preposterous. Your concoctions won't work! You'll never defeat me!"

Arathyn fires the arrow at Ganharen. The tincture explodes on impact in a shroud of mist. We look on in desperation as it eventually clears. Ganharen is embedded with Silverwisp, his ward fractured into frozen pieces scattered about his body.

Arathyn gulps before racing over to Ganharen.

"She … will come for you … Enmaran."

"And I will be waiting."

"What … are you waiting for … woman? Finish me!" Ganharen must be in excruciating pain, his voice is trembling.

"Believe me, lovely. Nothing would give me more pleasure than running a dagger through your heart but the curse has other plans."

Arathyn looks at me like he doesn't know who I am.

Arcura does strange things to people. Empowering things.

Without further hesitation, I give in to indulgence.

Damn the curse. Upon taking my dagger in hand, resisting a draining bond, I find his heart.

Twenty-Four

ARATHYN

I'm worried about Vexxyra, she certainly isn't the nurturing spirit I met on the coast. I still can't take my eyes off her, even in the midst of what might turn out to be our last battle together.

She has taken enough lives. Brewed enough deathly concoctions to make a witch content. It's only making me more fond of her. The same fondness she's finding in her deadly craft.

The feast is plentiful as Draygar devours what is left of Ganharen's energy. On my companion's back, I return to the others.

The stamina in these men is profound.

The Magmascythe is weakened, not from human blows, but from the demise of its master. It stops suddenly as it can feel my presence. *Enmara's presence.*

It faces me, running its gigantic paw across the earth that leaves flame in its wake. A fiery breath is let forth into the air. It seems to understand what I am.

Upon drawing my bow, the diamond within pulsates with such luminosity. As if it's a taunt, the goliath bounds forward in a rumbling assault.

Bolt after bolt crashes into its onrushing body as it stumbles and cries. The goliath's sheer size and strength is but only a façade now that Ganharen has perished. Further bolts find their target before its resistance is no more and its huge body comes to rest a few paces away. The beast has likely endured death once before, it does not deserve to endure it again.

Fire burns out. Husk smoulders. The goliath returns to bones once more.

"Once again, saved by my daughter. You're making me look weak." Vorathen inspects himself.

"A few burns, a mere inconvenience." Henry comes to the aid of Bernard.

"What is that?" Vorathen points at the Magmascythe's bones: a ruby shines brightly in its skull cavity.

"I am certain there is one person who will take an interest in it." I pry the ruby from the skull before depositing it into a small satchel beside Draygar's saddle.

"We are not far off civilisation." Henry casts his eyes over small stone-constructed shacks in the distance. Not all too different from Turinfall, except in its material.

"I bet we have their attention now." I lead us north toward the establishment. Nothing is left to the imagination. Just bone-hard ground with the odd stone wall jutting out.

"This is eerily quiet." Vexxyra's cautious words catch my ear as we near a solitary shack.

A fire lies smouldering. Shawls lash against the stone at the front of the domiciles as a breeze rushes through. Empty armament racks, scattered to and fro. This place is prepared for a quick exit.

Pushing away the shawls one by one, the sight of personal belongings scattered amongst the small, insignificant dwellings draws an immediate picture.

Bernard rubs the back of his neck. "Looks like we've just missed them."

"Scour the others. Leave no stone unturned."

They're gone, it's completely abandoned. Likely why no one came to Ganharen's aid.

I scratch at my head. "They're definitely up to something. Their own crusade, perhaps?"

"She may be searching for you too, Arathyn." Vexxyra is right. By now, she would definitely know of me. The easiest way to find someone is to seek them out.

However, we have fought enough deranged Kygeerans for one day. "Take a rest. Henry, take the first watch. This barren land is vast, should they return, we'll spot them."

⁕

Ahead. Smoke, thick and obscuring. The Kygeeran establishment far behind as we rush ahead. Barren land becomes grass underfoot, snow not too far off. A stiff breeze whips up as we throw ourselves into the confines of a pine forest. Navigation becomes difficult, but it is not too long before we find the source of the smoke. An ancient archway loops over us, with a cave that tunnels down into the mountainside.

Trees around us, blackened. Some have burnt right through and collapsed. Whatever did this, can't be too far away.

The smoke thins … Breathing is manageable. My vision clears.

Something brushes against Vexxyra's leg in a hurry. "Woah!"

Our eyes trace the figure's movements, a strange, boulder-like creature races out of the large opening and flees down the hill behind us.

Peering back into the abyss in front of us, torches grace our hands. We descend.

A winding path cuts into the earth beneath Mount Moradar. A strong smell of smoke still dominates the air. Blackened terrain and singed objects line our path as we traverse further under firelight. Incineration has decimated the entire cavern. Stumbling forward, a horrendous smell insults my nose. Bodies are everywhere, burnt to a crisp.

"Murder." Vorathen rolls bodies aside with his boot, revealing no weaponry.

Examining further, I try to find marks. Turning the palms of each, they're all the same. One by one, I feel a piece of me being torn apart.

Enmarans. My knees buckle under huge emotional weight. "I have failed them."

Once again, I'm the target of a comforting grip. "How were you to know that they were here?"

"May they rest in peace." The brothers kneel in the wake of my tirade, offering their condolences.

Suddenly, I am dressed in anger. Breaking free from Vexxyra's vice-like grip, I scream at the roof and the others step away. "They had no hope! I am sick to death of the unknown! When I find her, I will destroy her! Her head will rest high upon a pike in the Vigil!"

No one replies, no one dares. My voice still echoes about the chamber as they stand there questioning my character.

A large crack echoes behind us. Followed by several more as the damaged timber supports give out. Boulders crash to the ground and a blast of air hits us in the face. We are trapped.

Vorathen laughs. "Your revenge will have to wait. You may not have the brawn. But why do you need it when your voice hits like a catapulted rock?"

It's ironic that all I need to refocus is one of Vorathen's sarcastic remarks. "There is a cold breeze, there is a way out somewhere."

It is almost completely dark. Bodies are burnt so badly that Draygar is unable to siphon any remnants of life. Finally, firelight glistens off a wall and we trace it to find a slope with trickling water. A draught drops from above. It's our only option.

Fortuitously, the slope is easily scalable with careful footsteps. We unpack to cover up with extra warmth.

Snarls cause us to stall. *Now is not the time.* It's treacherous enough that one misplaced boot upon ice will send us sprawling. A recess in the cold stone wall up ahead indicates a den.

As we climb, six glistening eyes mirroring the torchlight gaze at us. One beast leaps out viciously, slamming into Henry, knocking him over. Shards of ice protrude from the beasts' skin above a thin layer of fur before crystal fangs lash at Henry as he rolls away.

Vorathen swings his blade at one which does nothing more than chip off a segment of bodily ice. A steel-tipped arrow from my bow shatters the beast's body, causing it to stagger, and Bernard takes an opportune moment to land a fatal blow.

Henry gets to his feet and another one leaps over him, crashing into a stalactite on the roof. It cracks and falls, shattering into pieces behind him.

"We need to get out of here!" Vexxyra's voice is amplified in the confinement. We ascend quickly. Luckily, the ravenous beasts do not follow.

Natural light takes over. Heavy snow envelops our boots as we escape onto a rock shelf. *The rock shelf.*

The monument stands nearby. We have returned.

Our near-death experience with the yeti-like behemoth comes to mind. A stark reminder of how lucky we are to have made it this far.

Sunlight beats down upon us. Wind subsides. A relative ease comforts my body as thoughts tug at my mind. *Is she off to the Vigil? Does she know where it is? Does she even know about it at all?*

As I reach the monument, my hands brush away fresh snow. Six sigils etched upon its stone surface glow in the colour of the relevant spirits. All except for one.

Kygeera.

The mysterious one has colour. A purple hue. Not fully luminous like the others, but it is there.

Vexxyra points at the unidentifiable sigil. "What do you make of it?"

"I think it's a sign of the growing presence of death."

Casting my eyes westward, there is no further sign of Kygeeran movement. The one we seek is out there somewhere.

"We head north. We must finish this."

Twenty-Five

ARATHYN

A determination runs rampant, fuelled on from the scores of slain Enmarans below. There has been enough death, enough fear. *I hope that one day soon, life as we knew it will return to normal.* But that just feels impossible.

We descend Mount Moradar, across the beautiful white slopes, through jagged crevices until we reach the pass. *Enmara's Vigil. Could it be?* I don't want to delay any further to find out if she's reached it. She's close, I know it.

Snow begins to recede, exposing cobblestone. A path slaloms its way toward towering spires of granite that rise above all that surrounds. My eyes make out steel constructions within the grounds. There once would have been civilisation here too. Once again, the smell of freshly torched material hangs in the air. Long abandoned, however, except for the bodies that call this place home within freshly dug graves.

"Menithren. The heart of the mountain. A bustling and thriving settlement. Now it lies in ruin, like everything else." Henry confirms my thoughts.

I keep my focus, we're on the hunt for the most notorious yet. "A flame can't hide its char."

On the north side of Menithren, we reach the hinterland. A sleet dresses the grass. Pines rise high as straight as arrows. We press on towards the crest. Hopefully, answers lie on the far side.

An answer that may come sooner. A small figure stands atop, leering down at us as we climb. As we draw close enough, it's the face of whom I have seen before.

Then, she speaks. "Have you changed your mind on that coat of yours? I'd still like to buy it from you."

"It's burnt and slashed, I'm afraid."

"That's just my type. Tell me … have you taught Draygar some manners?"

"Did you murder my people?!"

"Oh, no pleasantries? A shame. There aren't many of you, turn around now and I'll show you no harm."

The deflection of my question infuriates me further. "Aren't I the one you're after? We aren't leaving until you're dead!"

"*Dead?* The Saviour of Arcura wants me dead?!"

Vexxyra steps forward. "You're past any point of redemption, woman."

"Where there is smoke, there is fire. I guess I'll have to take care of you myself then."

Vorathen steps in front and laughs. "You and what army?"

As she strides forward, hundreds of men and women carrying banners, accompanied by beasts, emerge from beyond the crest. "This one?"

Vorathen is completely undeterred as he takes in their formidable presence. "That is my type too!"

Posing briefly, she assumes a powerful position. "You should've taken me with you. You didn't even ask for my name, so let me give it to you. You face Ellerica, the Kygeeran Spiritmaster. All things aside, it is wonderful to finally meet again. I'll even let you have the first move."

Hundreds of eyes watch us. My steadfast gaze finds the others. "Enmara will protect you, with Ellerica dies the curse. Let's finish this crusade."

Marching toward the Kygeeran army, our steps are full of desire and confidence. Now is not the time to show a single weakness even though we are hopelessly outnumbered.

My mind wanders briefly to Argora and her Rangers. We could certainly use them now.

It's too late for that.

"Surround them!"

They obey unequivocally. Within moments, we are surrounded by the mass of Kygeerans.

"The legend foretold, quivers before me. You'll make marvellous fuel for my beasts." The horde of Kygeerans approaches us. Step by step, our demise treads closer. There is a hesitation on their part though, surely the curse is still on their mind.

Within the satchel at Draygar's side, the ruby begins to brighten. A red glow penetrates the burlap exterior. Ganharen commanded the Magmascythe to siphon power from others, although I have no idea how.

Sacrifice? There is no better time.

Setting my hand upon the gemstone, I thrust it above.

Ellerica points at me. "A Ruby of Rebirth … Where did you ever find that? Bring it to me!"

I knew there would be one *interested.*

They all look on as it brightens further. Ellerica grows desperate, crying out as the stone begins to pulsate in my hand. *I just hope I'm right.*

Suddenly, streams of flame connect the stone with those nearby, ripping energy out of their bodies and they fall lifeless. Growing far too hot to handle, my grip releases. Fall to the ground, it does not. The Ruby of Rebirth forms into a red mist that swirls above me. Searching.

Kygeera? It sure doesn't look like a beast.

Ellerica, she's too far away. However, by the time she realises and begins to rush over, it's too late. The mist becomes unstable, warping and bulging before it explodes into a ball of flame, spraying embers into the sky. The wayward souls of the Kygeerans linger above briefly before they shoot into me. Much like the ones at Hammerknell.

"Aren't you just full of surprises? No matter, you will not defeat me like you have the others! You will burn before me still!"

Her disciples are unwillingly drawn to her before they are sacrificed at her feet in a stream of fire.

Ellerica is the embodiment of flame, growing twice her original size. A drape of flame trails down her shoulders that ignites the grass at her feet. Flames dance at her fingertips as she rights a diadem on her forehead which blazes above scorching eyes.

"Kygeera! I shall burn Arcura in your name!"

In an instant, my aura grasps at our own. The power that my body has consumed is so great that the act does not diminish my own this time. Hundreds of souls course through me, feeding Enmara's spirit.

We stand four half-morphs, behind me. Vorathen is finally able to fight beside us, empowered in his earthen-serpentine form. My frame sits upon Draygar. Death redefined.

My diamond-encrusted eyes raise to meet my foe. "Destroy her!"

Ellerica twirls her hands graciously before scores of fireballs are launched in our direction. Our attempts to dodge are futile as they home in on us, bursting on our bodies, the force of which pushes us back.

Vexxyra and Vorathen shrug off the pain as flames lick them. Henry and Bernard deflect them aside. *I don't feel a thing.*

Vorathen rushes in with his daughter on foot. His Horror doesn't move an inch, subdued by the caustic heat. Vexxyra glistens ever grander as fire begins to weaken her armour. Crystalline liquid starts to run over her shard-like defences.

Waves of Kygeerans charge at us. Vorathen cleaves his toxic greatsword into the onrushing army, killing many. Steel impacts upon him as the red army beats away in a flurry of weapons. Weapons that instantly corrode upon striking his armour.

Others seize up as Vexxyra's aura grasps their muscle. With agility and elegance, she dances her daggers through frost-touched flesh. The brothers sweep aside resistance as they fight back to back, slicing their way through with sword and shield.

Taking aim, I fire. A surge of white energy chains through their ranks as a bolt that disintegrates my primary target.

"Release the Hellions!" Ellerica's command booms over the land as she watches her army crumble before her. Bones are catapulted from contraptions, landing scattered before her.

"Rise up, fiends!" Pillars of fire shoot up from the ground before dispersing into menacing beasts.

Gritting my teeth, I urge Draygar into action. We storm through a faltering resistance of Kygeerans like we are stepping over small stones. Leaping high into the air, we crash down upon one of the hellions. Draygar sinks his fangs into its fiery body before it breaks free. Lava spills to the earth from a gaping wound on its back.

The battlefield ignites. Trees burst into flame. We find ourselves inside a raging inferno.

Blasts of intense heat strike us as pyromancers cast powerful spells over a barrier Ellerica has conjured to hinder our advance.

"Give me all that you've got! Not even a scratch!" Vorathen stands like a god atop a pile of corpses enveloped in bulging vines.

With a flick of the Kygeeran Spiritmaster's wrist, Hellions speed towards the reptilian warrior. Vorathen raises his sword in the air before taking a defensive stance with a battle-hungered smile upon his scarred face. "Let them come!"

Vorathen crouches, and with the might of a thousand men, he cleaves one in half as it leaps to its death. The Hellion's magma-filled innards spill over him, searing his body to the tune of painful shouts.

Vexxyra is quick onto the act, throwing a tincture at her father. Magma hardens and cools at its touch, beginning to encase him in stone. There is little respite, however, as another fire-drenched beast moves in for the kill.

Taking a deep breath, I switch my focus from Ellerica, waiting for the right moment. Enmara's power vaporises the beast, inches away from Vorathen as the bolt strikes.

"Finish her … lad." Vorathen's words slip out through laboured breaths.

Vexxyra retreats to tend to her father. Newly acquired strength aids in throwing aside the smouldering remains of the dismembered Hellion. Her aura, waning under the intense heat, does enough to keep the flames from devouring him. Vorathen cries in pain as she lays her hands on him.

"My Champions, we have a spiritmaster to tend to." Questioning gazes look on. *How can they deal with her immense power?*

Draygar and I turn away before racing to the base of the hill, leaving a great distance from her barrier.

"Fleeing like a coward?!" Ellerica's voice shoots down the hill.

No. I would never.

"Come on, boy. You and me." Our desires are at one, invigorated by a bond unrelenting. Springing forward, the landscape is but a blur. A wall of fire lashes before us, seemingly impenetrable.

Pressing my body flat against his neck, we lunge into the barrier. A flash as bright as the sun briefly obscures my vision before we land upon a line of conjurers who are hurtled through the air from a concussive shockwave. Draygar roars in cacophony, consuming the lives of numerous helpless Kygeerans nearby.

Empowered beyond belief at the expense of hundreds of Ellerica's followers and a torrent of energy from Draygar beneath me, I stare dead into the spiritmaster's firelit eyes. "Your reign is over. No one will die further at your hand!"

"Oh! Are you so sure?!" Laughs ring out as the ground shakes violently.

I fire beyond her as Draygar struggles to stay on his feet. Air around her ignites. What's left of her following groan and grimace as they are pulled toward her against their will in an ultimate sacrifice. Ellerica grows brighter with every second. Heat becomes unbearable. Fearing that no manner of power will protect us from what's coming, we start to back away.

A silence sets in. Time seems to stand still before nothing more than words break it. "Arcura belongs to beasts!"

"Get down!" A monumental blast of heat launches us through the air.

—⊰❖⊱—

Draygar circles around me, staring as I lay upon scorched terrain.

"Enmara. Thank you." Gathering myself together, I gingerly rise to my feet. Not a single tree remains standing. Not one blade of grass green. The crest, level. A blast so monumental, it has carved out a section of the mountainside.

Kygeera's spirit lies defeated nearby.

"By the light, you're alive!" Henry's echoing words carry a mutual feeling. His battered body sits up against a granite monolith. Slowly, I climb onto Draygar who treads cautiously as we travel upon newly carved earth.

"Go and claim it. I'll search for the others." Henry turns my attention once more to Kygeera's ruby-like spirit. *The others*, of which there is no sight of.

Kygeera's spirit doesn't move at all as we approach, until we get close enough that it can't resist. How it managed to endure her brazen use of its power, I'll never know.

To one last flash of light, a sharp snap echoes a great distance. Looking around as the last spirit is consumed, I search for something, anything. Purple gloom begins to emanate from the vicinity of the monument upon Mount Moradar.

Our doom?

"Over here!" Henry's voice splits apart my thoughts. His finger points down a sharp slope beyond where trees used to stand. I rush over before carefully traversing the descent.

Vorathen, Vexxyra and Bernard sit upon a grass shelf with their companions nearby. *Moncera*. Vexxyra has her arms around her companion, who has returned to its master in the aftermath.

Just laying my eyes on her has all my worries fluttering away into the furthest recesses of my mind. She takes the sight of me in, gasping as if she can't believe I'm standing before them.

With a tear-fuelled vigour, Vexxyra races over and throws her arms around me. The heartfelt feeling is mutual. "Our luck had it that we were sheltered. The trees were there one second and gone the next. I feared the worst."

"How is he?" I run my eyes over Vorathen.

Tears roll down her face. "He is badly burnt. I have done as much as I can. The rest is up to him."

"And you two?"

"Unscathed. Unbelievably." Vexxyra checks herself over once, questioning her judgement.

"That blast. I thought that was it." Bernard is in disbelief.

I turn my attention back to Vorathen. "Can we move him?"

"He needs rest and lots of it. When he wakes … if he does … I hope …"

Her heart must be wrenching.

⁘

Is it over? I look again to the mountains above. There is no doubt that the Eldest One will be seeking me soon, if it hasn't begun already. The answers I seek, I'm not going to find here.

"I carved that thing in half, lad." My gaze shifts to Vorathen who lies motionless nearby.

With a beaming smile, I shake my head. *Does anything exist that can kill him?* "That you did."

"You are crazy!" Vexxyra's words are born from relief.

"The more scars, the more a warrior. I assume as you sit here, the job is done?"

I study Vorathen over. "A monumental sacrifice on her part. Can you move?" *If he can, he will.*

"Strap me upon my beast, only a blade can spell my death."

With the assistance of the others, we move Vorathen toward his companion. Lifting his weight is like lifting two people. The Horror, which has returned from below, turns its head before emitting a sharp cry as it makes out its master. We approach cautiously in an attempt to not spook it further; however, it just stands obediently as we somehow bind Vorathen to it.

"Not too tight! I'd like to be in one piece upon our return. Keep my sword nearby, my arm still works."

We climb the charred slope, much of which has disappeared under a wintry sleet. Mount Moradar looks much different beyond a gloomy haze. *If the mountainside had eyes, they'd be staring at me.* There is no telling of what awaits us.

I stop abruptly as the rest ride by.

"Arathyn?" Henry questions my actions as they turn to face me.

A strange sensation washes over me, feeding on my bodily energy. Pale, I grow. A large streak of light expels from my chest forcing me to grasp at Draygar's mane to stop myself from falling.

Enmara's spirit forms from the light before my eyes, drifting elegantly down to the ground, landing on its ghostly feet. A towering half-opaque Diamondback Alpha, glistens in the moonlight. A mane drapes forth from a gigantic wolf-like head, kissing the frost below.

Vexxyra gasps as she suddenly realises what she is staring at. "Oh! What beauty!"

Dismounting Draygar in pure awe, I take a knee. Her everbright sigil upon my arm forces the bowing of my head as I kneel before the presence of the Goddess herself. Peering at the moon high above, the spiritual beast lets forth a majestic cry. Ghostly haze trails from its mouth.

Beams of moonlight brighten its lingering breath as the spirit looks on. Intense flashes draw more and more light before the mist recedes into a shaped diamond. With the eyes of the Protector looking on, another cry wails as the stone pulls in her spirit. The diamond drops to my feet, her power within. The gemstone sits like a beacon upon charred earth.

Gazes are fixed upon the gem. One by one, the others begin to kneel.

"Your time has come." Vorathen's voice carries over the weight of expectation. Somehow, his body has shifted into a position to look on.

"Do us the honour, Arathyn." Bernard lays his sword across his knee, peering at the sleet encompassing his boots.

Now is not the moment to leave anyone kneeling.

Walking toward the glistening gemstone, peaceful thoughts fill my mind. Tranquil and clear. I hear my father laugh, followed by the sound of childish giggling as I close my hand around the diamond.

My muscles clench as the power takes hold. My veins fill with a white substance which shoots up my arm. Energy travels further, through my neck that acts like a vessel. Finally, it expels through my forehead. Hands feel the shape of a crown and the Moonlight Diamond that sits recessed within. Pure white hair falls over my eyes from the crown's edge before it curls around my cheeks. Crystallised stone drapes down my back like a cape. Steps leave a ghostly trail in their wake as I turn to examine myself further.

The others look on in awe as I mount Draygar who no longer morphs at my touch. *A soulless touch.* His mind, no different.

"That's strange," says Vexxyra. She is not the only one who has that thought.

My diamond-like figure throws forth a command. "We must return to the Vigil."

⁕

I have developed a new sense, death, and it lingers around every corner. Cackles and shrieks originate from the peak, cautioning me, spurring me on. I feel gloom tracking, turning my gaze repeatedly to survey our trail as we reach the eastern side of the Feygoran Mountains.

Vorathen is tightly bound upon the back of his bounding Horror. It isn't a comfortable ride for him, that's for sure. We race by Hammerknell, of which something looks out of the ordinary. The tomb has been sealed shut. Crumbling debris lies in waste before the entrance. Numerous decaying beasts are scattered about.

"Do you think they were attacked?" Henry's words draw nervousness.

"They felt the need to close the tomb. I trust that there was good reason."

Fearing the worst, my thoughts drift into distress. *Has the Vigil fallen to a deathly onslaught?* Our final approach home feels that of a chase.

⎯⎯⬥⎯⎯

Enmara's Vigil rises grandly before us, my worries dissipate as I make out Rangers atop the wall.

"They've returned!" A Ranger spots us as others run to her side with bows drawn. *They've returned. It's not us they were expecting.*

A wall of swordsmen stands beyond the gate. Bows are lowered as we are identified. *As much as I can be identified.*

"It's … Arathyn." There is a hesitation as that conclusion is drawn. Many of my people haven't witnessed what I can truly become.

The portcullis is hastily raised and we stride beyond before it closes abruptly behind us. Immediately, everyone stops as if my mind can be read, almost as if they are being beckoned. Argora stands proudly upon her balcony high on the ridge as if she never doubted my return.

It gives me great pleasure to see that my people have prospered under her guidance. Nothing seems amiss.

Descending the stairs, she walks over. "Still in Spiritkind? I do say. You look the part."

"Enmara's spirit graced itself before me. Her power does not appear to wane from my body any longer."

Argora's eyes wander before picking out the diamond set within the crown. "Fit for a king. Look at your people. They'd give their life for you, Arathyn."

I address the masses. "As will I … Take Vorathen and see to it that he recovers. He is extremely lucky to make it out alive."

Several people rush forward to move him from Delbura. There is no shortage of volunteers to carry him off, one of which is my mother, looking healthy and full of life. A kiss is blown my way before her mouth turns into a smile.

"Halt." Boots freeze as movement stops abruptly. Confusion lashes upon faces. Dismounting, I reach for my crown. Withdrawing it from my head, I place it upon a stone pillar. To everyone's amazement, including my own, a sharp flash of light expels from the diamond, ultimately forming a circular veil that encompasses the entire Vigil.

"She is a protector after all." Vexxyra's words resonate with my thoughts as everyone watches me return to my simple human form with just the clothes on my back and a bow by my side.

My mother wears a gleaming smile. "Aren't you just full of surprises?"

It has been far too long. Feet carry my emotion-riddled body effortlessly. I run toward her, as does she at me. We meet in a loving embrace as I throw my arms around my mother, tears beginning to well in our eyes. The curse that has hampered this moment for so long, will no longer. Not a moment of it I let pass too soon.

"Oh. My boy. Your father would be extremely proud. I love you with all my heart." Now my tears are flowing.

"I love you too, Mother."

After a long embrace, she rights me and I take a step back.

"Do not worry about Vorathen, my boy, I will give him the best of care." My mother rushes off to join those carrying him.

"Any word on attacks?" I cut straight to the matter at hand, aiming a question Argora's way.

"Two. Nothing we couldn't handle. Creatures of the like I have never seen."

"The hordes of Death, you wouldn't believe what I could tell you. And Hammerknell?"

Argora's look turns serious. "They were tracked there. I sent a scouting party, ordering the demolition of the tomb. The entrance was sealed, we have not seen them since."

"Excellent. Although, I fear the monument upon Mount Moradar signifies a grand assault. This filth is drawn to me."

"The monument?" The mention of it goes right over her head.

"Upon the defeat of the Kygeeran Spiritmaster, it burst forth a gloom which I believe is the beginning of an end." *I just hope it isn't our end.*

"Incoming!" Right on cue. People disperse, seeking refuge wherever they can.

We race atop the rampart to gain vantage over *what* is arriving. Creatures of death teem down the mountainside in their thousands, bearing down on the Vigil's walls.

"Good lord. It was not like this." Argora gasps as the rest of the Rangers make their way over. My Champions are at my side.

"It is because of Enmara's presence. They are here to destroy her."

A veil as pristine as moonlight obliterates them in their droves as they try to pass through.

"I'm glad you removed your crown," Henry jokes. *It isn't one. He is certainly right.*

Bernard runs a hand across his jaw. "Are you certain it will hold?"

"It will hold. My concern lies with the Eldest One."

Time passes slowly. Thousands upon thousands of smouldering husks pile up upon the extremity of the veil before their assault lessens and finally stops. A moonlit barrier, still gleaming at full strength, shows no sign of faltering.

"What do you propose?" Argora once more has me on the receiving end of a difficult question.

"Enmara has bought us some time. We will stay here for now under her protection. The Eldest One's next visit, I need to prepare for."

There is a warmth in being home. Our travels have taken us far and long. Within these walls and now her veil, it feels the safest place in Arcura. *Safest.* Nothing will be truly safe while the Eldest One is still out there.

We retire for the night. Rangers return to their positions under torchlight. I divert via the butcher, heading towards Argora's quarters for some rest.

"Here boy." A slab of meat is thrown at his feet that will keep him occupied for hours.

Death is at the forefront of everyone's mind when it raises its ugly head. With Draygar, it couldn't be further from it.

On a bed on the lower floor of the commander's quarters, I lie awake. The comfort brings great relief upon my weary bones. Thoughts race across my mind. I know where to find the Eldest One. It is most likely waiting for me where it all began. Likely why I haven't encountered it since Sylvora.

Removing the veil could be disastrous should I harness all of Enmara's power for myself. But then again, if I choose to return to the Ruins of Highgarde with the Moonlight Diamond, the Vigil will most likely be safe as death seems to follow her. *Me.*

Argora walks in. "Oh, you're here."

"The mind wanders. Any word on Vorathen? I will visit him soon."

"Elraetha cares for him like a child. Put your mind at ease, Arathyn. You'll be the first to know, should something require your attention."

I can't sleep, Argora has dozed off upstairs. Pulling myself to my feet, I exit, stepping onto cold mountainous terrain. Crossing the training grounds to check in on Vorathen, I find him sound asleep.

"Get some sleep dear, for I am about to do the same. Vorathen will be fine. His body just needs to rest." The anguish lifts and my mother disappears through a shawl into another section of the large house she calls home.

As I wander back outside, my steps are interrupted by a soft female voice. "Over here."

Vexxyra whispers just loudly enough so I'd hear it before offering me entrance to her room. Without even a moment of hesitation, I walk right in. The last time I was in here, I was scalded with a strange mixture of reagents. I awoke with a feeling of uncertainty, much like how I'm feeling now.

Her hazel eyes glisten in candlelight cast by a flame dancing above rows of glassware. "What do you plan on doing?"

"Travelling alone to Highgarde and facing it myself. I have no doubt it's waiting for me there."

She rolls her eyes. "*So serious*. With me, silly."

It hits me that this isn't a matter of business, I find myself unable to speak. I just stare at her, making out the curves of her body pressed against silken garments, the golden-sapphire pendant resting against her skin.

My feet don't work, either that or I'm stunned by her beauty. She pulls a hairpin and her brunette hair drops behind her.

"I'll let you curse me with your kiss." Her words strike at my hesitation. Footsteps full of desire make their way toward me. Her eyes gaze into mine, awaiting a reaction. My own drop to her lips. Her warm hands connect behind my neck as she kisses me and I oblige.

My emotions get the better of me, forcing me to continue out of indulgence. She lifts my tunic over my head, discarding it onto the bed and her wanting eyes don't leave mine for a second. Acting on nothing but impulse, I unstring her blouse and throw it to the floor before pulling her to my chest.

Vexxyra's lips move to my ear as I plant a kiss upon her bronze skin. "Lay with me."

We slip under the covers, throwing off what's left of our clothing. Above the most beautiful woman I have ever laid eyes upon, I raise a hand to extinguish the flame burning with as much desire as us. I seek her waiting lips once more as I run my hand across smooth skin. My fingers force an exhale before pinching the flame, covering us in darkness.

———◆———

I stare out through a glass window, completely naked beneath the sheets. People are bustling about once more. *Is some rumour going around?*

Quickly, I wash and dress myself before heading outside, looking above at nothing but a white false sky under the cover of the veil. Vexxyra waves at me from afar before aggressively picking at an assortment of pre-cut plants. I just want to go over and kiss her, that was a night I'll never forget.

Why not?

"Ah! The light graces me once more. My enemies still have to deal with me yet." Vorathen's voice booms across the grounds, his body cutting the figure of a weakened man.

That's why.

"I hope you have seen the worst." My eyes pick out numerous welts and scars that cover most of his arms and a portion of his body.

Flickering eyes gaze up. Belief is questioned. "That's a strange-looking sky, lad."

"It's all that stands between us and annihilation."

"One would guess you're off to the east." His mind is certainly still sharp.

"I will travel alone, we must not weaken ourselves here."

Vorathen takes a sword to welted hands before staring with intent. "Then you must know that I will be in your footsteps. That is not a choice."

Arguing with him would be futile. We started this together. The only way I would be able to convince him otherwise is to throw the question at his dead body. *Even then, would that be enough?*

But I try nevertheless, placing my hand on his shoulder. "Are you certain? We are likely heading to our deaths."

"As much as I can walk on two feet and swing a blade."

Seriousness returns. "I feel we have a few days' respite from their assaults. We must waste no time."

"Here." Vexxyra hands her father a potion.

"Ah, I knew this time would come. Am I to die at the workings of my daughter?"

Vexxyra smiles at me before glancing distastefully at her father. "I guess you'll find out."

Vorathen forces the mixture down his throat in one gulp before coughing. Tense joints crack as he flexes his body, shrugging off the effects of the remedy. "Ahh. That hits the spot."

"Firebloom for the fire at heart," says Vexxyra before disappearing beyond the wall.

Climbing one of the watchtowers on the southern fringe, I carefully examine my surroundings, more so the mountainside. Burnt husks have been thrown around by a stiff breeze. Many remain littered about despite the best efforts of others to clean up the mess.

I flinch as a lean arm is thrown over my shoulder, followed by a kiss upon my cheek. "Take this, it will be painless. Should you need it." Vexxyra places a vial in my hand and closes my fingers over it. I take her warm body in my arms before planting a kiss on her lips.

Her eyes hold mine. "Will I ever see you again?"

Her words tie me up inside, there is no doubting her question. She has just handed me a lethal concoction. "It is my duty to keep my people safe. We're Protectors."

She knows as much as I do that I would sacrifice myself for my people, but I can't bring myself to say it. *I don't need to.*

"Then let's get you ready."

As we make our way back to the crown, a smile is shared at the sight of a grand hall. An apothecary hall still under construction, surrounded by lengths of timber and quarried stone. I whistle before Draygar races over. Carefully, I place my hands on the sacred piece of finery as eager eyes look on. Upon removing it from the pillar, it finds my head. The veil dissipates as the power transfers to my body, morphing me into Spiritkind once more.

"Fear not, for death seeks me. It may be days before we see the likes of such an assault again. Under the watchful eye of Commander Argora, Champions Henry and Bernard, you will be safe here. I shall return when this is all over."

Hands are raised in a show of respect, my mother's and Vexxyra's included.

"Come, Vorathen, it is waiting." The rejuvenated warrior, clad in buffed plate, climbs upon his Horror before we charge out of the Vigil.

Twenty-Six

ARATHYN

It's everywhere. Not a single tree stands without the feeling of lurking eyes behind. An ominous cackle whispers on the ocean breeze. Arcura is in peril, an ever-present darkness gouges at its land. *I am its only hope of renewal.*

"You wouldn't know time is against us. It is peaceful everywhere one looks." Vorathen whips through the landscape on his Horror beside me, turning his head as he takes in the freedom.

You wouldn't know. Is he blind? Did Ellerica get to him? Lush forests are being swallowed up by a blight. Wildlife, nowhere to be seen.

The earthquakes, now the blight.

The Protector. An advantage of mine, and only mine, to see the desecration that is unfolding. *Oh, how I wish I had his eyes.*

"What is your plan, lad?" A hint of nervousness rides in his voice.

"The Eldest One is likely waiting with death at its fingertips. Follow Enmara's will and we will not fail."

Jagged spires of rock north of Highgarde draw us closer. Afternoon sunlight beams down. "We wait for nightfall."

Vorathen straightens. "You want to challenge it in *darkness?*"

Yes. "It may give us an advantage."

A day passed, a day prepared.

The moon is full, almost beckoning.

"A clear sky, I sense that will work in our favour." My gut has been right all along.

I am a beacon in the dark. A walking sphere of light. I have no doubt something is waiting to tear me apart. "Whatever happens tonight, know that it has been an honour fighting by your side, Vorathen."

"Focus. You speak as a man defeated." His glance brings me back to reality.

Our companions find the mountain path underfoot. One last bend, one last visit.

My mind wanders for a moment as images of my people dance through it. Children frolicking about, oblivious to Arcura's dangers. *It is no time to weaken myself mentally.*

You speak as a man defeated. I take a long breath as my mane brushes against my back. "Guide me."

Slowly riding into the Ruins of Highgarde, I sit poised on Draygar with my bow nocked. Moonlight beams down around us. Vorathen is right behind me, wielding his greatsword upon his Horror.

The shrill of a cool breeze nips at my ear as I approach the dais. The gaping abyss of the cave beyond takes my focus as the runes begin to illuminate.

The wind swiftly dies.

A faint outline of a figure lines the entrance to the cave. Staring, I reassure myself that it's not just my imagination. "It's watching me."

Firing a bolt into the dark, I watch on as the illuminated projectile outlines the walls as it sails deeper into the cave before disappearing out of sight.

The outline reappears.

"I see it too," says Vorathen.

Drawing closer, I study the runes… Fully energised, they cast colour near and far. Another bolt is fired to the same effect. Turning my gaze briefly to Vorathen to gauge his reaction, he immediately gestures for me to turn it back.

The figure is closer, several paces in front of the cave. Taking a position on the centre of the dais, we're encircled in colourful contrast. Draygar morphs into form as a mysterious energy underfoot seeps into him.

My body lifts as he grows, aiming one more time. "You will hide no longer!"

The Eldest One breaks its silence, draped in cloth as dark as the night from top to bottom. "They all grace us … once more."

My heart races. "Stop these assaults immediately!"

"Assaults? That is far … far … beyond my power … young one."

"I took you at your word! What peace do you see?!"

A laugh crackles in the air around us. "Enmara's will was to restore peace between the spirits … to protect the *beasts* … You have succeeded in that regard. Did you ever wonder—"

I'm sick of its attempts at manipulation. "The power within us, within Enmara, will drive away the darkness once and for all!"

"Arathyn … Enmara … could never *consume* their spirits. Something else … What do you think … harbours their power?"

Consume? Harbours?

Suddenly, I realise what happened each time a Spiritmaster was defeated. Rumours of the curse returning when I was separated.

They weren't rumours.

Draygar.

A hand of shadow shoots out of the ground and holds us in place.

"You brought them all back … for Me!" A hysterical laugh rips through me. "Now … Rise … Illora!"

The ghostly outline of the raging spirit of death protrudes out of Draygar momentarily, before receding violently back into him. The beast bursts into the form that savaged us once before and I am thrown off.

Vorathen thunders to my aid. His Horror barrels in, ramming into Draygar's Illoran form which does nothing but infuriate it more. A devastating lunge knocks aside the most stalwart of men and his companion like they are nothing more than a leaf in a squall.

I can't move, it is far too powerful here. No wonder it was waiting for me.

"You see, Arathyn … Illora … Enmara … Their energy was far too great … One could never consume the other … The spirits … shattered.

"I … suffered … without my Illora … after your mind … my mind … was detached … I wanted it all … power …"

My Illora? If Illora has a spirit, why is it on the monument and not at Highgarde?

The sixth, purple. It's not just a presence of death.

Wisdom keeps flowing and I am forced to listen. I need to *listen.*

"I have lived … an eternity … The beasts … perished. Their spirits … I kept them … for centuries …"

Jumbling everything around in my head, I forget about the pain and my body is starting to wear.

Olynero. Vordera. Ixxenira. Kygeera. Enmara. They all have Spiritmasters? My mind shifts to the spirit brands. Not a single person afflicted with purple.

No. Arcura. Illora was never a part of it.

This was never for peace … Illora was brought here to destroy it.

To destroy Enmara.

"But they were … too weak. Then *you* came … *here*. The first … human … to ever return. I should … thank you … both … for *feeding* them.

"Death … will … linger on … I shall usher in … a new age … And I will … command it!"

My connection with Draygar is shattered, much like his interest when death lurks. *Now I understand, why would it help me?*

The grip on my body releases, but I have no control over my companion whatsoever. His Illoran form turns to face me at its master's will.

Vorathen jumps in front of me, only to be bludgeoned and bashed aside. *I will not be discarded so easily.* An onslaught with extreme agility has me as a target. My feet are too fast. My companion's Illoran form sails by as a gust of wind throws about my crystalline hair.

The Eldest One knows it has a challenge. "I'll … defeat her … through you!"

My aura burgeons, hope rests inside. Darkness peers from all angles, searching for a channel to extinguish the light. We will not falter.

"Melt … away!"

Flaming claws burst out of Draygar's gigantic ghostly paws before thrashing at me, knocking me back as smoke plumes above.

"The cold hand … of death …"

Draygar shakes his head violently as fangs as long as swords crystallise into icicles before being projected toward me with enough force to split a man in two. Jumping back, they crash into the ground in front of me. Shards pepper my body that manage to pierce Enmara's aura. Sinking into me, I endure the pain, remaining focused as Draygar begins to crackle.

His Illoran form, surrounded by discharges of light, unleashes a barrage of energy that grips my diamond-laced body, sending a shock coursing right through.

The Moonlight Diamond dislodges from the crown, both of which tumble to the ground as I hastily recede back into human form. Numerous small pools of white plasma lie spilled upon the stone below.

"She … bleeds … Destroy her!"

Draygar dashes forward, catching me in his jaws … I'm about to be ripped apart.

My body is thrown around violently as I reach unsuccessfully for the diamond. Clench after clench, I don't feel myself weaken, in fact I grow stronger.

My companion, Illoran form, cannot succeed. Our contact begins to morph me into Spiritkind.

"Impossible!"

Your bond with Draygar is unlike anything I've ever seen. I can hear Argora's words in my head. A bond that channels our energy.

Upon gathering my newfound strength, my hands find the crown and diamond as they're plucked from the earth. I combine them once more.

Blocking death out, I focus on Enmara's cries reverberating in my ears. *The Protector. We do what we must to save humanity.* I gaze into Draygar's deathly eyes. "Forgive me, boy …"

Just before the beast's jaws slam shut, I thrust the crown down his throat. My eyes gaze upon the soulless beast that heaves and shakes as it struggles to eject them. I know he's in there somewhere, the thought of which draws a ghostly tear.

"No! No! How … can it be!"

White light begins to glow from under Draygar's ghostly aura as it prepares one final attack out of sheer determination. Elements outline the beast as it attempts to annihilate me, giving up on its plan to regurgitate its impending demise.

Knowing that this will be the last time I'll lay eyes on him, on his poor body manipulated and abused for so long, Enmara's veil explodes out from within. The purple rage dissipates in a violent shockwave as Draygar vaporises right before my very eyes, launching me far in the air.

⚜

Stumbling to my feet, I peer around. Vorathen is nowhere to be seen. Enmara's power on my body has waned.

The Moonlight Diamond has come to rest upon the middle of the dais, all but drained.

Suddenly, I'm grabbed once more and flung into the air. Held by a mysterious, invisible force.

"I was a fool … to choose you … Draygar … I never thought … you … could harness the power … of both.

"Illora … Eternity … I have waited … and … you destroyed it all!

"I will … torture you … as you have tortured… me."

A stream of moonlight connects the diamond. Vorathen's figure walks beyond before my eyes begin to fail me. It all seems a dream as the Eldest One inflicts excruciating pain on my human body. My twisted mind aches as flashes of memories pass by. My body wrenches as if death has its hands inside rearranging my organs.

As my vision borders on blindness, a sword coated in Enmaran blood touches the diamond and shoots into light. Vorathen suddenly hurls the blade with all his might that spirals through the air …

"Not on my wat—" The words echo and drop off as my vision darkens.

My eyes yearn to open once more briefly. My body, now upon cold earth. The grip, released. Pain, halted.

A sword in shining light is pierced right through the Eldest One. Blinded by hate and rage, the banshee-like figure emits agonising shrieks that sting my ears as it fights with forces that burn away at its form from the edge of the blade. The Eldest One starts to waste away as souls escape to wild screams into the sky above.

"You think… you can … defeat me?! There … will … always be … death!"

The dais begins to rumble. The Eldest One's figure splits into a wailing shroud of spirits, circling above. Vorathen's sword crashes to the ground.

Oblivion looms as the stone platform buckles and rises before me. The Eldest One descends, forcing further souls to exit through exposed cracks. Terrifying screeches ripple through the night from scores of escaping entities as they are drawn to death.

An umbral beam focuses, fixating on the diamond upon the crumbling mass.

For the first time, to human ears, Enmara's cry drowns out the screeching cacophony. Death is incinerated. Souls are vaporised in a teeming downpour of moonlight until not a sound remains but the slow beating of my heart.

***

Dreams of Draygar flood my mind. Get off my leg! He just wants attention. I chase him through the maze of Elderberry bushes to the north of Turinfall as my mother rouses us, ever-present at the foot of my bed.

He was my purpose. My kindred spirit.

Daylight beams through an open window as I gaze around disorientated, I am home. Vexxyra is sitting beside me with her head in her hands. My mother, likewise.

"Peace has found us all." I've never seen more relieved faces. Full of love and gratitude.

"Oh! I thought it was happening again." My mother grabs my limp body. "Your body ... tainted by darkness ..."

"You were alive ... but not yourself." Vexxyra's face turns from one of concern to uncontrollable relief.

Not yourself. I've been there before.

"My father spoke of you talking nonsense, shivering and cursing as he raced home."

Sitting up, I check here and there frantically. "Where is Draygar?" *His feelings are non-existent.*

Vexxyra throws her arms around me as she begins to weep. My mind isn't playing tricks on me. As it slowly reconstructs itself from the hands of torment, the delusions fade. I do all I can to hold myself together upon understanding.

Reality grips me harder than a vice. *Draygar's gone.*

I hang my head dejectedly. "Our bond blinded me."

I glance at my wrist, hoping that this is all over.

It's still lit; however, the Olyneran and Ixxeniran sigils upon the women are completely dull. The destruction of the Eldest One and Illora's spirit appears to have purged the effect of the sigils on humans. *Why is mine still lit?*

Having only seen drained sigils on corpses, perhaps this is a sign that the curse has finally lifted.

Vorathen's figure appears in the doorway. "It was that bond you shared with Draygar that defeated it, Arathyn. It blinded you both."

The words Vorathen speaks are true, Draygar and I harnessed the link between Illora and Enmara. I should have known something was amiss when the Vigil was first established. When I left Draygar alone, resulting in our spiritual connection faltering briefly, exposing the villagers once more to the curse.

Illora consumed the Alpha Spirits one by one but it was Enmara who manipulated them to hold the curse at bay. Our bond was the link that held humanity together, the *link* that ultimately betrayed Draygar.

My crusade to seek peace was driven in secrecy by the Eldest One for his own bidding. But it was not to be in vain: Enmara gifted me the Moonlight Diamond, for had she not, I'd likely be dead right now, if not all of humanity.

Further realisation grows. "That is the first time you have called me by name! How did I return here?"

Vorathen walks over and places his arm on my shoulder. "Thank my companion. I'm glad something else turned its ears to your incessant doomsaying."

He pauses for effect. "I am glad to see that you are alright, lad. Draygar was a fine beast. Don't ever forget that."

Vorathen turns to exit. A man of not many heartfelt words, but they're always the right ones. He gestures thankfully to the women before disappearing outside.

My mother gleams as she once again has to check me over. "Come. Argora knew you would prevail. Enjoy this moment, my son."

Rising to my feet, I raise my arms to straighten the crown, only to feel its absence. *Right.*

A large bonfire is prepared and for a moment I feel like I'm back in Turinfall. My emergence draws gasps as if my people have seen a ghost. Clearly, there wasn't much hope of my recovery. Looks of uncertainty turn to amazement as my name is cheered.

This time I'm not burying a lie.

Argora makes her way through a parting in the crowd. The Moonlight Diamond rests in her hands but it does not respond to her touch. "I believe this belongs to you, Arathyn."

Grasping the diamond, it forces my sigil into a slightly brighter state. Upon the last remnant of its energy transferring, it gleams no longer. Guilt floods within me and I let the gem spill from my hand to the earth below sending the gathering into stunned silence.

My heart grows heavy. "No. As much as this is a celebration of our freedom, Draygar held that vile spirit for too long. In his time of need, Enmara's power destroyed him. It may have been inevitable but tonight is a celebration for us humans as much as it is for my companion.

"The sigils you bear, the curse has left us; however, I believe I still have one last journey to make. But for now … Every single person that this curse took from us, the masses that were slain just because they were different. Chaos gripped the entire human race in Arcura.

"This is for them! *This* is for us!"

The bonfire roars into life as torches are hurled upon it. Jubilant cheers echo into the night as flagons are raised. Song and dance erupt, this is the happiest most have been in a long time.

There is one more journey that beckons. I climb up the southwestern tower, leaving the celebrations behind. Peaks upon the Feygoran Mountains glisten in heavenly moonlight over the crest of the nearby mountainside. Gloom appears to be gone. Mount Moradar looks as pristine as ever against the night sky.

⊰❈⊱

Celebrations have died down. The bonfire has reduced to dying embers.

"When are you leaving?" Vexxyra has snuck into the commander's quarters.

"First light. I have seen enough darkness."

Walking over, we meet in an embrace, her body smelling of newly-bloomed roses. "Would you like some company? Henry has offered Delbura to make your travels light."

A kiss finds her lips. "I appreciate the gesture, but this I must do alone."

Curiosity grips me. I stare at her arm, making out the powerless state of her Olyneran sigil like there is still some form of its energy that lingers. It's completely drained, but I ask the question anyway.

"Would you be willing to part with Olynero?"

"I do not think humanity will ever be free unless these sigils are banished. Nothing is normal about them."

Normal. The vast majority of our lives were normal. Yet, I now speak of the Alpha Beasts as if they are. She's right.

Vexxyra laughs. "I should not be here. I'll leave you to rest, if you can get some." A door shuts quietly behind her.

I can't stop looking at the foot of my bed and the floor beside me, hoping that this is all a dream and Draygar would suddenly coalesce when my true eyes open. The only truth, however, is one I don't want to accept.

***

Hammerknell. The Vorderans. The mountain pass. Striding forward through a dense cover of snow, Arcura feels peaceful once more.

A tailor has mended my coat, the warmth of which buries inside, keeping the chill at bay. Morathaen's pendant, my father's bracelet, I wear it all. Everything of significance to me, I have brought along. I grasp at the Moonlight Diamond within my pocket, drained of all energy. Dull and lifeless, maybe it has served its only purpose.

There is no telling of what dangers await me, but I can't put the others in harm's way. *I started this alone, I need to end it alone.*

Vorathen would have been impossible to convince, I didn't want to give him the opportunity. I have no doubt that as soon as he notices my absence, he will be after me. *He probably has his eyes on me right now, hiding somewhere within a subtle recess.* That feeling alone brings about a level of comfort.

The gloom, gone. A sense of relief washes over me. Snow begins to catch on the fur collar of my coat as I make my way through crevices on an inclining slope. Sitting high in the sky, the sun casts light over a land now free of death.

The monument and the rock shelf it sits upon come into view. Treading carefully, I swing my head in every direction with each step I take. Pushing aside fresh snow that covers the monument's inscriptions, I find every sigil exhausted except Enmara's.

A thought crosses my mind. *Do I even need to do anything?* Words Vexxyra spoke come rushing back. *I do not think humanity will ever be free unless these sigils are banished.*

Have they been already?

Reaching for my pocket, I remove the gemstone. Without further thought, I place the Moonlight Diamond over the now-identified Illoran sigil.

Nothing.

Then Enmara's.

Also nothing. There seems to be no connection whatsoever between the diamond and the monument. Like a child experimenting with things that one can only imagine, there is no understanding.

Studying the sigil on my wrist, an idea sparks. *The Goddess of Arcura. The Protector.*

Upon placing my open hand upon the cool stone, energy starts to release from the Enmaran sigil before spilling over the grooves, seeking other markings.

A hand that cannot retreat. My ears flood with the cries of what I can only imagine are the Alpha Beasts. The moment at which each spirit is outlined brings about a flash of light before my eyes until every marking shines in pure, white light.

The shelf rumbles. My hand, released. Ice below cracks as the monument begins to twist before embedding into the ground.

Two markings remain. Enmara's and Illora's, but both are white, seemingly glorifying the defeat of the Illoran spirit that wreaked havoc upon Arcura. *A sign of her victory.*

Suddenly, the monument ejects, rising once more to its original position. Leering at my wrist, I find Enmara's sigil still branded upon. Convinced of what I have done, I step back.

"I knew I would find you here, lad."

My body flinches. "Forgive me."

"I watched you leave. Even now, you still think you can slip by?" Vorathen follows with his signature chuckle.

"Well. There goes some fun." A jaded figure is cut as he examines his arm, his Ixxeniran sigil is no more. "I see that your blessing remains. As it should."

"Let us head back home. I am certain you've stirred everyone up again."

Taking one last glance at the markings upon the monument, the curse is gone. The Eldest One has been banished.

Arcura is free, its people in peace. A smile grows on my face. Realisation that I have succeeded sinks in. However, it appears as if my shatterbound reign will continue under Enmara's guidance.

Taking a deep breath, my mind is finally at ease.

Until … my sigil subtly flickers purple. An ear-splitting shriek rips through me as the ground beneath my feet begins to tremble once more.

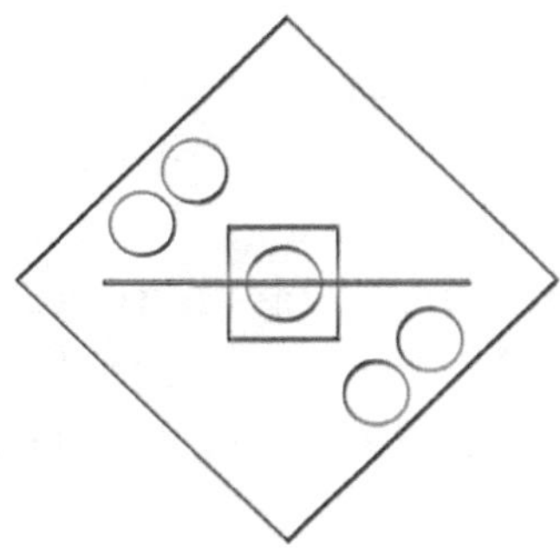

Acknowledgements

To all that who made this journey possible, thank you. *Shatterbound Reign* was a work in progress for a few years on and off until I finally decided to knuckle down and finish it. In that time, your support and kind words fueled my determination to complete my first novel. But that doesn't end here.

At the time of writing this, *Chronoborne Rage* is well underway and I'm thoroughly enjoying writing the second of the *Arcura Trilogy*.

Newcastle Interchange Train Crew: you all know who you are. Thank you so much for your support during the final phase of drafting and offering feedback. Dale, Col, Mal, Mat and Brie, thank you for your further insights.

AJC Publishing: AJ and Jenn, thank you for your offers, kind words and pushing me to make my story even better.

Busybird Publishing: Kev, Les and Joey. Thank you so much for taking me on board and transforming my work into something special. Sorry for all the questions!

Bookface Erina Fair: Alana. Having the chance to do something special for the launch of my maiden novel locally is something I could only dream about. Honestly, I didn't think I'd be lucky enough to get recognised anywhere so soon. You've made that a reality and I drove home over the moon. Thank you so much for taking a chance on me.

To my parents, thank you for reading several versions of the novel and providing very early critique. Without your help, I wouldn't have even made it to this stage.

And lastly, to my beautiful wife, Jasmine, and my son. Sorry for my incessant pestering. Your support and advice on how

I could make this a possibility will never be forgotten. You've constantly pushed me to be better and that in itself was all the motivation I needed. I love you all.

See you all in the next.

About the Author

Simon Leith is an emerging author from the Central Coast of NSW, Australia. With a passion for the science fiction and fantasy genres born from years of gaming, he writes, influenced by brands such as *Warcraft*.

He is a train driver by night, writer by day. With a loving family that supports his work, he looks forward to more releases in the future.

"Five years ago, I had a dream after playing *World of Warcraft* until an ungodly hour, one which filled my head with a story of great mystery. Later, I thought, how cool would it be to make this into an epic story? – a story that mixes beastly spiritual lore, human life and death, one with such circumstance and consequence. Would Arathyn know the magnitude of what he's really getting into? No."

www.simonleithbooks.com